# Carry
# the
# Sky

*—Kate Gray*

# Praise for *Carry the Sky*

"Many books about high school deal with bullying, but few explore the ramifications as deeply as *Carry the Sky*."
— Melissa Duclos, "11 High School Books That Will Take You Back to the Schoolyard," *Bustle*

"*Carry the Sky* is as intricate and precise as the paper cranes its characters fold. It comes as no surprise that Kate Gray is a poet as well as a fine novelist. Here we are surely in a poet's hands, her lyricism and attention to detail elevating the boarding-school narrative to something heartbreaking and truly universal."
— Cari Luna, author of *The Revolution of Every Day*

"Gray's dreamy, poetic language perfectly captures the languor, the sudden bursts of pain, the slow, subtle drowning that an isolated young adulthood can be."
— Julia Fine, *Necessary Fiction*

"The people in Kate Gray's intricate, visceral, and heartbreaking novel *Carry the Sky* armor themselves. Cocooned in sport, science, manipulation, power, privilege, or eccentricity, they face the fragility of their invented safe spaces when love, sex, violation, and obsession strip them to their most intimate selves. I can't say enough good things about this sizzling, deeply profound, poetic work."
— Davis Slater, author of *Selling Sin at the Hoot-Possum Auction*

"In the small, close world of a boarding school, three broken people circle each other, drawing closer to the tragedy that will move them all, finally, beyond their private sorrows. Three voices, three stories, and we are caught up in those stories as they are slowly revealed, like shards of a shattered mirror, one piece at a time. There is huge humanity in this novel. It is shockingly beautiful. Kate Gray is relentless."
— Joanna Rose, author of *Little Miss Strange*

"*Carry the Sky* is a dazzling narrative mosaic about innocence lost, the ghosts we grieve, and the emptiness of some forms of discipline and delineation. Kate Gray gives us a 'page-turner' in the best sense: you'll want to read both fast and slow, moving back and forth through this fearlessly told story, savoring."
— M. Allen Cunningham, author of *The Green Age of Asher Witherow* and *Lost Son*

"Gray's writing bridges the gap between poetry and prose with an undeniable literary flare."
— Gabino Iglesias, *That Lit Site*

"Lyrical, moving, and hauntingly beautiful, Kate Gray's *Carry the Sky* winds between two voices, Taylor and Song, both navigating the narrow lanes of St. Timothy's boarding school where they teach, both hitting the walls that surround them. One uses science to make sense of loneliness, loss, and desire—the other uses the beat of a rower's oar in water. Together these two outsiders struggle to move past mourning, to seek hope as they crack open their insular world. *Carry the Sky* is full of unforgettable characters and images, each word carefully chosen, like a perfect fold in a paper crane, creating a graceful neck, strong tail, and mighty wings, perched on the edge of the page, ready to take flight."

— Hannah Tinti, bestselling author of *The Good Thief* and co-founder of *One Story*

"The best writers find it a bit of a magic act balancing humor and heartbreak without showing how the trick is done. That being the case, this book is seamless sorcery. It rings true, raw and it will crush you. The best debut novels always do."

— Joe Kurmaskie, author of *Metal Cowboy*

"In *Carry the Sky*, two lonely hearts beat: Taylor Alta's in time to a cox'n's chant, and Jack Song's to the mathematical pulse of physics equations. Both are misfits in the moneyed, J.Crew world of St. Timothy's, an exclusive boarding school where the privileges of the old boy network threaten to trump right and wrong. This smartly told story kept me turning pages late into the night, and reaching for the book as soon as I woke up. Kate Gray's prose sings as she gives us schoolyard bullying, unrequited love, unresolved grief, adolescent desire running amok, and adult desire scarcely contained."

— Stevan Allred, author of *A Simplified Map of the Real World*

"Kate Gray's stunning debut beautifully shows us that grief is the great equalizer of our shared human experience."

— Edee Lemonier, *The Reading and Writing Cafe*

"Gray's poetic sensibilities crystallize in her prose. Under her careful hand, wild curls become a mask, hope is personified in the 'sunflower face' of a friend, and a lone goose in the sky evokes a blend of longing, loneliness, and loss. Often, her carefully rendered imagery and symbols purposefully repeat throughout the text, calling back to and layering on top of each other, slowly building mood and meaning."

— Alicia Sondhi, *Foreword Reviews*

*More reviews and coverage at forestavenuepress.com*

# CARRY
# THE
# SKY

# KATE
# GRAY

FOREST
AVENUE
PRESS
Portland, Oregon

© 2014 by Kate Gray

ISBN 978-0-9882657-6-9

Library of Congress Control Number: 2014936499

First edition 2014
Printed in the United States of America
by Forest Avenue Press LLC
Portland, Oregon

2 3 4 5 6 7 8 9

Distributed by Legato Publishers Group

Cover design: Gigi Little
Interior design: Laura Stanfill
Copy editor: Tracy Stepp

Forest Avenue Press is grateful to Literary Arts for the 2014 Oregon Literary Fellowship that helped finance this publication.

Forest Avenue Press LLC
6327 SW Capitol Highway, Suite C
PMB 218
Portland, OR 97239
forestavenuepress.com

for Katherine Venable Liddle
1960–1984

Will you ever bring a better gift for the world
than the breathing respect that you carry
wherever you go right now?

– William Stafford, "You Reading This, Be Ready"
from *The Way It Is*

# Taylor / **First Light**

ONE FOOT IN THE single shell like a blue heron lifting off water, I pushed off from the dock and lowered myself into the seat. In twenty strokes I cleared the cove. In twenty more strokes, I was full speed on the racecourse. No basic progression through arms, arms-and-back, arms-back-and-legs. Flat-out explosion on the foot stretchers, the balls of the feet, the body compressing and releasing, catching the water and gliding, recovering, the hands crossing, then rising out to the catch, dropping in, and feet pressing everything I had, everything I wanted, against the stretchers. Five hundred meters and my lungs cramped. My rating at thirty-eight strokes per minute, the sweat starting down my neck, between my breasts.

At 750 meters, Alex Jeffers, the boys' coach, passed me going the other way, halfway through his piece. His eyes glazed, his cheeks red and sunken, he was finishing. I was beginning. As we hurled ourselves in opposite directions, each body getting smaller, we gave one nod to the other.

Catch, release, my legs springing flat, my feet letting the seat roll back almost to the stops, I sprang. Sculling is repetition, legs driving the stroke, arms continuing momentum, each stroke an effort to overcome the body's want: to stop, to sink, to split in two. At the end of the lake, I let my shell run. My blades out of the water, hands crossed in my lap, elbows out, my abs holding my back extended at an angle, the scull glided. Bubbles rushed the round hull, no other sounds. With oars as wings, I flew over the water until momentum slowed, and I tucked the oar handles under my arms, bent my knees, and slid my seat up the tracks so I could hug my knees. I was a ball on water. A woman in a single scull. Alone.

No matter where I looked for you, you weren't there.

The cottonwoods made the air sticky, almost sour. The banks of the lake showed where water used to be. In late August, the banks of the lake were sharp drops in the mud. Little moved. First light spread into the far trees.

At the end of the lake, when first light made birches more yellow than white, I yelled, "Give. Her. Back."

# Song / **Skin Drag**

TEN MINUTES MORE. AT 10 p.m. I'm off duty. Usually I'm frantically grading fifteen lab books, but classes haven't started yet. The first lab books of the year, tedious, some disastrous. And here's a knock on the door.

"Door's open," I say. I don't get up from my desk.

"Mr. Song?" someone says. His voice is high, a Second Former. The door opens slowly.

"Mr. Harney, King of the Almost-in-Bed," I say. Maybe he'll about-face, go to bed. One never knows with the Second Formers what sets them off. They cry if I look at them. They cry for their mothers. They scream at their mothers on the phone. I can't believe the way St. Timothy's treats them: cubicles like rat mazes. Each boy behind a curtain, poster board for walls, one big, open room, the school too cheap to make real rooms. In all its wisdom, the school brings them here a week early to "bond," the littlest here along with the jocks who are never around, always out on fields and lakes, doing their jockly double-sessions. Thirteen-year-old boys, first time from home, babies really, packed like rats.

This one is more mouse than rat.

"Mr. Wrong," he says. Not funny. What is he up to? This kid. "I need help." He's in a gray turtleneck and gray sweats. His hair is sticking straight up. Bad personal hygiene, a bad sign.

"What can I do for you, Kyle?" I try his first name.

"You know physics, right?"

"Yes, that's what I teach."

"Then, you know stuff like how long it takes for a brick to hit the ground if you drop it, like from the second floor of the dorm, right?"

"Sure." Where did he get a brick?

"What about a feather?"

"Gravity is gravity, but that's a little different," I say, but before I can factor in wind and weight, he keeps going.

"What about a body? Would that be different? Would a body be like a brick or a feather?" Pointy face. Blue eyes like the eyes in the Wyeth mural downstairs, but smaller.

"Kyle," I say, "Mr. Inquisitive, what's a Second Former like you asking questions like this right before curfew? Don't you have books to read? Don't you have countries to conquer? Hasn't the sun already set on the British Empire?"

He looks down at the beige carpet. "Yes, sir," he says. His eyes look up for a second to check my eyes. "No, sir. The sun never sets on the British Empire." A little joke. A little smile. Then, he looks down again, says with a big voice, "I'm Imperial. I'm a Light Brigade."

"Okay, then, General Light Brigade, to bed."

He turns around, as if dismissed, a soldier. His back straight, he clicks heels, the socks he pretends are boots. Pulling diagonal from a belt he doesn't have, he draws the royal saber he also doesn't have.

"Charge," he yells, and he hurls himself against the closed door, his arm still raised, his chin smashed to the side. A loud crash. Motion acted upon by imbalanced force. He has no sense.

"Mr. Harney," I say.

A jock down the corridor yells, "You okay, Mr. Song?"

"Fine, thank you."

"Sorry, sir," Kyle says. He makes a show of staggering back from the door. The saber in his right hand, he reaches for the doorknob with his left. As soon as the door is open, he leads with his saber, yells, "Charge" over and over, "Charge" as he runs down the corridor. "Charge" again and again. Down the corridor the boys from their rooms respond "Shut up" and "Dweeb" and "You're dead." The school year has certainly begun.

The door doesn't shut.

Carla passes through the door before it shuts.

"Carla, you can't," I say. She closes the door. She is motion unimpeded.

"Before you say anything," she says.

We didn't see each other over the summer. I could have written her, but after Rehoboth, I had no words. Now she is a Sixth Former, eighteen years old. Is she taller? She's tan. She's thinner. Her curls are everywhere, hiding her eyes. From the door, she takes three steps toward me, puts three fingers on my lips.

Three fingers, cold. Her pale fingers, the last joint long. The pad of her middle finger crosses both my lips, fits into the crown of my upper lip. Cold and warm at the same time. Enough pressure to keep my words in my mouth. Something solid, no matter how slick, like a finger, meeting some vapor, like my breath, no matter how rapid, creates friction, and the boundary layer between the solid and the gas is the skin. The difference in velocity between the solid and the gas is skin drag.

She follows her fingers with her lips.

# Taylor / **Not Air, Not Water**

THAT MORNING BEFORE ANY of the girls in the crew arrived, I looked for you in the boathouse. You were in the fog over the cove, the wax smell of the boathouse after the bay doors swung wide, Kaschper eights and fours stacked, the light off their honey hulls. You were everywhere and not there.

If I could have talked with you, I would have told you about the cornfields of the Garden State before the long bridge into Delaware, how blond they were in the sun. I would have told you about the mud, how sludgy it smelled, all churned up and dry after John Deere tractors towed big, spiral blades. The flat pastures after the Delaware Memorial Bridge stretched a long ways, so different than the rolling hills in our college town. A week ago I had driven down a flat black driveway through maple trees, through lawns cut close, to a place I had never been before, a job I had never done. This year, 1983, you and I had talked about the U.S. and the Soviets aiming straight for each other full speed with warheads fully loaded. And we knew there was nothing we could do. And even though I told you about this job when I got it, my first teaching job, there was already so much more to tell. At the end of this driveway in Surrey, Delaware, the main building of the boarding school, St. Timothy's, was stone block this way and stone block that way. The campus was stone buildings, slate walkways, and lawns sloping down to a lake. A lake shallow and wrong. After one week, this job felt like hurtling headlong at something hurtling toward me.

Sixty years ago the Du Ponts built this lake. The Du Ponts built this school for farm boys to learn Chaucer, to learn rowing, to learn ways of tending corn. I was hired to tend both the boys and girls whose families now owned those farms. I would have told you I didn't know how to tend.

When 1983 began, we were both twenty-three years old, and if you had been in the smell of the wax on the rowing shells, in the still air this morning, I could have let loneliness be its own thing.

But you weren't there, and I kept walking to the end of the dock.

Two years ago, you and I sat back-to-back at the end of a dock like this one, jutting out into a different lake, Lake Onota in Massachusetts, where our college crew practiced. At sunset the lake turned from turquoise to jade to black. It was so still that night that the air and water were the same: same color, same temperature, same texture. Your long, strong back lining up with mine, our shoulders wider than hips. Rowers make unusual girls. Usual girls have hips wider than shoulders. That day we had raced and won. That night we talked well into dark. The only difference between the night air and the water was stars.

"Did you see it?" I said.

"There," you said. You pointed where the shooting star had been.

It was no stretch to imagine the wish you had. The tall and blond Mark, the type of dancer people circled on a dance floor, his Michael Jackson moonwalk a perfect blend of grace and mechanical motion. Your first date you ran to my room to tell me. For months we talked about whether or not you should sleep with him until one day you stopped talking about it, one day either you did or you realized how the possibility killed me.

Around us that night on the lake in Massachusetts, there were tiny ripples against the dock, a bird's call, cars in the distance. It was May, unusually warm for New England, muggy.

"I thought I was going to die today," you said.

"Around 200 meters?"

That's the usual place when we go into oxygen debt, like there's a plastic bag over nose and mouth, and our lungs almost burst, and everything in us wants out.

"When we took the power-ten on Smith," you said. "I didn't think I'd keep going."

"I couldn't tell."

"Good thing," you said. Leaning into me, you thanked me with your back.

"Hey," you said. You got up, and I could barely see your skin against the dark water, the dark night. "Try this."

Getting up and walking beside you, I knelt the way you were kneeling. The length of my thigh, the same length as your thigh, kneeling.

I couldn't see a thing, not the edge of water, not the edge of night.

Then, I felt your wet hand on my skin. If I didn't breathe, maybe your hand would stay on my arm. "Tell me when your hand hits the water."

Your fingers, all grip and sure, the calluses on your palms scratchy. And you pulled my arm down to where the water was, but I couldn't see the water. My skin couldn't feel it, either. The temperature and texture of the air completely matched the water. My skin in air, my skin in water. No difference. It was the ripple on my forearm that meant water. I said nothing so we would stay like that. Your hand on my arm. But soon something changed, and you let go.

This morning I couldn't tell. This morning on a lake with fog on warm water, a lake built by Du Ponts for rowing, for farm boys to learn rowing, I watched my wrist submerge, and only my eyes could tell what was air, what was water. My skin couldn't feel the difference.

"Checking the temp?" someone said behind me. There was a curl to her words.

A student faced me at the other end of the dock, a tall girl, black curls falling over her face.

"Bath water," I said. The dock rose and fell with each step I took toward this girl. Her eyes moved from my top to my middle to my feet to my middle to my top. I wanted to cross my arms. Her legs spread, lycra shorts, maroon and gray tank top, her skin was tight on muscles and freckled and white.

Before I reached her, I said, "You're Carla?"

"In the flesh," she said. Her steps toward me, like a mannequin, her hands a different pace than her elbows, her forearms at odd angles to her shoulders. The previous coach, who left for a rival school, warned me that this girl was both impulse and force, the type of rower who could win a race with her drive or lose a race with her recklessness.

"I've heard about you," I said.

"Who me?" She turned toward the water, her curls covering her eyes. She turned her back, her shoulders wider than her hips.

She was not you, not even close to being you. But there was a jab in my chest, the place that cracked when I heard the news about you.

Other girls walked down the dirt paths from the dorms to the cove where we were. A breeze came up and sent the fog over bare legs.

# Song / *Ls Are the Hardest*

I DIDN'T USED TO be skin drag. In San Diego as a kid, I was
uniform motion. A pool in the backyard. Dad, Mom, Kim, me.
Five years old when we moved from Korea. My sister and
me, as soon as we could swim, we were always in the pool,
on the bottom, crossed legs, talking bubbles. One hand on the
ladder to keep us down, one hand moving quick left, quick
right, to make bubble-talk like real tea parties. We throw back
our heads, laugh loud. Bubbles fly out our throats. Lots of air
through open throats. Appropriate force through appropriate
opening. We swim to the surface and gulp up air, then head
back down to the bottom, hold ourselves down on the ladder.
Cross-legged on the bottom, talking through bubbles, I could
say anything to Kim. Our bubble-talk was animated and loud,
more bubbles, or intimate and soft, few bubbles. Wish I could
bubble-talk with her still.

At six years old, there were no more bubble parties. Dad
said no more. Dad was bigger than Newton. Bigger than Mao.
About as big as Lech Wałęsa. "No more pool until English perfect," except he said it with *R*s for *L*s. Smart guy. Chemist.

So, every day that pool, that kidney shape taking up the yard. I sat in the living room with the tutor, Mr. Chan, Chinese, yelling over the oscillating fans. The day we met I thought he'd have a long, skinny beard and slippers. He was younger than my dad. Raced bicycles. Smooth legs. Smelled like sprinklers.

"Golf," he said. Some weird sound came from way back in his throat.

"Guff," I said.

"Guh," he said. And he opened his mouth with his bottom jaw first. My sister's face at the bottom of the pool behind bubbles and gibberish. I about laughed.

"Gruh," I said. I talked bubbles, a language Mr. Chan couldn't speak.

After Mr. Chan left, I told my dad, "It's too hard," and my dad said too hard equaled staying in North Korea, Communists, and praying in secret. He said hard was moving whole family to United States. What did I know about too hard?

Each night late my mom and dad came home, put Elvis on, opened cans of Bud. Mom and Dad sat on the front porch of our adobe, and they picked paint off their arms and legs. All year long, seven days a week, one house after another. Paint in their hair, on their eyelashes, on their teeth. Dad was no chemist any more. They spoke Korean to each other, laughed so loud their heads knocked the wall behind them. I tried to listen, but by seven years old, I lost Korean. If they heard me coming, they switched to English. And their cheeks caved in, their mouths didn't open so much, and their throats didn't hold low notes. English words pushed through their mouths, but their mouths resisted. Wave drag was English in their mouths.

For months from the living room window I watched Kim splash in the pool. "No more pool until English good," my dad didn't say any more. Didn't need to. Mr. Chan's wiry legs stuck out of his shorts. We sat at the card table practicing. My English still bad. Sometimes I gave him my homework folded in a rose, sometimes an elephant.

"Thank you, Mr. Song," Mr. Chan said. "Now say, *letter*."

Always the Ls: *letter, last, too late.*

When Carla slips through the door, when she puts her lips on mine, I lock the door behind us. Off duty, 10 p.m., the Kings of the Dorm put themselves to bed. The jocks back early showed the babies, the Second Formers, the routine. The summer didn't drain every ounce of order from their jock brains. For three months of summer I tried to exert force and block the energy moving through me. Twenty-eight-year-old man shouldn't fall for a girl, a student, no matter how smart or self-assured. The greater the distance the less the attraction. But no distance right now means great attraction.

Lips and mouths hook together, hands grabbing backs and clothes, we shuffle to the couch, fall on it. I'm on top, and there is no me. One light by the rocking chair lights up half her face, her curls falling to the side. Her eyes, big and dark, and she looks at me as if I am the world, and she barely has a hold on the world, and she presses up, meeting equal and opposite force pressing down.

I slide off. One loafer drops, then the other. At her middle, my fingers on her zipper; at her feet, my hands tug at the end of her jeans. She puts her hands behind her head and lifts her hips off the couch. She says, "Don't you want to talk about, like, inertia, maybe centripetal force?"

"You're funny," I say, and her jeans come off.

And she gets still. And when my hands feel how soft her thighs are, when my hands cup her hips and draw her down the couch, I forget time and age and dorm rooms. I spread her legs, like paper I will fold. And I kiss her, kiss down her thighs. And she arches up, and we are objects in motion with the same speed acting in a balanced force. We are Newton's first law.

But then her breath gets shallow, and these sounds out of her mouth are like a baby, and she makes sounds like she's hurt, like I'm hurting her. The sounds are high and rapid, too much air through too little space. And I stop, stop kissing her, stop before anything else.

Then she turns animal, wild, kicking, and I'm already not

touching her, and she says, "No, no, no," and I land on my butt. Tears shoot out of her eyes; she gets sweaty and curls up, puts her fists between her legs. She rolls away from me and turns her face into my stinky cushions. She keeps panting.

*What have I done?* is all I can think. What I haven't done is this before. Talk was all we did, ever, and the force between us of negative and positive charges, the electricity in our walks around campus. What I've done tonight, the undressing, the kissing, is too much. So I say, "Carla, Carla" to her back, really quietly, but she doesn't move. She rocks a little. Her hair is soft; her curls straighten when I put my fingers through them.

When I see her shake, I tuck a blanket around her. Out of my mouth comes the song my mother sang to Kim and me when we were new to San Diego, little, fresh off the boat. I don't even know what it means. It's the only Korean I have. My mother sang it to us to go to sleep, sang it to Kim in the hospital when she was weak.

Back in my rocking chair by the one light on in the room, I rock forward, backward. This young woman who holds on to the world through me, who opens before me like something raw and faultless, some equal force, is a girl. An eighteen-year-old girl.

Mr. Chan taught me to say Ls: *lewd, loser, lecherous.*

# Taylor / **Out Loud**

THE FIRST WEEK OF crew practice was the week before the rest of the students arrived and before classes started. The first week of crew practice was also the first faculty gathering at St. Timothy's. The lawn party was beige: khaki pants, cotton button-downs, ducks embroidered on belts with D-ring buckles. It was late August, and the lake was too hot. The smell in the breeze was cottonwood. It stuck to the back of my throat.

I looked for you. It wasn't the first time I looked for you in the wrong place. If I had found you at the party, I might have told you about the ways that scotch singes on the way down, like you think love might, but all it is is desire. You see, I needed you to be there for that evening and for the rest of the story.

There's a crack I carry around, and the only thing that fills it is you.

The dining hall was behind me, the one with the mural inside, all the white boys turned the same direction. Andrew Wyeth painted it. He used the same face for every boy. There wasn't one face with brown or green eyes, just blue, and in every face, there was boredom in the corners of the eyes.

Outside the dining hall, the first table with a white table-cloth was the bar set up. An older African American man waited for me to say what I wanted to drink. "No, thank you," I said, and kept walking as the lawn sloped down to the lake, the muddy lake. Teachers talked in little circles. Women in skirts, men in pants. Men with short hair, women with long. New teacher, dyke in khaki pants. The seventeen-page St. Timothy's dress code meant I left my jeans and flannel shirts tucked behind the new L.L.Bean and J.Crew clothes, the brands specifically named in the dress code. In my apartment attached to the dorm, in my bedroom with a dresser issued by St. Timothy's, the soft clothes I like to wear were tucked in the drawers, and the stiff clothes I have to wear to be a teacher stuck to me like plastic wrap.

Some old teacher walked up so close I could smell his clothes. His checked shirt, stretched over his belly, was orange peels in garbage cans. He said, "Don't you drink?"

"Excuse me?"

"You will," he said and nodded. His chin moved farther into more chins. He turned and walked away.

My button-down shirt felt unbuttoned, a breeze in my breasts.

As soon as the smelly teacher walked away, Dorothy White, the headmaster's wife, turned from the little circle around her and gathered a small flock of older teachers, dragged them up the lawn.

"Taylor Alta, English, Geography," she said a few feet away from me, "I want you to meet Tom Francosi, Mathematics, Stuart Applebaum, Economics, and Reverend Bill Moose." Trailing behind her in a line, each man wore khakis, button-down shirt, tie or collar.

Tom Francosi said, "Nice to meet you." His handshake was a short up and down.

Stuart Applebaum said, "Glad you're on board." His handshake matched mine, and his blue eyes softened as we shook hands.

"My, my," Reverend Moose said. "What do we have here?" He bent back to take a big breath. "A rower, by the looks of her." The steps up the hill winded him. Reverend Moose was slow curves, an arc from neck to knees, a profile like Alfred Hitchcock's. The softness around his eyes, in his belly, made the faculty party spread out on this lawn much easier. I could breathe.

"Yes, sir," I said, "I've rowed." They knew I was on the 1980 national team, the one that didn't go to Moscow.

"Taylor, it occurs to me," Mrs. White said, her head shorter than my shoulder, "that girl, the rowing coach who drowned in that accident on the Schuylkill last week, did you know her?"

She knew I did. She was drum roll and clashing cymbals. Her blue eyes were denim, old-people blue, the people who say things too loud. Tom Francosi's eyes were blackboards. Stuart Applebaum's were glass. I couldn't look at Reverend Moose.

"Yes," I said. "My friend."

Stuart said, "Did they find the body?" He leaned his question toward me.

My button-down shirt was cellophane. The crack in my chest was dark and deep. The crack came with the phone call last Wednesday night from our teammate. I didn't know how she got my number since I had been here only two days. But that's not what I asked. I asked her twice if she was kidding, but she wasn't. I fell on the floor in my apartment when she told me you drowned. The carpet smelled like mildew.

Mrs. White said it out loud, in front of people. She said you drowned.

"If you'll excuse me," I said.

Uphill was quick. I swung wide the door to the dining hall. The slam of the door, the dark of the dining room, and the stares from white boys in the mural were sucked into my chest instead of breath. Both my palms hit the girls' bathroom door, hit the stall door, stopped only by the tile wall. My knees went to the floor, and my hips slumped between the toilet and the wall. I couldn't crawl under the toilet tank. In one breath I brought cold toilet, ceramic bowl, and tile down into my lungs. The cold was quiet and good.

The quiet turned to a soft sucking sound. The bathroom door pushed the stale air inside.

"Taylor?" a man said from the bathroom door. My cheek resting on the stall wall, cold and damp.

"Taylor, it's Alex Jeffers. I know the guy who tried to save your friend," he said. The door to the girls' bathroom closed behind him. "He's fine. He made it. I'm sorry about your friend."

"Thanks," I said. I sat back on my heels. I was church-kneeling inside a bathroom stall. When you went to coach the novice crew that day, you had the crazy autumn current and a waterfall meters away and your youngest high school girls being swept toward a waterfall. That's what you had when your motor conked out. Alex's friend had tried to reach you in the river, tried to keep you from going over the falls, but his motor conked out, too. He and his boat went over the falls. The river didn't keep him, just you. You were caught in the turbine of the falls. And they didn't find your body.

"Mrs. White is a pain in the butt," he said. "I was coming over to see how you're doing. I heard what she said." He stood outside the stall. "I'm sorry."

My hand on the toilet seat, I pushed off the floor and stood up. I turned around, and there was Alex's blond cropped hair above the stall door. No eyes, but hair. I opened the door to his pink polo shirt, collar up, his arms crossed over his chest. His forearms were layers of muscle laid one on top of the other. He opened his arms to me.

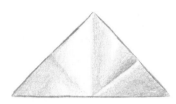

# Song / **Newton's First Law**

IN THAT WYETH MURAL in the dining hall the eyes of each boy with brown hair and blue eyes follow me around. Wyeth wasn't paid enough by the parsimonious Du Ponts. Thought he'd fix them, paint the same face for every boy.

Every good boy does fine. Sound waves in parallel patterns. Every good boy does not come out of the girls' bathroom. Two new teachers together? Been here a week, tops. Rowers, both of them. Excessively tall. There's a big wet spot on his pink polo. Over his heart. How touching.

They split directions, she somewhere else, he to the faculty party. Skip Newton's second law and go to third. Equal and opposite reaction. You can't touch without being touched.

Old Mr. Leonard, the one black face at this party, wears his white apron, tends bar. "Afternoon, Mr. Jack."

"Five years here, Mr. Leonard," I say, "and you can't call me Jack?"

"No, Mr. Jack." Delaware is hardly enlightened. The Mason-Dixon line is too close.

"You are the King of Courteous, Mr. Leonard. How was your summer?"

"Same as my spring," he says. There is no irony in his voice.

"And your family? How are the grandchildren?"

"My pride and my purpose," he says. At the thought of his three granddaughters and five grandsons, Mr. Leonard shakes his head and smiles. He has worked at St. Timothy's as a custodian and sometimes bartender for thirty years or more. To the few black students, from Philadelphia and Wilmington, he is preacher, father, mentor, and coach. He knows more about the goings-on inside this little bastion of turpitude than anyone else who works here.

"Just so. For this occasion, I better have scotch, don't you think, Mr. Leonard?"

"Fine choice," he says. Mr. Leonard's hands are swift. His hands, dark like my father's, are lined from hard work.

"Hey, Jack Song, where have you been?" Herbert, the librarian, has spotted me. Can't believe he stinks so badly. I nod to Mr. Leonard whose return nod tells me he's seen too much of Herbert this afternoon.

"I've been prepping for classes, of course," I say to Sir Herbert of the Unwashed.

"Not in my library you haven't," he says. "That's the problem with education today, no real research." Herbert's jumping on his soapbox.

"Now, Herbert, you know I won't neglect your precious books." He nods, and his chin has white stubble. His checked shirt is tight over his paunch. No bathing or shaving.

"You should see the new set of encyclopedias," Herbert says. His eyebrows, so disheveled, lift up. His focus shifts. He fixes on my glass. "Hey, Song, what are you doing with a drink?"

"Relaxing?"

"You know you Orientals aren't supposed to touch the stuff." Sir Herbert draws a breath.

"Not quite, Herbert. We Asians do math, remember? Research, man, do your research," I say. Herbert sways. He looks down at his now-empty glass.

Before he decides to ask Mr. Leonard for another drink, I say, "Have you met the new teachers?"

"Not the rowers," he says. He leans too close. "I saw the girl earlier. You know, she doesn't drink?"

The sad sack. Entropy is taking its course. "No, really? An athlete who doesn't drink?" I say into his bloodshot eyes. "Herbert, how will she get on?"

He leans. "Well, she won't," he says. "That's the point." He walks off in the direction he was leaning. Downhill.

I'm late. The circles have formed. The Sciences, the Humanities, and Rev. Moose pontificating. All East Coast. All white. Mr. Leonard and I stand out, and I'd rather stand with him. But now Mr. Rower-Man joins the party, bends down so Dorothy White, the headmaster's henchwoman, can talk in his ear. She's probably speaking softly so he has to lean his hard body in close. Hello, Mrs. Robinson.

Will you look at that? Those kids can run. Two boys, one girl, right across the lawn, holding their clothes over their faces. And there's Sir Herbert raising his glass to naked kids. Fit kids. That girl, unmistakable, that's Carla. Nobody runs like that. Carla with no clothes. Long, lean. Those angles. I sweat. Every good teacher does fine. I've done fine not to see her all summer, but I am no good boy. Her fingers against my breath, the couch, my lips on her. The stress that shifted plates, stress too great causing slippage, slippage creating body waves and surface waves of seismic proportions. Earthquakes emit energy in all directions, and Carla streaking releases seismic energy.

Everybody's cheering the streakers.

Carla has the lines of a treehopper. Different than a grasshopper. Smaller folds. I can fold one in about an hour. Origami, a good way to learn patience. A good discipline. Practice waiting. I keep telling her we'll wait until after she's graduated. Carla calls her graduating class, "19-fucking-84." She has a way with words, that one.

A couple of petal folds, a couple of rabbit ears, and I've got a treehopper made. What treehoppers do is they camouflage as thorns. Can't tell when they're on a quince. Carla's like that. She adapts. How will she adapt to an earthquake inside her? How will I look at her again without seeing my own fault?

Darwin is amazing.

# Taylor / **Eight Moving as One**

MINUTES AFTER MEETING CARLA on the dock where water felt the same as air, I walked inside the boathouse. The varsity St. Tim's crew, second-place finishers in the Stotesbury Regatta, the biggest high school rowing event in the world, were all over the boathouse. Three racks of eights, their honey hulls upside down, their riggers sticking into the air, most of the rowing shells were the boys'. The girls' program was pitifully small: just a varsity and a novice crew. Like so many schools, St. Timothy's wanted girls to win magically, to spring from some ribs and row. The eight varsity rowers and their cox'n were looking at the seats upside down, talking together and pressing their elbows as they laughed, walking over to the oar rack, the girls tipping their heads to look at the maroon and gray blades, thirteen feet up. These girls were muscle, long limbs, sure.

"Good morning," I said. The girls in clusters made a circle inside the center bay. They knew who I was from the letter their families received over the summer. Not just anyone could coach St. Tim's girls, but never had a woman been a St. Tim's coach. The parents expected the Stotesbury Cup, nothing less. By 1983, women had competed in Olympic rowing exactly once, but because the U.S. had won, parents of rowers expected their girls to be Olympian. I didn't know what to expect. Sure, I knew seat racing and time trials and 500 meter splits, but I didn't know Delaware, the mansions of Wilmington, the elite families whose men commuted to D.C. and Philadelphia, whose women ran charities and prepared their girls for politics. These girls, their bodies muscled but soft, their teeth perfect in their perfectly-timed smiles, were smart, the type of smart that gets ahead, that steps over or on. This type of Adam Smith smart works against the selflessness needed to win the Stotesbury Cup. Rowing is the fierce abandonment of self in the service of winning. St. Tim's hired me more for coaching than teaching, and coaching was all about pushing girls to abandon what they knew in their heads for what they could overcome with their limbs. The trick was willing the body to go past the limits of the mind. Magician as coach. Pulling a winning crew out of a hat. Magic was not what I knew.

"Let's start," I said. "Each of you introduce yourself and describe your workouts over the summer." Two girls rolled their eyes and giggled into each other.

"Never mind," I said. I faced the two girls full on. "Say your name, and lead an exercise that everyone else will do. You two go first." I backed away from the eye-rolling girls.

It went around the circle: jumping jacks and Emily, Buttons Daley and crunches, and Carla and real push-ups.

After hands on waists and bending at hips and breathing, breathing, I said, "Starboards this side, ports that side." The girls separated to either side of the bay, into an even number with a cox'n in the middle. "Any strokes?" I said. One girl stepped up, and another girl was pushed by her pals.

"Okay," I said. "Most noble strokes."

You were our stroke all four years. There's nothing a crew won't do for a stroke. Our backs match the pace and angle of the stroke's back. All we watch is the pace of her body moving up the slide, her back, her blade. We'd die for her.

These two were both thin, not as tall as the others, one eager, the other shy. "We'll start with Buttons, and try Amanda this afternoon. Everybody else pick a seat, and let's get hands on the boat."

"Okay, Alicia, cox them out," I said. Last year Alicia had been the cox'n for the Junior National eight, and her voice alone could take the girls to first place. The other girls started chanting something I couldn't make out.

"Coach?" Alicia said. She stood four foot ten, probably ninety pounds. The chanting grew. "Everybody calls me Rambo."

"Okay, then, Rambo," I said, "cox them out of the house." Eight girls lined up along the shell in the rack. They faced Rambo, their backs to the open doors of the boathouse, and waited for her command. Rambo saw the girls, the boat in the rack, the riggers jutting out, the door where the girls would carry the boat, the dock beyond.

"Count down when ready," Rambo said.

From bow to stern, each girl called her seat number, "Bow," "two," "three," each number said high or low, soft or mocking, each a measure of the girl.

After Buttons said "eight," curt and sure, Rambo said the next commands, "Hands on. Slide the boat out of the rack. Gently." And the hull moved slowly out of the rack.

"Easy. Watch the riggers," Rambo said. "And up." As if the eight were hydraulically powered, the boat rose with eight girls beneath, four on either side.

"Face out of the house." All the girls turned.

"Walk it out," Rambo said. The boat with its eight pairs of legs moved toward the port side of the dock.

"Way enough," Rambo said. The girls stopped. They put both hands on the shell. With the cox-box and extra clothing in her hands, Rambo ran to the bow of the boat. She said, "Ready to lift, and lift. Up over your heads, and up."

The boat didn't move the way it was supposed to move. Three hundred pounds and thirty-six feet long. As soon as I saw the boat hesitate, move an inch up, then down, I ran. Under four seat, I grabbed the sides, bent my knees, and pushed. When I straightened my arms all the way, my spine took the load. The boat rose above our heads.

The two lines of girls stepped together beneath the boat, lifting three hundred pounds of wood, fiberglass, and metal overhead.

Rambo said, "One hand in. Roll it to waists."

And we did.

"Way out. Gently," Rambo said, "And down." All nine of us lowered the shell, bent with the boat.

The thirty-six-foot shell, the composite Kaschper eight came down one end first. It landed on the water with a smack. It didn't crack, but that smack wasn't safe. The girls in the bow couldn't slow it down. Some girls stood up, ready to get the oars.

"Again, Rambo," I said. "Do it right, Saints."

The girls stopped, faced me flat. I looked at them. This was the moment to win them. They didn't know what winning required. They turned to their places on the boat. I leaned into the shell, took hold.

Rambo said, "Ready to lift, up and out of the water."

Then she said, "Lift to the waists, and lift."

"Up over the head," Rambo said, "and up." We pressed the boat up. The boat over our heads, the girls' arms shaking made the boat shake.

Rambo said, "One hand in. Back down to the waists, and down."

"Set it down, way out."

And the boat came to rest on the flat water.

No sound.

"Good job," I said. Bow four jumped to their feet. Altogether, they made the Nadia Comaneci both-hands-in-the-air, backs swayed, hands above their heads, four girls, breasts to backs, first facing bow, then spinning at the same speed to stern, butts to laps, falling into giggles. Bow four was always like that.

"Coaching gymnastics?" Alex said behind me. His voice

was a stiff wind. "We don't have all day," he said. And then I saw all three boys' crews in the boathouse, boys with hands on hips, boys on the ground, all boys staring at the one girls' crew.

"Adjust seats on the water," I said to Rambo. To Alex, I said, "Guess you boys better get out of bed a little earlier."

Rambo and the crew tightened oarlocks. Away they went. I stepped into my launch and started the motor and took off. I wanted to wake the dock.

We didn't practice much that day. Five hundred meters down the course, I called, "Way enough," and Rambo echoed the command. I killed the motor in my launch, floating beside the eight. What I had seen was an accordion, girls opening backs at different times and at different angles, girls bending their knees and rolling their seats up the tracks at different speeds. They were supposed to be one girl, eight moving as one.

The middle of a lake with no roads or motor boats nearby got quiet quick. Sounds fell away like a cloak, and the girls' Varsity eight and I were left with the splash of the waves on the boats, the slosh of fuel in the tanks, a coffee cup rolling in my boat.

On the Friday before, I took the launch out and filled the lake with the roar of the motor. There were no students, no impatient boys. You had died two days before. August 24, 1983. With the throttle open full, I made white water crash into cottonwoods on the banks. The race course on the lake, the sheltered cove, the starting platforms, the grand tour was pretense. I made wakes. I cut the lake. I carved your name in water.

"That's enough for today, Saints," I said, and the girls broke their formation to look at me.

After Rambo had turned the boat around, she let the boat come to a stop. Then, she said into the PA, "Sit ready." All the oars moved to the catch position. The girls slid up to the start, rolled the blades up, and buried them.

"Ready to row," Rambo said, "and row." The blades dug into the water, burying too much of the shaft, and the eight moved slowly past me. The girls bunched, and the boat lunged side to side. We had work to do. In each of us, we had to find the compassion, the willingness to sacrifice ourselves for each other. We had to find the heart in order to win.

# Song / **Earth Calling**

FOLDED A BRONTOSAURUS. DINOSAURS are cake. Folded a water beetle.

Carla and her bugs. Sometimes I leave little ones in the tree outside her dorm room. Only at night. Sometimes I leave them on the trail to the boathouse. Left one yesterday after whatever it was that happened in my apartment. Somehow she made it back to her dorm without the dorm parent noticing. The start of every year can be a little rocky.

After her practice with Excessively Tall Alta, Carla should find the bug I folded. Newton must have rowed. Take a rowing shell moving across the surface of a lake. Take eight oars and a bunch of overachieving girls, and what do you have? Uniform motion.

The major source of resistance in rowing is drag. Misfits of Science know the idea as wind resistance. Think badminton shuttlecock versus baseball. The shuttlecock has greater drag. Now, think rowing shell. The surface of a rowing shell, the tiny slivers and divots in the shellac, the grain of the wood, creates friction, hinders the movement of a solid through liquid. The viscosity of the surface moving through the liquid or gas is the skin.

I'm all skin drag. I'm resistance. I'm the thing that slows movement. What I've done to Carla. What I did to Kim when she ran to catch the phone. What people do in relationships. Drag. The force that weighs down, works against the uniform motion of objects in action.

The lab reports I was working on, the lab I hoped the Misfits of Physics would grasp, was Newton's First Law: *An object in motion continues in uniform motion unless acted upon by an unbalanced force.*

It's like this. A person is strapped into a vehicle, therefore one with the thing. The vehicle moves, the person moves. So, if a person is stupid and doesn't wear a seatbelt and the vehicle hits a wall, boom. Person and thing are no longer one. A person becomes a projectile. Bye-bye.

People are supposed to be smarter, make choices. Asians are supposed to be smarter than anybody. In a relationship, both people are strapped in. If one stops, the other goes bye-bye.

Planes being blown out of the air are a different thing. Say, people are flying to Seoul. Say they're moving 500 miles an hour on a Korean airliner, and boom, a Soviet missile hits them. Imbalance. They and plane become a million pieces. All 269 lives shattered. Bodies in pieces. Nothing to bury. Koreans caught in the Cold War. Who knows what Reagan will do. But the U.S. and Soviet Union? They are a different law: equal and opposite reaction. Can't touch without being touched.

Carla and me? We hurtled a million miles an hour together for an instant, but then, I stopped. Imbalance. She is now a projectile, and no origami bug will help her. And it's like this: No one who causes her pain can help her out of pain.

Newton is amazing.

First time our paths might cross is dinner. That mural in the dining hall gives me the creeps. Truth is, light reflecting off paint can't make eyes follow the viewer, but that one boy in the mural follows me to my seat at the dinner table.

I'm assigned to chaperone dinners with the rower, Taylor, Queen of the Tall Girls, cross-dressing tonight, skirt, pressed shirt, Eddie Bauer jacket, no tie. Good thing. A tie would make students talk. They'd call her weird but wouldn't have the word for the other thing. Tall, no boobs, deep voice. Got to be. Newton never had a law for that. Sir Herbert of the Encyclopedias could look up laws. What do you call a woman who dresses in sweats, runs ten miles a day, and has no boobs? Doesn't take a rocket scientist.

But what was she doing with Mr. Rower-Man coming out of the bathroom at the faculty party?

Of course, Sir Alex of the Tall Boys swings by our table tonight. Positive and negative valences. Attraction. Predictable.

"I don't think we've met," Mr. Clean-Machine Alex says to me. He sticks his hand across the table, and his hand is the size of a shovel.

"Yeah, Jack Song, Physics," I say.

"Hey, nice to meet you. Never could figure physics." He thinks he's being cute. He turns toward Tall Girl and flashes a Mr. Clean grin at her. The two of them are teeth and meaning.

Since she's been here, Tall Girl has been wave drag, slow and steady friction, something heated and magnetic and sad. She's barely holding on and leaving a wake. She's how I was after Kim. Grief is like that, dead weight in the water. Maybe rowers know that type of drag. Maybe Mr. Clean knows it, too. Whatever they have between them, the kids at the table are watching. In a moment they'll make two and two go five.

"Tommy Underwood," I say, "Prince of the Untucked Shirt. Dress yourself, young man." My voice comes out big, low frequency, air pushed through appropriate passage. Tommy looks quick, like his fly is down, turns toward the mural, undoes his belt, unzips. He tucks front-left, front-right, tucks back-left, back-right, zips up, tightens his belt, and turns quick around. He's blond, and his fat cheeks are burning red. The boys on either side jab him.

The bell. Dorothy White, Mrs. Headmaster, dings her dinner

bell. All heads drop. Except Taylor's. She's looking around. I catch her eye, blue eyes, big circles, grief reflects in the face, and my head exaggerates bending.

Dorothy White's voice is flat, crackling, not enough air through not enough throat, "For what we are about to receive . . ." and I catch Carla watching me two tables over. Does she think no one is looking?

At that god-awful weekend in Rehoboth, with a towel around me, I came out of the bathroom with another towel to dry my hair, and there she was in bed, looking at me, assessing. The sheet draped over her, it showed her feet, her hips, flat stomach, breasts. Her one arm up over her head on the pillow, her muscle and freckles, her curls all over her face, the pillow. She looked at me, those brown eyes following me out of the bathroom, magnetic, in Rehoboth that one weekend, the weekend we slept in separate beds, slept with no sex. Couldn't do it. Too often I forget Carla is a kid even though she's eighteen. Her brown eyes tonight are different. They're small, a child's. I am Mr. Lecherous. Mr. Loser. I am now wall, the unbalanced force. She is motion, projectile. Bye-bye, Carla.

"Mr. Song," somebody at the table says, and I don't even know everyone is sitting down but me. "Pass the potatoes," the kid says. Eating machines. Taylor looks straight ahead. Nobody's home.

"Whoa, whoa, ladies and gentlemen," I say, "this is not the feedlot. Put your forks down. Now, each person turn to your colleague on the left and your colleague on the right, and say your name and what form you are in. That's it," I say, "Commence," and it's a race. The younger the student, the faster it goes.

"Marty Kraus, Fourth Form," he says to the kid on his left. "Marty Kraus, Fourth Form," he says to the kid on his right, and Marty Kraus grabs a dish.

Taylor Alta, still not there. She turns to the student on her left, opens her mouth, but nothing comes out. Earth to Taylor.

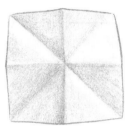

# Taylor / **Fresh Water Pond**

THEY LOOKED LIKE BIRDS, but in rows. Six tables in three neat rows, an aisle down the middle, two birds per table. The tables hid wings and feathers, revealed necks, beaks, and beady eyes barely above books and pencils and three-ring binders. The ones who sat alone were the only girl in the eighth grade and a boy who looked at the wall. At St. Tim's they called eighth grade Second Form, ninth grade Third Form. There is no First Form. Something like the British schools. Something else prescribed, like what to wear and what brand. The boy who looked at the wall wore a wool tweed coat with elbow patches and a tie bumpy in its knot. His hair like electric shocks, he could have been Einstein if he weren't a baby bird stuck behind a table.

You would have known what to do. You had already been teaching a year in Philadelphia before I ended up in this birds' nest, the faces turned to me, their throats exposed.

"Miss Alta?" the small blond boy in the front row said. He was more tree frog than bird, bright green.

"Yes." His name was sure to be on a list, but I was all gills and scales, no hands.

"How many tests will we have?" the frog said. "How much are they worth?"

If we had been swimming, little frog and fish, if we had faced each other suddenly in a slow pool, I would have un-locked my wide mouth and swallowed him.

"Well, now," I said, "your name?"

"Jimmy O'Brien," the frog said.

"Jimmy," I said, and evolution caught up with me. I was a fish with legs and walked to his table. My hands sprang from gills, and I reached a hand to him. "Pleased to meet you," I said and shook the clammy hand he extended.

I went around the room, taking each eighth-grader's hand, Second Former's hand, and wrapping mine around theirs. I stood, and they sat. I found my bag and lists, my three-page hand-written notes for an hour-long class. I found my spine and hands and voice.

"We're starting this term with South Africa," I said. "Does anyone know where that is?"

And David in the second row, on the left, his glasses making his face a dragonfly head, raised his hand straight up.

"In southern Africa," he said, and he looked to his left at Tommy Underwood, and they giggled.

"Right," I said. "So, what's going on in South Africa right now?" Ask open questions, said the articles I read on teach-ing, the only teacher training I had. My undergraduate English major didn't include Education classes, and learning to propel my body over water and lifting weights were more my world than witty conversation about Mr. Darcy. Perhaps Jane Austen would have served me better.

From the back row, the desk with one bird, the tweed coat and wild hair, a voice fired words like a typewriter.

"A-par-theid, the in-sti-tu-tional se-gre-ga-tion of the black ma-jor-i-ty by the white mi-nor-i-ty," he said each syllable, and he moved his head like the platen of a typewriter, jerky, quick, turning one direction, until his head reached his shoulder, and he said, "Zip. Ping." And he spun back to the other shoulder, and started the typing-speech again.

"Kyle, is it?" I said. His name checked on my list. He nodded machine-style, precise, up and down. "How did you know that?" The other birds turned toward the back row, and all I saw were heads of hair, blond, brown, tight-curled black.

"Don't know," Kyle said. His metallic voice flat, keys striking. He looked down, his chin almost tucked into the knot of his tie.

You wouldn't meet my eyes at our graduation. Your last name in the middle of the alphabet, you marched in line before me, the As at the end, and stood while the rest filed in. In the black cap and gown, the white of shirts and the white skin of most of us, our line cut the lawn into green halves. Two classmates handed out pink, green, blue balloons, and you didn't take one. I did. The balloons said, "Apartheid kills," in big black letters. Our college had not divested. When I passed by your row, I tried to turn your head my way, but you were looking at the bleachers for Mark and your family.

When my family saw my balloon, they shook their heads. My family believed communists were at work everywhere, especially in South Africa. Workers organizing and rising up were a sure sign. They feared Martin Luther King Jr., feared Gandhi. They couldn't say "Soviet Union" without whispering it as if the devil's name might draw the devil out. Your parents pointed at you, snapped pictures, waved. Mark beamed at you, and you waved at him.

Kyle didn't move. His arms slack at his sides, his head almost to his notebook, he was no longer typewriter, dictionary definition, words. Two boys leaned into each other at one desk and whispered.

"South Africa," I said, "is one of the wealthiest nations in the world, and one of the poorest nations." Two days I had spent researching and rehearsing great paradoxes and twists of language. I heard none of the *oohs* and *aahs* I had expected. The entire class was pond-bottom sludge. Lecture was what I knew. College. This school the Du Ponts built, stone by stone, had teachers from the finest colleges in the country. What we knew from our training in those fine colleges was analysis, how to take a Geography class and break it into countries. How to take a country and break it into statistics. What I didn't know was eighth grade. Second Form.

The bell at the end of the period was spring.

Birds became bodies, and Second Formers scraped chairs on wood floors, slammed notebooks, stuffed books into bags. They slung bookbags on shoulders and ducked by my desk at the front of the room. Almost in the hall, they spoke loud and bumped shoulders and elbows. They had five minutes to find their next class, and I had an hour before Fifth Form English.

As they left, I heard, "Did you hear him?"

I heard, "What is wrong with that kid?"

"Weird" was the thing I heard that could have meant me.

# Song / **Flight**

GEESE ARE DISGUSTING. ST. Tim's is on the flyway, goose poop everywhere. Every evening lines of geese flying low over our heads, and every morning there are green globs all over the lawn. Geese aren't even good fliers, but they are good for explaining to young Misfits of Physics things like aerofoil and parasite, profile, and induced drag. It's easy, really. Air passing over the top of a wing is faster than the air passing below it, causing less pressure above, causing lift. Flapping helps. Sometimes.

When I wasn't inside practicing English, I sometimes went outside to play with Kim when we were little. Tea parties in the pool stopped when I was five, but not flying. I was the pressure below her wings; she was the bird. Carla said she and her brother Doug did the same thing sometimes. Different culture, same culture.

Carla spent a lot of time with her brother in the summer, told me her dad would make Doug work the peach orchards, "make a man of him." As soon as she could get away from her mom and dishes, she found Doug in the trees. A few years older than Carla, he'd be hauling limbs bigger than he was, carrying a tree saw in the other hand. Brother and sister transformed into bug-hunters, and that's where she found her love of bugs. And she told me that sometimes when they couldn't find bugs in the bark or leaves, Doug rolled up his sleeves, made an offering of his flesh to mosquitoes. He got them fat in a second. But he kept flexing. And the bugs popped. Blood bubbles. He got four going at once sometimes, that was, until their dad found them. Carla said their dad could come up really quiet, smack Doug on the ear, topple him. Doug never said a word, though. Tough guy, her big brother.

Doug and Carla were tough. Their dad thought he was so *avant garde* with performance art he sponsored in his gallery, goat blood poured on walls, and the artists all in black. Carla told me about one who smeared blood on her breasts, and that was too much, so she and Doug snuck out. They ran into the fields surrounding the suburban gallery.

She told me they tried goose calls. Doug was better at it. Somehow his throat opened up, and his jaw unbuckled so his voice went hollow.

Then they tried flying. His back flat on the dirt, Doug took off his shoes and lifted up his feet. "Here," he said to her, "lay on my feet."

"You sure?"

"Yeah, I'll lift you."

So she put her belly on his socks. His toes tickled a little, but then she moved forward and he pushed up, and she was in the air.

"Put your arms out."

And she did, like Kim, and she was a goose flying south over the Delaware cornfields, and he made the noises geese make from the back of his throat, and he lifted her higher, way high, and his eyes were right in her eyes, except her body was in the sky. And she leaned a little too far to the left, and his foot slipped out from under her, and wham, gravity, she was on the ground. Her nose was blood and her eyes not seeing for awhile.

Doug kept saying, "I'm sorry, Carla. I'm sorry," and really, it wasn't Doug's fault. She stuck her finger under her upper lip like her dad did, and pretty soon it stopped. There was blood all over her shirt and Doug's shirt and on her face.

"Your turn," she said.

"Not even, I'm too big."

"Are not."

"Am, too."

"Scared?"

On her back she lifted up her legs and her skirt went up and her panties showed, but she felt safe because it was Doug. It's funny the things she told me. He lay his belly on her feet. At first he was heavier than she thought, but pretty soon she got the hang of it. Her feet, she said, might have gone right through him, but his bones stuck. He put out his arms, and she held him up. She couldn't do the goose noise. His eyes were in her eyes, and her eyes were in his eyes, except his body was in the sky. I can see them because we did the same thing, except Kim never lifted me.

Carla is strong that way. She adapts.

It was bugs that drew us together. Flying bugs: mosquitoes, dragonflies, flies. Not too long after she arrived at Tim-Tim's as a Third Former, she was out staring at shrubs. This girl with her curls going all over stood in the middle of shrubs outside of classrooms.

"Excuse me," I said. "You okay?" In between classes, I had a stack of lab books under one arm and walked up to her sideways.

"Better than you," she said. She didn't even look at me, kept bent over looking at a dragonfly, a blue-spotted brown one that stayed still on a big leaf.

"What do you have there?" I said. Two steps closer, and she jumped and turned at the same time, came down in a crouch. Her arms out, her weight low, she was ready to tackle me or run or slap me silly.

"Whoa," I said, "just curious."

"It's gone," she said. "Thanks." And the dragonfly was no longer framed by the green leaf.

"Sorry."

"*Aeshna juncea,*" she said.

"Sedge Darner," I said. And that's when she looked at me.

After that afternoon, we walked many afternoons, all over campus. I told her about how dragonflies move, and how some bugs live in water until a certain age and then fly, and about inertia and entropy and turbulence. She told me the Latin names of everything, about larvae and spiders and how she can see the web shake when a fly feels the spider approach. As a fifteen-year-old, she was the type of scientist I could never be: She was outside doing it. As a Physics teacher, I was inside thinking about the outside.

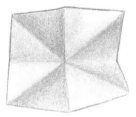

# Taylor / **Small with Him**

THE CHAPEL, ITS SEMICIRCULAR arches intersecting, the power of Romanesque architecture to overwhelm with the sheer weight of stone, is a tomb. Nothing in the contract required me there, but expectations in boarding schools are like ribs; the bones don't show, but they confine every breath. The cornfields surrounding St. Timothy's were mud and motion and spiraling bugs this Sunday in late September. Cut short, the stalks stuck up like a bad crew cut. My feet, out of my shoes, were quiet in the warm mud of the path, and the flocks of geese didn't know I was there. The fog in the morning helped get me into the middle. The geese snuffled while they dug down. In the middle of the brown field with black and white and gray geese, feasting on grain and honking, I was one of them, a member of a flock, following heat and wind and food. Four swans in the far corner of the field, a clump of white interrupted the brown, and the geese didn't mind.

In the middle of the field was a red patch the size of a moving box or a cooler or a sleeping bag. It wasn't the color of mud or cornstalks or geese. If I tried to check it out, the geese would launch.

In the first days after I arrived at St. Timothy's, I made them. I sprinted right into the middle, ran flat out. The birds took off. Their wings pounded, and their voices went up an octave.

That's what happened just then, but not because of me.

The red thing moved. First a hand came out, then it sat up. The geese went mercury. The red thing was little. Its stretch scared them. It was that student, Kyle, the one the other kids called weird, coming out from under a red blanket. His hair was sticking out, and he stretched his arms way above his head, let out a monster yawn.

And after the yawn, he dropped his hands into his lap and turned into a rag doll. After looking around, he looked straight ahead, and my maroon-and-gray windshirt stopped him. He didn't move. The birds were rising and swarming into the next field.

Then, there was light on dark. His white hand moved back and forth, right-left, right-left, in front of the red blanket. Quick little waves. His hand a little curled.

I waved back. Something small in me was small with him.

And I stood there in my windshirt. The whole world went mud and cloud and swirling birds.

Rolling forward on his knees, he put his hands into the mud and lifted himself under the red blanket to his feet. Wrapped in the blanket, he walked toward me, a cocoon walking itself.

I stepped over the crew-cut stalks, and we met in the middle of the field. The geese still frantic and folding into each other. Plenty of fields, corn and soy, and they got mad at this one. This was their field, and this kid was in it.

"What are you doing here?" I said.

"Praying." He said it to the dirt, and then looked up at me. His eyes were blue, the pale blue when clouds burn off the sky.

"Then why aren't you in chapel?"

"Why aren't you in chapel, Ms. Alta?"

"Hey, attendance is mandatory for students," I said.

"Attendance is mandatory for all chapel services." He quoted the school catalog. The blanket made a circle around his head. He repeated my words the way I said them.

"Enough."

"Enough," he said. My sisters and I did this too often growing up. I took a big breath in.

"Look, you're going to get in trouble if you spend the night out here," and he started in, repeating me.

"Cut it out," I said, and I reached for his shoulder. As my hand was about to touch him, he jumped back and toppled over. Landing on his butt, his feet in the air, he almost did a backwards somersault. He's so little and light. He didn't say anything, just rolled on his side and curled in the blanket, his head tucked in, the blanket over him, like he was waiting for something else from me. Maybe a kick. I bet older kids kick him. And his peers, Second Formers. Kids from elementary school. Everybody.

Stepping to his side, I squatted down. "Hey, Kyle," I said. He didn't move under his blanket. He's so little, little like a bug curled up, a curled-up bug a bird would pluck whole and swallow.

"Kyle, what's wrong?"

He didn't say a word.

The fog had already passed over this field and left everything wet. I sat down cross-legged, next to Kyle. He was a red lump in the brown of the field. He didn't whimper or sigh or shiver. Pretty soon my butt got wet, and the backs of my jeans got soaked. Pretty soon the geese settled into the next field, and Kyle and I were the only two people in the world.

"Sorry I tried to touch you," I said.

He didn't move.

"This is a great place. I go here, and I can leave everything behind," I said. Why I was talking to this weird little kid I didn't know, this thirteen-year-old wrapped in a blanket in a middle of a cornfield. "Everybody's always around. There's no place to think. I can think when I'm rowing, but it has to be in the middle of a lake when everyone's working hard, when every-body's pulling so hard the boat feels light. I can really think then."

A beetle crawled from under one of the pieces of cornstalk. It waddled because it was so big. Its brown was so brown, like the middle of eyes.

"But I can't make that happen when I need it," I said. "Today I need to think." The beetle crawled under another pile of grass.

"About what?" I heard from under the blanket. No movement.

"About everything," I said more to the beetle than the boy. "Well, we have a head race in a few weekends in Philadelphia, that's a three-and-half-mile race, and the Schuylkill's where my friend died, and the crew isn't rowing together, yet, like Carla isn't matching Buttons' back, Carla's really strong and all, but the whole boat has to move uniformly, and anyway, I have your papers to grade." I've said too much.

"Don't assign them," Kyle said under the blanket.

Smart kid. "You're funny."

"Am not." The blanket was red over the lump of his head. "Do you like Mr. Jeffers?"

I couldn't see his eyes, if they went clear like he knew noth-ing, or if they smiled like he knew something about Alex and me in the bathroom at the faculty party. Maybe his eyes didn't land on anything, and he was dropping depth charges, seeing what came up.

"Yeah, right," I said. "No."

"Mr. Song?" This kid is younger than I thought.

"I like all the faculty, the men and the women." My stomach felt gray like the sky right after saying that. "But not in the way you're thinking."

"How do you know what I'm thinking?" His voice came out quiet from under the blanket.

"You're right. I don't."

"Mr. Song likes Carla." There was no question in his voice, kind of a statement like a stalk laid out in the cornfield.

"And you know this because . . ."

"Like, at dinner, he looks where she's sitting. They walk around a lot, sometimes at night. And he folds things for her and leaves them in trees."

"He does not." It's weird what this kid sees.

"Does too." He sat up, stripped the blanket off his head. "A week ago, I saw Mr. Song put one in a tree by the boathouse. It was a dinosaur. I got it." His face was red. His eyes were big now, not squinty.

"You took it?"

"Yeah. I didn't think it would get anyone in trouble. I just wanted to see," he said. He looked at me square. His eyes were close together. "Honest, I wouldn't have if I'd known."

"No one's in trouble," I said, "but you said he left it for Carla."

"It was a good guess after you talking about her rowing and uniform motion," he said. Under the blanket something rustled around. Then, a hand reached out, and a tiny dinosaur was in it, the tight folds, the bright colors of paper, almost silk. "I put two and two together."

His palm was a sweaty pillow with brown in the creases. The origami dinosaur looked soft when it should have looked crisp. The purple pattern wasn't distinct against the white background, the white not so white in Kyle's hand.

"Yeah, well, don't jump to conclusions," I said. I leaned toward him and gave the side of his arm a little tap. I wanted to grab the dinosaur, ruin any evidence that Jack and Carla were something. And I didn't know why I wanted to shut the little guy up.

That touch on his arm shocked him again. The dinosaur launched out of his hand. I ducked, and the dinosaur landed in my lap.

"Kyle," I said, "it's okay." And I picked the dinosaur up. "Why are you so jumpy all the time?"

His eyes looked where the dinosaur was. He said, "There's no time left."

"What?"

"You don't have much time when a nuclear bomb goes off, like if you're within two miles of the epicenter!" He was talking really fast, like he was six years old and saw a car crash. "A few seconds," he said. "That's it. Ninety-eight percent of the population will be wiped out. And if you live more than a mile away, you don't stand a chance, either. Death comes slower, and you wish you died quick. First, you go blind from the flash, and then, the wind, and then, the skin starts to drip off."

"Gross."

"Yeah, and listen." His eyes got bigger. "You should know. You gotta be ready. You got to do something." He leaned toward me as if he might grab my windshirt, hang on, shake me.

This kid is weird. But when he talks about death, he's like a sculler at the start line, total focus.

"So," I said, "we're all going to die."

"Not like that. Imagine Mr. Song, with radiation boils all over his body, and if he and Carla got kissy-face, his lips come off on her lips."

Horrible. This kid is creepy.

"Wow, Kyle," I said, "you're out of line. What's going on?"

A breeze came down the crew-cut rows. It didn't move the stalks and grass; it moved strands of Kyle's blond hair, the strands that weren't stuck to his greasy head.

"I'm scared," he said. "I don't want the geese to die."

The flocks of geese in these fields made the ground come alive. Their way of feeding and calling made a hum, something steady. "Why are you talking about death?" His face jerked left like a machine, then jerked right. Without looking at his face, I put the dinosaur on his blanket.

"Why do you like rowing?" he asked. The question was drum roll, cymbal crash, horn.

I didn't answer because I didn't know.

It was something to do with not wanting to feel pain but wanting to know pain. Like wanting to know fire. You light it in front of you, the colors all over the place, the heat all over your skin, but you don't want to burn or anything. I don't know, but I understand him a little more in the middle of that field, with geese all over everywhere, geese getting along with swans, and all of us finding a place to land.

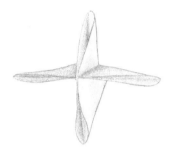

# Song / **Balance**

THE QUEEN OF LATE-TO-CHAPEL stands in the back, by a column in this cave. Tardy. Too many tardy marks gets study hall. Early in the school year Carla's starting her yearly bad-girl accumulation. The bad girl with bad curls.

Rev. Moose sermonizing, already? The cartoons Kim and I watched as kids when we first got to this country, they pop in my head. Charlie Brown, the teacher in the classroom talking, "wah-wah-wah-wah." Can't help it. But today, Moose's words break through.

"In an age in which shuttles carry the first Afro American into space, humans triumph over bigotry and oppression, send our dreams of equality into space, for all cultures everywhere to see and replicate. Guy Bluford Jr., a young man from Philadelphia, went to public high school, received a B.A. from Penn State, then served meritoriously in the Air Force in Vietnam. A month ago, he launched into orbit and history with the Challenger. With this vision, this drive, you, too, can harness your education for the benefit of America and the good of mankind." Rev. Moose looks out over the Tim-Tim blazers and skirts.

"In this age," he continues, "there is also evil. When science is used to create missiles, ones launched by our enemy at innocent Koreans flying home, when the jetliner is struck out of the sky, that, ladies and gentlemen, is a blow to mankind, to progress and pluralism. It is your moral imperative to work for peace, to intervene on behalf of innocents, and to invent for the betterment of men. Use your education for good. Use science to propel men into new realms, where no man has gone before."

Students explode. They giggle, poke each other. A couple flash Spock's "live-long-and-prosper" sign, the fingers split two and two, a V in the middle. Rev. Moose is not usually *au courant*. Popular culture, a good device to hook students. His equation: science + democracy = peace is flawed but plausible. Another equation: science + evil = destruction is right on. Here is a chapel talk for me. Episcopalians always connect to politics. Not so with Catholics. No so with Buddhists.

Our family was very practical. We chose the practices suiting each situation. Church on Sunday, rice and banana offerings on Lunar New Year and Autumn Moon Festival, prayers of healing from our priest, fortune-telling from the shaman. No need to hire wailers when Kim died. As the oldest son, the only son, my wail started the ceremony. The wail came loud, the right opening for the right amount of air. Before the ceremony, many ceremonies. The Korean funeral home in San Diego gave us three days to wash, prepare, dress, collect, and bury her. Not anywhere near our grandfather's fields in Korea, but in a tomb looking east.

Three years ago. Year one I kept picking up the phone to call her. Year two I expected her to call. Year three is this year. Every good boy does not do fine. Bad boy with a girl's bad curls.

In church sometimes Kim and I mixed American games. Rock-paper-scissors for the daily bulletin. Fist-on-palm, fist-on-palm, paper. Fist-on-palm, fist-on-palm, rock. Whoever won got to use the paper for origami. Not very pretty, but practical. I usually won. Give me a piece of paper and twenty minutes, and I can make about anything. Kim sat back on the pew and watched. The priest would wah-wah-wah, and I'd face the opposite direction, kneel on the floor, and lean on the pew, use it as a desk. Squash folds are cake. Each week I won I'd try to fold squash different ways. Start with a waterbomb base. Bring the top flap over, pry open the paper, and flatten to make the squash fold. Before the "This is the Word of the Lord," I'd hold the squash in my hand for Kim to see. She clapped. Every time. Our mother looked down on the pew at the two of us, Prince and Princess of Distraction, and she'd shush us, but I could see something else in her tired eyes. Pride is more than light reflected.

No fortune-teller told us what cells would unfold in Kim's veins. And when she was sick we made offerings to our ancestors, to the sun and moon and Newton. Nothing helped. My father, the chemist in Korea, me in physics, science was in our blood. Mom insisted on candles and incense, on offerings and tithing. There are things that can't be explained. Einstein knew that. How about the exact size of the moon to fit the sun perfectly for eclipses? How about the perfect way that rays of the sun bend in our atmosphere so they do not sear our flesh? Something designed the universe so that we can exist. No amount of science can explain everything. No amount of religion can, either.

How can I explain what exists between Carla and me?

# Taylor / **The Pair**

LOOKING FOR YOU IN the library was easy. Your carrel was third floor, left from the staircase, right at the end of the stacks, left at the corner of the inner courtyard. It was prime real estate, the sunken desks right by the windows, Beach Front, we called it.

"Let's go," I said. I was ten steps away. The people around us looked up.

Your brown hair hung slightly below your shoulders, and your head was bent over history books. A ten-page paper due tomorrow.

You didn't turn around. "I don't hear you," you said.

So I was tiptoe and quiet sign to the girl studying behind you. Stepping on her desk, between her books and notes, I launched over your head, landed on your desk. It didn't break, but the sound was bigger than breaking.

You jumped. Everyone on the Beach Front yelled "Hey" and "Cut it out" and "Grow up." You grabbed my arm and pushed me into the stacks.

"What are you doing?" You tried to be quiet.

"Studying," I said.

"Yeah, right," you said. Too long hair and bangs swooping up like horns, your face was hidden behind glasses too big. You stuck your face in my face like if you got closer to mine, you'd understand.

"Let's go," I said to the glasses and hair.

"Where?" Your hand was still on my arm, thumb and forefinger light on my tricep, the grip through my flannel shirt. My hands took both your shoulders. They filled my hands, the muscle of so much rowing. I turned us in a dance in the library stacks.

"Tell you when we get there." I turned you down the stacks toward the stairs.

My light blue VW wagon started like a lawnmower, pull, pull, turn over. You in your stained sweats, me in my flannel shirt and sweats, we sat there waiting for the engine to warm up. That Sunday morning in April was cold and blue, and the blankets from the back seat were all the heat we had. We wrapped up.

The drive to the lake was away from Mount Greylock, the highest point in Massachusetts, which made you laugh because in Colorado, you lived at a higher elevation than the mountain's peak. Then we passed alongside the Taconic Ridge, which the farmers called the train of elephants, one hill, the mother, touching the next hill, the child. The hills rolled for miles in their slow New England train. We didn't talk. The crocuses in clumps in front of farm houses. Cows standing in a foot of mud. Ice still in the marshes.

No one was at the boathouse. The dock stretched into the blue-black of the lake, turning the green hills of the nearest shore into purple on the surface. I lifted the cinder block to reach the hidden key.

"How did you know where that was?" you said.

"We have ways," I said in my best imitation of Colonel Klink on *Hogan's Heroes*.

The handle of the big bay turned clockwise, kicking the lock open. After we lifted the door up, the smell of wax on the eights was honey around us. The April morning light was a thick yellow line down each hull stacked on the right-hand racks. The smaller shells were on the far left rack. I headed left.

"No way," you said. Standing in the bay put the dock and the lake and the reflection of green behind you.

"Come on. Just because we both row port doesn't mean we can't row a pair." A pair takes a perfect balance of port and starboard. One of us switching sides meant rolling the blade up with a different hand, like writing with a different hand. We could flip.

"Surely you jest." You were taking Shakespeare.

"Hands on." I gave the command. Since you knew I'd carry the shell by myself and smash it if you didn't get there, you ran to the rack.

Once out of the rack, the shell rested on our shoulders while we walked to the dock. Up and over our heads and up, we rolled it down to the waist and down, and down to the water, no splash. We got the oars, tied in, and pushed off the dock.

Stroking was what you were born to do. Your back read like the scriptures you included in notes to me: "Love one another as I have loved you . . . greater love has no man than this, that a man lay down his life for his friends." Your notes were shoreline, evening light, moon. How we talked to each other was stream. This note with this Bible verse was the one I read over and over, memorized, as if its moon shadow would lead me where I wanted to go.

At the catch position, you sat up, your back a V-shape. On command we set the blades and pulled, but we tilted left, then right. I barely got my blade out at the finish of the first stroke, my right hand unsure how to roll up, my left hand unsure what to do with the handle of the oar.

By twenty strokes we were beginning to move together. When I dragged the oar or when I caught water with the tip, you said, "Oh?" like "Are we going in?" But through the dips left and right, your back was sure. Your back was part of something bigger, bigger than the pair, the lake, Mount Greylock in the distance.

"Hey, kiddo," you said, "we're getting it."

"Oh yeah, Olympic trials, next stop," I said. It was hard to talk and row.

We rowed past the cove we used for practicing starts. We rowed past the boys' camp used in the summer. On the other side of the lake, I steered us to a dock.

"Way enough," I said. The angle wasn't right, and we were coming in too fast.

"Hold water," I said. You dug in your blade. We turned into the dock without crashing the bow.

"Nice landing," you said.

"Ready?" I said and put one foot up to stand on the dock.

"For what?"

"Your turn."

"*Nyet.*" You were taking Russian, too.

"*Oui, si,*" I said, "whatever." I knelt down to hold the pair off the dock.

With one foot under, you stood up on the dock. You said, "Okay, you asked for it." One step to get behind me, one step to bend down, the shove was not too hard, but enough to throw me off balance.

The way a girl learns to dive, kneeling at the edge of a pool, pointing her alligator arms at the blue, then rolling, I rolled far enough out to miss the pair. The water was ice. It was blue slivers in my lungs. I came up yelling.

Hard laughs made you hold your thighs. I kicked up from the water, used my arm as a bat, and batted the water to cover you with spray. Drenched, your hair was no longer horns; glasses dripping, you took them off and put them on the seat in the pair.

"You're in big trouble now," you said. Your knees came up into a cannon ball. I had enough time to take two strokes to the dock, so when you came up, I was sitting on the dock.

"You brat," you said when you saw me waiting.

You gave me your hand to get help out of the water. Even with the cold of too-cold water, your skin held its tan from summers out west, in the Canyonlands, in the Grand Tetons, the desert. The water rushed down the T-shirt, rounding your breasts.

You stepped into my arms. The hug was water to water.

"There," you said, "in case you weren't wet enough." Stepping back and shaking your hair in my face, you wanted to be double-sure. I still felt the press of you on me.

A breeze turned our bodies to ice. We ducked down and stretched out on the warm planks of the dock and lay on our backs like we might make snow angels, with feet apart and arms away from our sides. But it was April, and the sun felt new.

Maybe it was a draft or a leaf. It was something covering my hand. Maybe a shadow. That something was your hand covering mine. I didn't move my hand in case your hand was a butterfly and flew away.

"Our Father," you said, "who art in heaven." Your words were slow and sure.

My eyes were the April sky. I was supposed to join in, but my mother was the last person I prayed with and back then I was four and held her hand at Mass.

"Hallowed be thy name," I said. The words were a tape recording, lines rehearsed. The words were goose bumps. But I warmed into the words.

We said the Lord's Prayer on a dock on the lake, a long ways away from Mount Greylock. The words were different with you lying next to me, praying together in wet T-shirts. Your hand on my hand, our words together, I let the sun into a place in my chest.

That place was the place for forever.

"For Thine is the kingdom and the power and the glory, now and forever," you said, but I didn't. That part wasn't the Catholic part, so I stopped.

"Amen," you said.

"Amen," I said.

This was the closest to forever I had come. The place in my chest where the sun had reached was a place that was now and always. We were bigger than this lake, our families, Mount Greylock in the distance.

"It's cold," you said, and you sat up. Your eyelashes did that thing they do: They made stars.

"Okay, then," I said and sat up, hugging my knees to my chest.

"Ready to row bow?" I said.

You grabbed your glasses, and I held the shell for you. We pushed off the dock. Never had you rowed behind me. Never had I stroked. We both sat in new seats.

It wasn't until the middle of the lake that we began to work together. Our blades at the catch, our feet pushing off, our hands nearly the same height, we found the rhythm we needed.

"You know what?" I said. The words sounded too loud over the slap of oars on water.

"I'm bad at bow?"

"Not bad."

"What?"

"I can't say it," I said.

"Breathe," you said.

The words I wanted to say were not on this lake. They were not passed in church through a mother's hand to a daughter's. The words were not a prayer. The words I wanted were about wanting, the opening in a chest, the loneliness.

"I love," I said. The oars pulled through the water. "This." My skin under the wet shirt shivered.

"I know, Taylor," you said, "I know what you mean." Your voice was sure, like flat water and a cox'n and all the crew behind you. But you didn't know.

The slap of the oars, the wheels of the seats up the slide, the breeze. In my chest there was a forever place. In all the world, there was no love bigger than this lake, us two, and the highest mountain in Massachusetts.

# Song / **Specimen**

THE NIGHT WHEN CARLA snuck into the dorm when only the Second Formers and jocks were in their rooms, I had turned out my light by my rocking chair, and Carla was wrapped in my blanket on the couch. Long after curfew, few sounds down the hall. But then from the rat maze of cubbies where the Second Formers live, I heard a mewing, like kittens, too much air through too little throat. Hungry, hurt kittens, and when I pulled back the curtain and took one step inside, Kyle was curled up on the foot of his bed. "Kyle," I said, "what's wrong?" He was no longer the Light Brigade, no longer conquering lands for the British Empire. The mewing grew rapid and loud. If other boys heard, they kept quiet.

"Talk to me, Young Sir," I said, but he said nothing. At the foot of his bed, curled up and crying, he looked feral, a specimen removed by force.

Behind me the curtain moved, and Carla stood in the space where I pushed the curtain back, and Kyle stopped. Carla watched and said nothing. Whatever she had been through was through with her. I said nothing.

Kyle started to snore, pretending to snore, louder than crying, and when I looked back at the space in the curtain, no Carla. Who knows what Kyle saw.

# Taylor / **Birch Bark**

AT SIXTEEN, FIFTH FORMERS are birch trees, bending any way the wind blows, bending to get out of breaking. When I say the ghost is real, they nod. When I say the ghost is a malevolent device of Hamlet's psyche to cope with grief, they nod. It wasn't until I showed the Olivier movie that they had shape.

Shannon McDaniel said, "Look at his face."

Gerry Frankel said, "Yeah, he's so expressive."

Then Donny Zurkus said, "What a faggot."

It took me a few steps to get to the light switch. Everyone winced and went overdramatic: "Ouch." Then I walked right into the movie, Sir Laurence Olivier moving on my body, the black and white images on my button-down shirt. I walked from the screen into the cone of light, found the stop button, and the projector clicked, and the movie film drooped slack, the Fifth Formers shouting, "Hey, what happened?"

"Donny," I said, "what did you say?"

I stood in front of his desk, his legs sticking out from under it. His head almost touching the backrest, he was so far slumped in the chair.

He brought his feet under him and slid his body up the chair. With his forearms flat on the desktop, his shoulders flexed, he could stand at any second. If he stood, we would look into each other's eyes. He was my height, but thinner, raw, all muscle. The only things holding him back were the desk and his grade.

"I said he looks homosexual." His cut jawline, hair clipped, his face all angles, turned flat at me. His eyes were not birch bark.

"And what," I said, "does homosexual look like?" My voice was metal, my heart liquid.

"You know," he said, "like that." He pointed at the screen. "Lips all pooched out, wrists bent, all floozy," he said. And he bent his wrist, said the words, lisping the *S*s in *wrists*. A couple of boys near him turned in their seats away from Donny, and a few boys bent their wrists and touched their eyebrows with light fingers. The girls' laughter was high and icy.

"You don't know your history, do you?" I said.

"I got an A in it."

"Then you must know he married Vivien Leigh." I was river around stone.

"So?"

His chin lifted, and I could see the muscle tighten by his jawbone. We looked at each other, and in his eyes, he was hiding something, like a small boy hiding a jackknife he's not supposed to use. He was trying not to be scared, trying not to poke fun.

"So," I said, "it's unlikely he was a faggot, especially since a faggot is a piece of wood." The girls giggled. The boys looked at Donny.

"I know what a faggot is," he said.

I took a step toward him. "Then," I said, "you know that derogatory terms will not be tolerated in this classroom." I stopped before his desk. I stopped before my hand could do anything but say, "Stop." The muscle by his jawbone flexed, released, flexed, released, and I turned and walked back to the movie projector. The projector stuttered, and the film caught in the sprockets. When I went back to my seat, the film made

Olivier walk on my back.

No one said a word. There were no squeaking desks, no sighs, nothing but birch bark faces in the light of the screen, nothing but film clicking through sprockets.

I was still river.

When you and I watched the French film, *Ménage à Trois*, at the movie house in our college town, where they showed the artsy films in the early eighties, I was waterfall in the dark. You were sitting next to me, snug in your ski jacket, the one with the white stripe that ran up your left across your shoulders then down your right on a blue background. When the two women made love on the screen, I wanted to put my hand in front of your eyes. The movie light washed out the color of your face. Shouting "Fire!" would have made everyone run. If only you were someplace else. But you were there, and I was on the screen. I was kissing a woman and you were watching and everything was wrong.

Walking back along Spring Street after the movie, we didn't say anything. We both watched our boots on the icy path, the narrow part slick and gray from other people walking. We went to my room, my room in Kruger Hall. When we walked in, I apologized for the mess as I always did when we walked in my room.

You said, "It's fine. It's you."

I said, "It's not fine."

You tipped your head up from where you were sitting on my unmade bed. I couldn't sit by you. I couldn't sit. Your brown eyes with those little flecks were as big as eyes on a movie screen.

"I'm not fine. You didn't like the movie, did you?"

"Of course not. Did you?" You leaned forward, and your eyes got narrow like they were trying to see in the dark. In the dark, afraid of the dark, I was walking blind in the mess of my room.

"No, no, it was gross," I said. My head moved back and forth, a searchlight.

What if I'm afraid of the dark, but I walk into a dark room to see that there's nothing there? It's one thing to walk in and out, and nothing happens. It's another thing to have someone I care about be there, hiding, and jump out at me. What if the thing I fear comes true?

"Why did we go to that movie?" you asked. You put your hands between your thighs, squeezed your shoulders together.

"Because," I walked toward the door. I turned back, "Because the film is me." I couldn't stop. My arms at my side, I bent over you as I spoke. "I'm one of them. Homosexual." My head above your head, my body before you. "If you can't handle that film, you can't handle me."

My voice was walking into a dark room without turning on the light.

You said nothing.

Your eyes were not trying to look in the dark any more. The part in your brown hair was a clear white line. Your hands came out from between your legs. You stood up and said nothing. You turned toward the door and said nothing. Three steps. The white stripe on the back of your jacket, a U upside down. The door closed.

Boo.

And Hamlet stabbed Polonius on the screen at the front of the classroom, and the Fifth Formers said, "Gross!" Donny said nothing.

"Okay," I said. "I don't want to give all of it away." Olivier, his lithe body, moved on me until I reached the projector and shut it off. Lights on, the Fifth Formers stretched their arms above their heads.

"Miss Alta," Rambo said, "is the ghost really evil? I mean, if he is Hamlet Senior, wouldn't he protect Hamlet Junior?"

From the front row, Gerry said, "Not necessarily. What if he just wants revenge?"

"He could do that without Hamlet," Donny said. "He could get the other minions to do his dirty work for him." Donny leaned on his forearms.

Rambo said, "But who else would have access to Gertrude's chambers?" She looked at Donny, then at Gerry, then at me.

"Maybe Ophelia. She's wacko. She'd believe anything," Donny said.

"Interesting," I said. Leaning back against the desk at the front of the room, I crossed my legs at the ankle. "Hell hath no fury like a woman scorned. Is she crazy, or pissed off?"

The Fifth Formers shifted in their seats. Teachers weren't supposed to say "pissed off."

"There's nothing like a girl with a grudge," Frank said. He sat in the third row usually with his arms crossed over his chest, his eyes down at the desk. The boys' laughter was low, foggy.

"Seems to me there's nothing like King Hamlet coming back from the grave," I said. "I'd say he has a grudge." My weight shifted to my feet. I pushed off from the desk and stood before them.

The girls said, "Gotcha."

"Freud would interpret this a different way," I said. "I know you read *Oedipus* in Second Form, so you know about the marrying-the-mom-and-killing-the-dad thing. Maybe Prince Hamlet secretly wanted Gertrude, and he feels so guilty that the ghost is his subconscious haunting him."

Donny's desk smacked the floor. "No way, Miss Alta. King Hamlet isn't coming back to kill Prince Hamlet. He's coming back to kill Claudius." Donny's desk was a gate keeping him in.

"Donny, you haven't read the ending yet. And maybe the subconscious is more powerful than you think. Maybe Hamlet feels so guilty for wanting his mother that part of him wanted his father dead. This is Freud talking, remember?" I looked from Donny to Gerry to Rambo to the rest.

"I still say that's crazy," Donny said. "Freud was a freak." Donny crossed his arms and slumped back in his chair. A little boy practicing with a jackknife.

"Freud is one way of looking at things."

All at once the students leaned over to pick books off the floor, close their books on the desks, stuff their book bags. When dismissed, the Fifth Formers turned sideways to fit around the projector in the aisle, their one arm on the backpack strap, the other arm out almost rodeo-rider style for balance. They passed me in pairs, the girls touching forearms with their girlfriends, the boys turning their heads to the boy behind them so their necks flashed at me as they passed single file through the classroom door.

Rambo said as she passed me, "See you later, Coach."

Before class, before rowing on the lake alone, I woke up crying.

In the dream we were in college, but you were about to die. In the dream we both knew. We were in Kruger Hall, on my bed, your back against the headboard. I was leaning on one elbow at your feet. You told me about a new guy you liked, not Mark, since I knew Mark was already seeing someone else. I didn't know if you knew; that secret was knotting my stomach up. Your new guy's name was Richard, curly red hair, studying to be a minister, same Episcopalian as your Episcopalian. And I encouraged you to see him, even though we both knew you were going to die.

The knotting of my stomach turned tighter, and I curled into a ball, laid my cheek on your shin, the jeans soft on my cheek. My other hand fit around your other shin.

I said, "You know, it just isn't fair." And the knot cinched inside me, and my knees contracted toward my chest.

I never finished the sentence. I never said, "It isn't fair that you're going to die."

Books closed and stacked, stuffed into my briefcase, I zipped the bag. The desks in the room were bigger without students trapped in them. Gertrude's voice, not Hamlet's, lingered in the classroom.

"All that lives must die, passing through nature to eternity." Is it natural to have no body, to die for no good reason?

The movement in the halls was the rapids of students changing class.

# Song / **Torch**

A KOREAN GIRL IS a living paradox. Two things at once seemingly contradictory, but apparently not. Hard and determined to achieve, soft and eager to fit in. Closed to distraction, open to culture. Flowering, wilting.

Carla is little contradiction. She is singular in her conviction. American girls exceed their bounds. In the letters Carla wrote me she told me she could feel wherever I was, what chair I was sitting in. She wrote that she was that chair, could feel my legs on her legs. Her imagination was scary detailed: the hairs on my legs soft, my butt going onto her, the curve of her lap, a perfect fit. She imagined so much heat between her lap and my butt, we were both slick. I almost slid off her, my chair. Her letters over the summer held no ambiguity, no contradiction. I cannot imagine my sister imagining such a thing.

Never write things down. Could be used against you.

Five things needed for class. Associate one thing with each finger. Thumb is bowl. Index finger is cold can. Third finger, the hand that's needed for the demonstration. Fourth, the mouth that's needed. Fifth, soap with glycerin. Bowl, can, hand, mouth, soap. Move the fingers as I walk down the hall to the lab, and I won't forget.

"Mr. Song, Mr. Song," Tommy Underwood yelling. "Come quick." His shirt untucked, his hair every which way. What a crop of Second Formers.

The sound of something, air, a torch, the compression of gas through small opening, loud, getting louder. Tommy opens the door to the lab. The metal stands on the table, little crosses. The hoses for gas. The beakers and dishes and stink of formaldehyde. Donny Zurkus and his minions. They pinned Kyle to a lab table, a frog.

Safety goggles across Donny's face. Blowtorch in hand. They rigged something up. Blowtorch to glass funnel, glass funnel to stand, object in funnel, dripping, funnel to tube to Kyle's ear. He's spread out on his back. Five kids pinning him.

"Boys," I say. Two kids holding his legs down, they look up.

"Zurkus," I say, and I walk up behind Donny, grab both his shoulders. Clammy in his dress shirt, big muscle boy. Don't spin, don't aim that blow torch somewhere else. I hold him in place. His head pops up. Busted.

"What the hell?" Donny says. He turns to look over his shoulder, but he can't see me right behind him. Between my hands, his body twists. You're not going anywhere, Mr. Shit.

"Zurkus. Turn the torch off."

"But we're working." His voice louder than the torch. He looks at the other boys. They look at the table. Kyle is laid out on the slab, pinned, but no hands pin him.

Donny Zurkus turns the knob on the blowtorch, flame off. I let go of his shoulders. He takes his goggles off. I about flatten him.

"Mr. Zurkus," I say, "What do you think you're doing?"

"English. You know *Hamlet*?"

"Don't give me that."

"Honest. You know, the part where Claudius kills Hamlet Senior? No way you can kill somebody through the ear like that. We were checking the real world implications, you know?" He looks at his minions. The boys in his minion look down. Kyle doesn't move.

Donny and the lingo. Admissions tours. Brochures. Tim-Tim's ambassador.

"We were only using wax. See?" And Donny gestures with the blunt end of the blow torch, now turned off, to the glass funnel with wax melting in it.

Nothing moves, and everything else is in the shelves along two walls, the Pyrex measuring glasses, the thermometers, Petri dishes, all the tubes and wire and balls. Microscopes on their stands.

"Bull, Mr. Zurkus," I say.

"But it's true, Mr. Song," Donny says. "It's not fair. You're not giving us a chance." His voice gets girly.

"Report to the headmaster, all of you."

"I'll miss practice."

"Mr. Zurkus, you may miss many things. Go." I look at Kyle. Safety goggles slide across the table. Donny Muscle-Boy with Big Moves. Door swings open. He probably flips me the bird. The other boys go out the door after him.

Good riddance.

Inventory of the shelves. Still everything looks in its place. I have to clean this pigsty. Mr. Lazy Song. Mr. Disorganized. Not like Kim.

We never had to share a room, not like most FOB kids. Old Korean clothes, cramped American quarters. Our parents worked hard to get a real house. My room, messy with books. Kim's room, dolls in boxes, matching outfits. Pink bed made perfect.

When she started to bleed, got the purpura all over after falling, playing at foursquare, when she didn't stop bleeding, I folded her clothes for her, made stacks in her drawers. Older brother. Nothing much I could do.

Kyle still stretched on the table. The same position. His face tipped away from me. His khakis dirty. His tie pulled tight to the side. One flap of his collar up. He could be a rag doll, nothing Kim would play with. Too dirty.

"Mr. Harney," I say, "time to go." The kid must be shaken. No chance against the others. Five Fifth Formers pinning him down. Almost torched his grease for hair.

"Okay, Mr. Harney, you can get up now," but he doesn't move. Inertia. He's always pale, so this is nothing new. But he's extra white. Better check.

I step up to the table, and the cold top presses against my waist. Black stone, the best Du Ponts could get for scholar boys taking lab science. Du Ponts know labs. These labs made perfect once Sam Omura graduated. Sam the wonder scientist, the best Tim-Tim's produced. My hand goes for Kyle's forehead.

"Kyle," I say. My hand two inches from his forehead.

His eyes open, and my hand catches his forehead as he jumps. He starts up with a scream. A whole lung full of air shoved out his throat. It's animal. Sweaty skin, I press his head down with my hand. I keep his head down. His head about to explode under my hand.

"Kyle," I say in the middle of his scream. "Kyle, it's okay," and I have to get loud. His back straight, his legs kick out, bucking on the lab table.

Three screams, and he stops.

He falls back on the lab table, flattens. This time his face turns toward me to look, really look. His frog eyes open. He could be in formaldehyde.

"Come on, Kyle," I say. That scream at any moment. "Time to see the nurse." Kyle drags his torso up. An old man. Shifts his legs to the table's edge. Waits. "As if," Carla might say, "as if a nurse can fix him." His legs dangle. A little boy. His feet not even close to the ground. He leans forward, his hands on the edge, his arms straight.

Kim and I, we sat at the edge of the pool, feet in the water. I threw stuff in the pool. She told me not to, Dad would get mad. Sometimes Americans thought we were twins, not two years apart. She caught on to English much quicker than I did. She swam in the pool more than I did, and when she got sick, I felt guilty for that summer I was so jealous of her.

"Kyle, let's go," I say. Third law. This kid can't be touched without touching. He looks down at his feet dangling, and he says nothing, makes no funny noises. What if there were a way to have motion without resistance, a perfect surface on which an object could be propelled? What if there were no drag or imbalance? What if kids could grow that way?

# Taylor / **Ski Jacket**

BUTTONS AND CARLA CAME and got me. They came to my table at dinner, the table with ten students and Jack Song. They were dressed more for practice than dinner, gray hooded sweatshirts and sweatpants, running shoes. The two girls knelt down beside me. Their breath was strange. They told me I had a phone call. They had to have been in my apartment to know I had a phone call. In my apartment. They thought the call had to do with my friend.

I ran.

In my skirt, the one that doesn't let me run, I ran away from the mural with all the boys looking the same, and all the students in the dining hall looking.

The distance from the main building to my apartment was less than a race, maybe 500 meters, and my skirt almost ripped when I ran.

The receiver was upside down on my desk, the lights on in my place. The screen door slammed when I picked up the phone.

"Hello?"

Every time the phone rings, I think it's you. I think you might say, "Just kidding," or "I'm a covert agent, operating in the Soviet Union." I keep thinking someone on the phone will tell me you're fine.

"Taylor?" Your mother's voice was long and smooth.

"Yes, ma'am." My stomach was hollow.

"They found her jacket, Taylor, a mile downstream. With her wallet." Your mother's voice was Colorado-long vowels. Her voice was a lot older than it was two weeks ago.

"Her ski jacket, the blue one with the stripe?"

"Yes, her jacket and wallet. That's it." Your mother's voice was an echo.

"Nothing else?" My stomach was a drop of water falling.

"No, honey, nothing else. But I want to ask you something about that, Taylor."

"Ma'am?"

"You have to be honest with me about this."

My stomach filled with ripples, and I thought about Mark cheating on you, and other things I hadn't told. Maybe your mother knew that I loved you more than a friend loves a friend. Maybe she didn't want me at the memorial. Maybe she thought I was bad for you.

"Taylor, we need someone there who can identify her," she said, "whenever they find her body. We would if we could, but we're in Colorado Springs." Her voice was a wind in a canyon, a sound tight and soft at the same time.

There was a white mass floating in the pool in my stomach. It was bloated, and it smelled. The bile built in me.

"Yes," I said.

"You'll do it? Good girl. I told her father you'd do it."

"Okay."

"We'll talk soon. I'll let you know if there's anything else," and then the phone line clicked. The sound after it was gray.

My skirt ripped on the way to my bathroom. My knees landed on linoleum. The bloated thing in my stomach burned on the way up my throat, out my mouth, my nose.

After the sink and water on my face, the hand towel to my nose and spitting, the cold of the bathroom linoleum against my calves, the cold of the bathtub against the blouse on my back felt iceberg. I wanted ice, to fall into blue and cold and sleep.

My legs stretched out in front of me, I ripped the rest of my skirt off. The rip echoed in the bathroom.

It's been twelve days since your motor cut out. That's when the straps that were supposed to save you, hanging from the chain link fence across the Schuylkill River, got caught in the motor of your launch, the launch you borrowed from the university to coach the girls, to coach them away from danger. Those straps hanging down from the chain link fence that spans the Schuylkill were there for scullers to grab and tie to, but since the water was so high, the straps hung farther in the water, perfect for snagging and stalling a motor. That's when you panicked after you pulled and pulled and pulled the motor cord. You jumped into the river, only 750 meters from the falls in the river, the big falls that created a turbine all year long. You went over the falls. The girls in your crew watching from the dock, watching you who knew how to tend the girls in boarding school from the minute you stepped on the campus. They called you Coach, they called you Miss, and the names they used were the right ones. The rowers you tended didn't see you come up. That's what they told the reporters. That's what everyone read. So it must be true.

Your mom told me you were wearing your ski jacket. It must have been heavy in the water. It was a good coat, warm enough for the cold two weeks ago in Philadelphia. It wasn't supposed to be cold in September, but wind can change everything.

That jacket, midnight blue with a white stripe up one arm, across the shoulders, back down the other arm, stood out. Across the freshman quad, across the snow between the student union and the library, I could spot you all four years we went to college together.

It was your jacket they found a mile downstream, not you.

On the bathroom floor, sitting like a schoolgirl, legs together, hands folded in my lap, my back straight against the porcelain tub, my legs in stockings were as brown and unnatural as my mother's.

"Stockings were invented by men," my mother said in a rare moment to my sisters and me. "They are hideous devices to keep women from running away." My mother never ran away. When my father moved out, she divorced but stayed "married in the eyes of God." She wore stockings and heels and girdles and red, red lipstick and rouge and everything I knew nothing about. When I told her I wanted to row, she told me the last thing I needed was more muscle on my shoulders and back. When I told her you died, she said she wished I never rowed.

My long brown legs, my penny loafers upright, my calves soaking the cold from the linoleum floor, I didn't get up when the door opened.

"Miss Alta?" Buttons said.

"Come out, come out, wherever you are," Carla said.

"Be right there." I rolled toward the toilet on my knees. My legs touched stocking to stocking and sounded like zippers as I got up. My ripped skirt stayed on the floor. Walking in pantyhose from bathroom to bedroom, the air between my legs, the swish friction of stockings, I was naked. From the entryway outside my bedroom the students couldn't see me.

"Miss Alta, you okay?" Buttons asked.

"Just a minute." My clothes all over the floor, I put sweats over the stockings, and my legs were prickly. With blouse over sweats and stockings in penny loafers, I walked out of my bedroom.

"Nice outfit," Carla said. "Dress code à la Alta." She was curl.

The taste of vomit, the bloated body that used to be you, the phone answered in my apartment, all went red inside me, and I couldn't stop.

"Carla, what were you doing in my apartment? What were you and Buttons doing?" I stepped toward the girls.

Carla kept her face flat and shiny, but raised her eyebrows.

Then, she smiled.

"You said we could?"

"I said you could skip dinner and answer my phone?"

"Yup," she said. She spread her legs to make a solid base, put her hands behind her back, like she could take a blow and keep standing. Buttons' eyes were down.

"What?"

"You said we could come see you anytime. We came to see you. You just weren't here." Her curls fell forward in her face, so her hand pushed them back behind her ear.

"So you waltzed into my apartment? What else did you do?" I hadn't looked in my living room, in my kitchen. My legs rubbed nylon against sweats when I walked into the living room. No beer cans. No ash trays. No mess besides my own.

"Out," I said before I turned around.

"Out," I said when I turned around.

Buttons twisted from her hips and caught her balance with a hand on the wall. Then she reached the doorknob, and pulled open the door. She didn't look back. She was out the door when she said, "Sorry, Miss Alta." The screen door slammed behind her.

Carla didn't move.

Carla squared her shoulders to me.

"You look so cute when you're mad," she said.

In two steps I reached her shoulders, dug my fingers into her upper arms and turned her toward the door. Her shoulders were muscle. Her height almost my height. She twisted back. Her face was swinging toward my face, her curls almost in my face, and the smell of scotch in my eyes.

"Get out," I said. "Now." I pushed her toward the door, but her body went lead. "Carla, get the fuck out of here." My voice went high, like brakes on a train.

"Bad phone call?" she said. She covered one of my hands on her shoulder with her hand. I pulled back. "Bad day?"

"Carla, you reek. Don't make this hard. Get out." She didn't move.

Carla's back to me, I turned to the wall, walked up to it so I could rest my forehead on the white paint. My eyes closed. The wall didn't smell. There was no sound, only the cool, hard wall on my forehead.

Carla started talking soft like someone telling a story at bedtime.

"That look you just gave me, it was like my dad. Just like it. My dad hated bugs. More than anything he hated the bugs in the peach orchards. He inherited those. Between petal fall and shuck fall, we walked the trees, checking for bugs, all kinds: stink bugs, oriental fruit moths, Japanese beetles, green June beetles, and western flower thrips." She moved closer to me. My forehead was rolling on the cool white wall. What I wanted was to be paint, to be white on a white wall.

"Dad had his beating tray, and we pounded branches. He was sure our neighbors' soybean fields were a breeding ground. My dad hated bugs." All I could see was your jacket and its white stripe.

"I loved them. The best are green stink bugs. They have this shield for their body with little pointy heads, and they're like emerald. They shine." I turned my head toward Carla, leaned my shoulder into the wall. She made a point with the tips of her fingers over the top of her head, like a rooftop, like she was a giant girl sitting under a miniature roof. Then, she leaned her shoulder into the wall, and we were two feet apart facing each other.

"One time I'm nine maybe, and it's June. My brother, Doug, sleeps in. He's a teenager and way into cars, not bugs. That morning the ground smelled like wet grass, you know? Dad and his red-and-black flannel shirt.

"'Come on,' Dad says. 'If you're going to come, come on.' He goes out the screen door without me.

"'Wait, Daddy,' I say. His black, curly hair bounces away from me." I see Carla now, not your jacket, little Carla with curls like her dad's.

"My yellow rubber boots make sounds when my feet finally

go in like squeak, squeak. Running in rubber boots is hard, you know, but I run to catch up with my dad. His legs are long. The canvas beating tray is in one hand and a mallet's in the other. I run and fall behind, run and fall behind. He keeps going. I'm little. The only reason I catch up is that he has to catch his breath. He's a wheezer." Little Carla with long curls bouncing up and down, running to catch up to her big dad.

"The dirt along the road is red. We walk along the orchard, the trees starting to bud out, the peaches about so long." She held up her hand, her thumb and index finger open to an inch or two.

"Really cute. About halfway, he turns and walks in about three trees. To kneel down really close to the tree, he clears a place. Branches stick out. Where my mom cut his hair around his ears is white compared to the rest of him." She squinted and looked away.

"'Carla,' he says, 'come here, hold the tray.' He puts the canvas beating tray under the lowest branches of the tree. Dad uses a painting he doesn't like, flips it over and uses the backside for a tray. It's an awesome bug catcher." She's little in the story, in this room where the phone rang and she answered it and came to the dining hall and got me.

"'No matter what falls,' he says, 'hold tight.' He looks at me with the look that says, 'I mean it.' It was kind of like the look you gave me just now.

"The grass doesn't feel good under my knees, so I push my ankles out and sit back on my boots. But then I can't hold the tray very well. I sit back up on my knees and lean on two sides of the tray. I hear his thick breathing. His shoulders go up and down even when he's kneeling still.

"Dad takes a branch in one hand and raises the rubber mallet with the other. 'Ready?' he says. He gives me that look again." She reached out with one hand as if holding the branch, and used an imaginary hammer with the other.

She looked at me as if I were little Carla in the story, as if she were her dad.

"He whacks it three times. Two bugs go *plop, plop* on the canvas. Nothing else drops except a couple of leaves.

"I bring the tray up. The bugs are slow and emerald. The light on their shields makes them glow. I bring my face close to the tray so I can see them. 'Two,' I say.

"'Just two,' he says. 'Are you sure?' He never believes me.

"'See?' I say. With a hand on both sides of the tray, I lift it up, but he's bending down at the same exact time. *Bam!* goes the tray, and the two bugs fly up in the air." She's pantomiming the whole thing, and I'm there in the orchard on my knees with her.

"'Damn it,' Dad says, 'damn it to hell.' And he takes the side of the tray, and he shoves it, and his arm catches my head, and I fall and roll over. I'm like a potato bug and curl up.

"'Look what you've done,' he says. I look. The beating tray is red and dirty.

"'I didn't do it, Daddy,' I say. And I'm still on the ground.

"He turns, and his face is red, red like stoplights. 'What did you say?'

"'Your hand hit it.'

Dad's head blocks out the sky. "'Don't you talk back to me,' he says, 'ever.' He puts one hand on my shoulder and rolls me into the dirt. He pushes my shoulder down hard. My cheek scratches against the grass and dirt." She rolls her cheek into the wall as if the wall were the ground.

"'Yeah,' I say. And my cheek is smooshed." Her mouth flattens against the wall.

"'Say yes,' he says. His big hand presses my shoulder into my ear. Dirt and sticks press hard into my ear and cheek.

"I say, like, nothing. He stands up. But then, he leans down, and his hands move fast. One hand goes between my legs, pushing my legs open, his whole hand on my butt, and one hand grabs my shoulder, and my body goes up in the air. Like, really fast.

"'Get up,' he says. I go up above his head, and stay there for a second, like he's thinking whether to throw me, and then I go down, and he puts me on my feet. His eyes are big holes. The place between my legs stays achy. His voice is like thunder.

"We do it again. Tree after tree. Lean down, take a branch, *whack, whack*. We find bugs. Green, beautiful bugs. Each time we pound the branches, he says, 'Damn it, damn it to hell' like there shouldn't be any bugs, like I have done it wrong."

Before me was a little girl. Before me was a girl shaped by a mean parent. It took a few moments for Carla to return to my apartment. It took seconds for me to remember you. I can't handle all the meanness, all the want.

"I'm sorry, Carla," I say, "you have to go."

The step she takes back looks as though I hit her with the beating tray. She turns on one foot and reaches the door. The sucking sound of the door opening came before the screen door slammed.

The sound after the slam came from the place at the top of the throat, but deep. It started little, like a kitten cry, and I covered my mouth with the palm of my hand. My other hand covered my mouth, too.

The bottle Alex had brought me to celebrate the first day of classes, to apologize for being a jerk the first practice, was unopened in the cupboard over the sink. The whiskey was still the only thing in the cupboard. Carla and Buttons hadn't gotten it. The scotch on Carla's breath came from somewhere else.

The corner of the whiskey bottle fit well in my hand, the glass cool in my fingers. I twisted off the cap. The smell was spicy, and I almost sneezed. My glasses were juice glasses from the dining hall, the little ones that fit inside the green squares of the dishwasher trays. I tipped the liquor down my throat. The Jack Daniel's was fire down my throat, and I tried to spit what I could into the kitchen sink.

But it spread. The next glass didn't burn so much. And the next tasted great.

And after the next, I called you at the boarding school where you taught, but the phone rang and rang.

# Song / **Pressure in Contained Area**

THE HALL TO HIS office reeks. His smell happens way before he happens. Wyatt White, Mr. Head Honcho and his damn pipe.

"Mr. Song, thank you for joining us," Wyatt White says. Big voice. Puts his pipe in a tray on his big mahogany desk. The leather armchair gives Donny Zurkus a stage facing the headmaster. King of the Bullies Zurkus.

"I'm glad you asked." I can do polite. I can do rude better.

"Mr. Zurkus was telling us about his English experiment, weren't you, Donny?"

"Yes, sir," Donny says. Mr. Bully transforms into Mr. Goodness, smiling deferentially, maintaining eye contact. Gag me.

"Go on."

Facing Wyatt White, two leather wingback chairs. The kind with studs down the arms, the kind I see only in school administration offices. Persian rug. Dark built-in bookcases. Pressure in this office builds at an exponential rate.

"Yeah, so consequently," Donny says, "we figured there's no way someone could die by pouring something in his ear, you know? Unless it was acid or something. But that's not what Shakespeare said."

Wyatt nodded. His elbows on his desk, his hands together, big fingers touching each other.

"Just curious about the reality of it," Donny says. Like this is a good thing. Like Wyatt White might reward him. There is no end to the shallowness of youth.

"Give me a break," I say. Donny and Wyatt are vectors at forty-five degree angles from me. Connect the three bodies, and you have isosceles. The arrows are pointing toward me. Wyatt's eyes are packed with nothing, and Donny's are packed with shit. Layers of shit compressed in his dark eyes. Too many times Donny has gotten away with his big-man antics, Mr. Muscle Mean, because teachers are afraid of his donor dad, the big money the big man brings. Too much. Bad-Boy Zurkus has done too much.

"Mr. Song," Wyatt says, "let the boy explain." Wyatt's neck is red. Back to my corner. Maybe he's playing Donny. Back, back away from the bully, everyone entitled to fairness, a hearing. My eye.

In five years at St. Timothy's I've never seen a student more raw. Kyle, Mr. Embryo.

One hundred yards beyond the windows behind Mr. Headmaster-with-Oral-Fixation is the lake. Practice time. Carla. Perfect sport for her. Not much drag on a rowing shell, almost all that work converted to uniform motion, balanced energy.

In five years at St. Timothy's, I've spent three years bumping into Carla after crew practice. Not since the couch. Folded a dinosaur for her after that night, but never heard back. No looks at dinner. No letters. What happened with touch caused an equal and opposite reaction: no contact. Sometimes I see her in the dining hall, and her shape, the muscle of her, is more a visceral recognition than cognitive. I sweat. Mr. Obvious. But no one notices, and now that I'm Mr. Indiscretion, I walk away.

Damn the body. Praise the mind.

"You know, Kyle said we could. He volunteered. Absolutely, he asked us to let him play the king." Donny looks at Wyatt, looks at me, looks back at Wyatt. Donny likes this idea. He's practically wagging. King of the Lapdogs. "We didn't hurt him. We did what he wanted." I about clock him.

"So, Donny," Wyatt says, "it is your contention that young Kyle wanted to have molten wax poured into his ear while pinned to the lab table?" Wyatt presses his hands flat together, palms touching, brushing his index fingers to his chin. Surprising he doesn't put his fingers in his mouth.

"Yes, sir," Donny says.

"And is it your contention that you were trying to apply literature to everyday reality?"

"Exactly," Donny says. He presses the knot of his tie, smooths the tie flat against his chest.

"Oh, please," I say. "This kid has had it in for Kyle since day one. I've seen it in the halls. I've seen it in the dorm. Other kids have told me."

"We can't rely on what other students tell us, Mr. Song," Wyatt says. He picks up the damn pipe, puts it in his teeth, keeps speaking while he puts his hands on matches. Sulfur. Flame. Sucks in the flame to the pipe. Sweet, fruity, Virginian tobacco. Makes me sick.

"Look, Mr. White, if you had seen Donny with the blow torch, if you had seen Kyle after I got the boys off him, you would know that there was nothing consensual or academic." Kyle, the mouse of him, wild, pinned to the table, pushes me, like forces opposed, the repulsion of like negatives in the room in their isosceles. Negative Zurkus + Negative White = Anger in Me. All body.

"All right," Wyatt says. "Mr. Zurkus, you can leave."

"But Mr. White," Donny says. He is not wagging any more. Both of our vectors are pointing at Wyatt White.

"We'll speak later, after I discuss this matter with your father."

Donny's eyebrows are rockets. Mr. Surprise. Mr. Shit-Will-Hit-the-Fan Zurkus. He-Whose-Daddy-Is-American-Textile.

"But why?" Donny says. He's leaning way at the edge of the wingback chair, his one leg bouncing from the ball of the foot.

"Because this offense may call for suspension. St. Timothy's will not tolerate bullies," Wyatt says. He takes the pipe from his mouth and sets it in a huge ashtray. His neck is sweating and red. "Now, dismissed." Mr. Head Honcho doing the right thing. And Mr. Union Textile may want my head on a platter. Big donor, old man Zurkus.

Donny gets up from the chair. He faces Wyatt's desk and doesn't move. He stands there. His arms are straight down, parallel vectors. He looks in the direction of the vectors. For a moment he looks like a sail, like something shapeless. Maybe he is a boy trying on wind. Maybe he is a boy too scared of his own shape. I'm sure there is little substance to the boy. Then he raises his head so that his eyes look at me from under his brows, and he smiles a little. He turns and walks out the office door.

"That's not the last we will hear from that young man," Wyatt says.

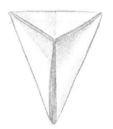

# Taylor / **Close Call**

MAYBE DURING COLLEGE AFTER a brush against Penn we stood on the Penn dock and held hands. Maybe I had my arm around you to keep you warm, but probably we stood there, shoulder to shoulder, shaking. It was late. It was raining sideways. The wind had come out of nowhere, and the current was driving the novice guys' four toward the falls.

Both the men's and women's crews had brushed that day against Penn. Too long. Too hard. Too many crews trying to get into the dock before dark made the crews more voice than muscle and bone. No lights on the boats. Just the light from inside the boathouse bays and the decorations for tourists, the white lights outlining Boathouse Row. Not much light cast from the open doors showed white caps on the water.

All of the women's crews were in. Drenched as we were, we ran to meet every crew, grab their oars, run them into the bay, run back and help carry the boat inside. There was no time to do anything but run.

One crew was still out there in the swirling water we could hear. Even the coaches were on the dock, not on the water. The coaches called directions from their megaphones. The cox'n was new, the rowers were novices, and we hoped they didn't really understand that 750 meters downstream something could kill them. None of the experienced rowers said anything. We knew how cold water strips breath away, wears down the muscles, gives swimmers a moment to wonder if they would be better off dead, should let go, and then the lungs kick in and everything inside craves air. Almost all of us have fallen in at some time. But none of us had dealt with cold water, wind, inexperience, and a fucking waterfall.

Two years later you did.

We stood there on the dock in the Schuylkill with water dripping down our windshirts, between our breasts, soaking into our underwear. We stood there without saying anything, wanting our words to be throw-lines the rowers could grab.

And somehow they rowed against the current, against the wind, and came close enough to the dock that we could grab oars and pull them in. They threw their water bottles and shoes at us so we could get their stuff more quickly. They got one foot up and out, and we grabbed their oars. And the bigger guys grabbed the boat and lifted it up and onto their shoulders, walked it into the house. The novices huddled in the house and dripped and shifted their feet back and forth.

The only time I heard you swear was then.

"Holy shit," you said.

Maybe we laughed. Maybe we slapped each other on our soggy backs as we walked into the boathouse. I wish I could remember. There's so much I'm forgetting so fast.

# Song / **Inert Force**

MR. CRAP ON MY Career. This Zurkus. Muscle-Boy, son of Union Textile. His daddy will have my head.

Carla's keeping her distance tonight. Equal and opposite reaction. In Rehoboth we were one, strapped in, but one of us hit a wall, and *bam*, projectile. Bye-bye. Can't talk to her. Can't explain. Be the wall.

Carla and Buttons are in trouble for coming to dinner a) late and b) in sweats. Walking up to Queen Alta, right after the blessing, Carla putting her arm around the Queen, the Queen turning and brushing her arm off.

"Get off me, Carla," Alta says too loud.

The whole dining hall stops. Carla pulls her arm away but doesn't drop it, her way of moving, all angles. Everyone stares.

"Mr. Underwood," I say, "what is your favorite sport?" Sports are big with Second Formers.

"Golf," Tommy says. Of course.

"Good choice," I say. "The game of royalty. Mr. Underwood, do you know how much work is done in the act of swinging a golf club?" The other nine faces are now turned toward me.

Queen Alta and Ms. Out-of-Dress-Code Carla are out of their sight.

Tommy shakes his head, looks at the fried chicken on his plate.

"Not much, Mr. Underwood. Let me tell you."

Dickie Trowbridge raises his hand. Like we're in class. Next to Dickie, Marty Kraus is stuffing his mouth with a roll in one hand and french fries in the other.

"Mr. Kraus," I say, "please try to take one bite at one time." Dickie is waving his hand so wildly in the air, he might have to use the restroom. "Ah, Mr. Trowbridge, yes?"

"Mr. Song," Dickie says, "the amount of work is related to the amount of force exerted on an object." Dickie is smaller than the boys he's sitting next to, voice higher.

"Yes, Mr. Trowbridge, that's true. And what is your point exactly?"

"I don't know. I thought that was the answer." Amanda McMartin, across the table, throws a french fry at Dickie. Lands on his plate.

"We'll have none of that, Miss McMartin."

"It just slipped," she says. She brings a napkin to her mouth to hide her smile.

I look up and Dorothy White is eye level with me. Didn't see her coming, Mrs. Head Honcho, she with no authority but lots of power. Her old-lady blue eyes are right there as I turn my head. I about drop my fried chicken.

"Oh, Mrs. White," I say, "to what do I owe this honor?" Mrs. Headmaster making the rounds? Lady Busybody come to find out about Alta, why the students dressed in sweats interrupted, why Alta ran from the dining hall? The students at the table are looking at me, at her, at me, at her. We'll see which inert force stays inert.

"Mr. Song," she says, "I'd like a word with you in my office after the meal." She doesn't make nice-nice. The gray roots of her too-red hair stand out tonight. Not enough cakey face makeup.

"Of course, Mrs. White, what a pleasure. Unfortunately, I have study hall after the meal. I'll make an appointment." I'm grinning. I can do nice. I do rude better. Yup, students see me grinning. Good show.

But my chest does that thing, like a big Japanese Taiko drum. The sternum is the drum, the waves of sound using the marrow to resonate. My ribs are a drum, Old Bat White holds the stick, and her words are the strokes of the drumstick hitting my ribs. Someone saw Carla leave. Carla turned me in. My indiscretion. The end of my career. "Suuu," the drummer releases air from her lungs, and uses her whole body to strike the blow. That thing sounds in my chest when I know I'm done for.

# Taylor / **Simplified World**

RAND MCNALLY GAVE EVERY mother in the fifties and sixties a sure thing, the Map of the Simplified World, color coded, complete. There were few contours: Antarctica had blue cliffs, Nepal gray peaks. One or two cities in each country were spelled out, like Minneapolis, like Guangzhou. Countries came in yellow, pink, purple, orange, tan, and blue, and red ran around them all.

My mother gave me a Map of the Simplified World. But in 1983, that map was wrong.

The right map had only three places: where you're from, where I am, where we were.

The Geography classroom smelled this morning of socks crammed in the corners. After a few weeks of teaching, I should have known which map roll was which, but I still had to reach above the blackboard for the metal handles of all the real Rand McNally maps to find St. Tim's copy of the Simplified World.

Yesterday I was in Colorado. But you weren't.

I looked for you in your sister's face, and she looked for you in mine. When she picked me up at the airport, she had to wipe the inside of her glasses, spotted with tears. Maybe I was a little taller than you. Maybe my glasses were tortoise shell and yours metal. Your sister thought you were walking toward her.

Your sister's blond hair doesn't match your hair, but her eyebrows are your eyebrows. Her eyelashes do that thing yours do, make stars when she smiles. She has your cheekbones. Maybe she is shorter than you. Definitely she doesn't row. Her hips curve, and her shoulders are round and soft, but she has your laugh, the hands that comb her hair back from her forehead. I thought you were walking toward me.

The footsteps behind me in the classroom were fast, and then two hands came over my face, pushed up my glasses, and covered my eyes. My sight went pink. The fingers were long and cold and thin.

"Hey," I said, "cut it out."

"Guess who," a girl said. Her breath came behind my ear. I twisted, but she pressed my eyes hard, and yellow and red circles filled my eyes.

"Carla, if this is you, you're in big trouble." I turned toward her, but she stepped in the opposite direction. As I moved, she moved.

"Oh, Miss Alta," Carla said. "You're doing that cute thing again."

"Carla, stop it." I stood still. "Take your hands off me."

"Not until you say you missed me." She leaned into my back, her breasts brushing. Everything about her was yellow.

"Now."

"Hey, Taylor," Alex said from the doorway, "sorry to interrupt. How was your trip?" Carla dropped her hands from my eyes. The room spun. When I got my balance, I saw Alex in the doorway. His hands were on either side of the doorframe, and he leaned his body in the door.

"Alex, hi."

"So, you okay?" Whatever he thought of what he saw, his face was all concern, his eyes on me, not Carla.

Alex and Carla in front of me, the smell of the classroom

where no air moves, a map with more than the places we've been, I couldn't keep the air in me. There was a leak.

"The memorial?" I said. "It was hysterical." Carla sat down at a desk. Alex took his hands off the doorframe. At St. Timothy's everything is "fine, thank you." I was supposed to say, "The trip was fine. Thank you."

"No, really, think about it. There's a coffin. There's friends and family and teachers and Sunday school classmates, and there's no body. There was nothing in that coffin." The laughing shook me. Carla's eyes were the peaks of Nepal, and Alex's eyes were the white Mojave. I was an ice flow separating. I was blue Antarctica.

Carla and Alex said nothing. The map of bright colors was behind my back, and I wanted to tell them that the world now had only a triangle of places you would never be. I wanted to tell them about the ice separating in me. I wanted them to tell me you were alive.

"Okay, really?" I said. "A good part was I got to ski." Both of them dropped their shoulders a little.

"Sounds great," Alex said. "Just thought I'd check in." He shifted away from the doorframe. Two Second Formers appeared, ready to squeeze by him on either side. His arms raised up, and the students passed underneath with plenty of room.

"Thanks, Alex, I appreciate it," I said.

Alex's profile was angles, his nose, sharp cheekbones, spiked hair. With those looks, he could model. He turned and entered the flow of students getting to class.

Carla angled out from the table.

"So sorry to spoil your special moment with Mr. Jeffers," she said. "Better get going." Carla used one hand to pull back the curls from her forehead. They fell again.

"Make way, make way," a Second Former said. He was a ball in a pinball machine, the doorframe a bumper. He crashed into Carla.

"Kyle," she said, "watch where you're going, punk." With both arms she exaggerated shoving him away from her. The shove she gave was soft, tender in the placement of her hands. I hadn't seen them together in the halls, but from this moment, Carla was playing tough kid and its flipside, protector.

Kyle exaggerated bouncing from bookcase to desk to person to wall to person to desk. The pocket he landed in was his usual desk in the back row. His stained backpack dropped to his feet, and he spread his arms out on the desktop. His head, with this greasy hair sticking up, landed on his arms. He pretended to pass out.

Carla turned to me at the front of the room. "Kids today," she said with a smile. Kyle had a champion. She walked out the door.

The doorway your parents wanted me to walk though led from the apse behind the sanctuary and altar to the packed congregation. Mark was behind me. The family was behind him. I was to lead the procession to the front row. The door opened to every church pew packed, and everyone turned to the door opening. I took one step, and there was your dark, shiny coffin, with you not in it.

Lilies and roses and tulips were all over the coffin and the altar and the aisles, and I stopped, stepped back. Mark bumped into me. Mark, who got to put his arms around you when you were dating, now put his rower arms around me. Then he bent down to my ear, said, "*Êtes-vous prêt?*" the formal commands to start a race, "*Partez.*" The two *P*s brushed my ear with his breath. That rest in his arms was enough. I walked into the sanctuary, past the altar, took my place in the family pew, the memorial service started with you not there.

"Miss Alta," David said, "why do you have that old map out?" His lenses were so big that the map became a globe, two globes on his face. Each student was a globe. Each globe had stopped spinning.

Tommy Underwood said, "We're leaving South Africa. Good riddance." He jabbed Peter Frankel on his right.

"Not yet," David said, "Zippo the Clown hasn't done his project." He twisted in his desk to look at the back row. Kyle's head was still turned and resting on the desk. "Looks like Zippy is dead," David said. "Good riddance." David leaned over to get a high-five from Tommy.

"Speaking of which," I said, "Kyle, how is your South Africa project?" I walked toward the back row. Kyle didn't chirp or bark or make any sound.

"Kyle?" His mouth was open, and his face was so relaxed that his cheek sunk in.

"Hey, Kyle, Zippy, Zippo," Jimmy said. "Wake up!" And he threw a crumpled paper ball. From all four rows of seats, white paper balls flew at Kyle. Even Maggie Anderson threw one.

"Enough," I said. "Everyone stop." I turned toward the class, raised my hands to my hips.

"Sounds like Zippo is teacher's pet," Tommy said.

"Am not," Kyle said. He sat up in his chair. His hair straight up. Kyle turned like a machine in one direction, "I am re-search-ing ur-a-ni-um de-pos-its in South A-fri-ca." Then he moved continuously back to start again. "Zip. Ping! Will re-port to-mor-row." Kyle dropped his head on the desk.

"That'll work," I said. "Can anyone tell me what *divestiture* means?"

Maggie raised her hand straight into the air. Tommy and David sat low in their desks.

"Maggie?"

"It means when you make water go a different way." Maggie said things louder than other students.

"That's diverting." Tommy shook his head.

"That's close," I said, "really." Maggie sat back in her desk. "Stopping where money flows. We already know that in South Africa, the white people do the owning and the black people do the working. And you need tons of money to do that. Where does it come from?"

"The gold mines, the diamond mines, the petroleum," Kyle said. His head back on the desk, his mouth was half flattened on the desk.

"The dead have spoken," David said.

"Yes, Kyle, good answer. But I mean American corporations who do business in South Africa." If I keep talking, maybe the students will leave Kyle alone.

Tommy said, "Why shouldn't Americans do business there?" Tommy Underwood's dad was the CEO of American Express. Tommy told us about limousines he'd ridden in Bombay and the rickshaws in the streets. He told us about Swiss chocolate in Geneva and bikinis in Bali. He knew a little about a lot of countries.

Maggie said, "Because they make money from poor people."

"Coca-Cola, Texaco, General Electric, IBM," I said. "Here's how they work. How many of you get a Coke every day?" Every hand went straight up. Except Kyle and Maggie Anderson's.

David said to Maggie, "You do too drink a soda."

"I drink Tab," Maggie said.

"Same difference."

"So, everyone drinks a Coke every day. How much do you think it costs to make one can of Coke? Sixty-five cents?"

"No way," Jimmy said.

"Twenty-five cents," David said.

"A nickel," Tommy said.

"So, how much does Coca-Cola make off you guys drinking Coke every day?"

"Tons," Jimmy said.

"Loads," David said.

"So what if they go to another country, and it costs two cents to make the Coke?"

"I'm moving there," David said.

"So they make a profit. That's what they're supposed to do," Tommy said.

"What if the white owners use their profits to run white schools but don't let black kids go to school or vote?" I said.

"That's not fair," Maggie said.

"So, if you don't drink a Coke today, the company won't get the profit."

"Yeah, right," Jimmy said, "like my Coke will make a

difference." He rolled his eyes and made a big circle with his face.

Terence Franklin said, "Kind of like VW in Germany." He never spoke. The one African American boy, he looked out the window most of the class. In his pressed shirt and tie, he always sat upright, his books arranged on his desk, his notebook open. He turned away from the windowpanes, the morning light flattening his face. "Like Volkswagen."

"Exactly," I said, "but no one divested." The other Second Formers looked at each other. Then they looked at Terence.

"What do you mean?" Tommy asked. "You mean the car?"

"Yup," Terence said. He looked down at his notebook.

"Want to explain?"

"Nope." He folded his hands in his lap. There was something sure in Terence, something broad and winding and a part of something big.

"Okay, then," I said, "Hitler wanted a car for German people, and he made Jews make the cars, and the sales of the cars helped kill the Jews."

And the words out of my mouth were light blue, the color of the VW van my mother drove. She packed us in, the side door sliding left, and one of my big sisters hauling it right. It never felt shut.

In 1964 my mother put up Goldwater-for-President posters on the doors of the VW van. She spray-painted big gold letters, "$RU_4 AuH_2O$?" She believed in everything he did. But no one in our town liked Goldwater. No one believed in the Red Menace. Everyone in our small town knew my mother.

"Hey, Taylor," a kid called at me when I waited for my mother at the Grand Union grocery store, "Are you $H_2O$?" He pointed at me inside the bus. I sat with my knees drawn up, my feet on the vinyl seat.

It was Charlie Delorenza from Catechism. He was in my sister's class. He never did his homework.

"Hey, Taylor," Charlie said, "your mother's square." I didn't know what that meant, but he said it like my brother said "cheater."

Charlie ran away when his mother came out of the grocery store. My mother and sisters came right after.

My mother loved that van with Goldwater on the side. She loved people flipping her off. They saw her coming down the country roads and veered toward our van. They rolled down the window and stuck a hand out, high in the air, the middle finger up. My mother beeped the bus horn. It sounded like a clown. Then she played chicken, steering toward the car. Just in time, she steered back. She laughed. My sisters ducked under the wraparound windows. I waved since I thought people were waving.

And my mother drew red lines around families she said were Democrats. None of us crossed those lines. And she painted the town in colors like pink and yellow and blue. She was the line around everyone.

There were few contours.

# Song / **Electric Charge**

THIS LESSON WILL BLOW them away. I'm holding lightbulbs in both hands, 120 watts each, my fingers wrapped around the metal part. I'm the socket. We do Franklin. Franklin was amazing. City of Brotherly Love right next door. But first, we go back.

"Okay, my budding scientists," I say, "where does electricity come from?"

"Clouds," "sockets," "Kyle's hair," they say. Everybody's a comedian.

"That's not it," I say. "Where does the word *electricity* come from?"

The Second Formers look at me like I asked them to graph relativity. Little Einsteins.

"How about *electric*?" As if that will help.

"That helps," another comedian says in the prime of his sarcasm.

"From *Elektron*," I say, and I have the discussion by myself. The budding scientists are dull today. As if they're bright on other days. "The Greek word for amber. 'Amber?' you say, and I say, 'amber.'" The Little Einsteins don't follow.

That's how Mean Dorothy White started the conversation with me the other day. Okay, not with amber or electricity, but with words that meant more than one thing. Each sentence was charged, and like-charges repel.

Her office door was open. The opening to some lair, the mother of the species, waiting. The Taiko drum hitting my sternum. Big beats. Not much breath in me. Ribs ringing.

"Mr. Song," she said. "Thank you for taking time out of your schedule to see me." Mrs. Headmaster Ma'am, always talking double. If I could pry her mouth open, I'd check her tongue for a fork.

"It's always a pleasure to see you, Mrs. White," I say. My mouth is full of crap.

"I've been meaning to speak with you," she starts in, folds her hands. The Whites and their wingback chairs. We're one green wingback facing another. At any distance the repulsion is inversely proportional.

"A student has been brought to my attention. You know it is rare for students of concern to be brought to my attention," she says.

But here it is. The dreaded. She knows. My parents will find out. Other people will talk. Gossip. Tim-Tim's teacher has ruined a young woman. Please, let me bring shame to my family. First born. Only son. Please, let me wipe the floor with my advanced degrees. Violating *hyo*. The Taiko beat is in my throat, and no sounds will come out of my mouth. Someone must have seen Carla slip in my door.

"His name is Kyle Harney," she says, and the Taiko mallet does not strike. There's air in the room, enough air in enough space. "His name," not "her name," is a valve opening, electricity jumping from fur to amber.

The Second Formers sit on the lab stools and spin. They wobble, and they lean. They turn around and face the other direction. The two lightbulbs I've been holding almost roll off the lab table when I put them down, and then I hold up the amber rod. It's a yellow-brown color, twenty inches long, almost transparent. Solid tree sap. The fluorescent light in here doesn't show it off.

"Masters and Mistress of Science, here is *Elektra*, amber, a holder of soul." Again, that look like I'm speaking relativity to them. And they are no Einsteins.

"Mr. Song," Peter Frankel says from the third stool on the left, "what do you mean, *soul*?"

One person is listening. The other students stop spinning for a moment.

"Fine question, Mr. Frankel. The Greeks believed that if an object could move other objects on its own, then it had a soul."

"So, a cue stick has a soul?" Tommy Underwood says. Mr. Underwood often plays pool in the rec room. He should be studying.

"No, doofus," someone says, "a cue stick doesn't move on its own."

"Why? I mean, not the cue stick." Terence asked. "Why soul?" His eyes already looked like he had static electricity in his system. Of course he does.

"Well, Mr. Why-Everything, the ancient Greeks thought that anything that seemed to change itself was the very essence of life. What other elemental things can change themselves?"

"What's elemental?" Tommy says. Reliable, that one.

"Basic," someone says.

"Maybe clouds?" Maggie Anderson says. Encouraging, this girl.

Kyle doesn't say anything. He turns circles on his stool. Once, twice, too many times. Mr. Harney, King of His Own Kind.

"That's just it," I say. "Water. It can change itself."

Terence's face is flat, like the lab table, dark marble. "Of course, liquid, solid, gas, but how does *soul* work?"

"Mr. Franklin, the Greeks believed that at the essence of all life was a force, an ability to transform, to metamorph, to move things without any outside influence. Let's try it."

Besides the two lightbulbs and the amber rod in front of me,

I have a rabbit's skin, gray and white, hair on one side, desiccated flesh on the other. The fur is soft, softer than skin, any skin. But fur has more texture than skin. Texture equals friction, and when an object is in motion through air or liquid, equals drag. Fur has more drag than skin.

"Is that real?" Tommy asks.

"Yes, and Mr. Underwood, you will be my assistant." He falls forward off his stool and takes a bow before his peers. In the few steps it takes for him to assume his role, he gets three high-fives.

"Take the fur and rub the rod."

Tommy turns his round face toward the class. One eyebrow goes up. Just one.

The boys erupt. Every boy in the class doubles over and spins away from each other, and Tommy Underwood is left with the rabbit pelt in his hand, and his face a deep red. Maggie Anderson turns red but doesn't laugh. Young Miss doesn't get it. But I'm the dumb one. Great way to phrase directions. Teacher of the Year.

"Okay, Mr. Underwood, enough of the gutter." The students can't look at each other without popping their faces, holding their sides, and spinning on the lab stools. "Go ahead, Mr. Underwood."

Tommy runs the rabbit fur along the rod. Some kids can't stop giggling.

"Enough, Mr. Underwood. Hold the fur two inches from the rod."

And all of a sudden, the hair of the fur stands on end, points to the rod. As Tommy moves the pelt slightly up or down, the angle of the hair changes. The hair is pulled toward the amber. To the Greeks, the amber moved the fur. This was soul.

"Now move the pelt closer to the amber," and sparks jump out. Tommy's round face turns up, Mr. Jubilant.

Budding scientists say, "Wicked" and "Wow." They say, "Let me try," and they grab for the amber, for the fur.

Not Kyle. He spins on the stool, one, two, three times. His

greased hair straight up. He says, "Loose electrons," and he keeps spinning.

"What's that?"

"Loose electrons." He keeps spinning.

"Exactly. Most people thought that the friction created the electricity. But Ben Franklin identified that every object has an electrical 'fluid,' and rubbing them merely transfers the fluid from one to the other."

The boys look at me and wait, like I could not possibly have said what I said. It's a second before they double over laughing. A couple of them fall off their stools. Yeah, Teacher of the Year. I know it.

"Now look, Students of the Gutter, I meant to say that Franklin identified that the action did not give one object something. He showed that there was a transfer in a particular direction. We now call the charge negative, and Franklin was the first to see that energy was conserved."

One student says, "I can get a charge."

Other students laugh and yell things like "Oh, baby" and "Hubba hubba." Maggie Anderson looks from one boy to the other and doesn't say anything. What can one girl do in the face of all these boys?

Kyle says, "Like charges repel and unlike charges attract."

"Exactly, Mr. Harney." Never has there been a student like this student. Never has a student been so quick to understand science, despite my unfortunate directions. Here is a true Student of the Year. Young Mr. Science. Kyle faces the front of the lab and doesn't spin any more. With the greased up hair and his gray sweats, he looks like a Conehead. I hate those shows.

Mrs. White starts to tell me about Kyle.

"Mr. Song, he is the boy who was pinned to the lab table. And we suspended the student who did that. But I've heard Kyle is wild, out of control. Student Ambassadors in the Admissions Office were talking about him."

"Mrs. White, let me assure you that Mr. Harney is no barbarian," I say to her from my wingback chair. I don't raise my voice, because a younger person must defer to an elder.

"Yes, I'm sure," she says, "but he's quite odd, isn't he? Makes strange noises, always alone, nearly antisocial." With each phrase she leans forward more. We're differently charged and there's a pull. It's a fact, not a desire.

"Yes, all of that is true, but he's an excellent student. I'm his advisor, his dorm parent, and his teacher. I know Kyle." It's the Korean in me that holds my tongue. If she knew the students, she'd know his brilliance. If she really cared, she'd build the Second Form boys their own rooms, she'd admit more Second Form girls, she'd have role models on the faculty for everyone. I'm the non-white, the token. Sure, it's good she keeps her ears open. At least, she asks and investigates. That's something.

"Why does he speak like a machine?" she says. "Does he do that with his parents, or other adults?" Dorothy White is leaning so far forward in her wingback chair she about falls off.

"Not that I know of," I say. At the end of the conversation, I promise to pay close attention.

"There's no telling what other students will tell their parents." There it is, the reason. She is about as concerned about Kyle as she is about a gnat. It's the blessed name of the school.

There's no telling how Kyle caught her attention. But he catches everyone's attention.

"Zippy knows everything," a boy says.

"Mr. Know-It-All," another says.

"Geek" was the final word.

Mr. Conehead Kyle puts his right hand on the lab table and pushes off. He spins to his left, and his knees fit underneath the lab table. One spin, two spins, he keeps spinning.

Together in this class, in the dorm, he and I have *inyon*. It's like electricity, like soul, but different. More events than can be known conspired to bring us to this place, this moment. We are connected. We are cause and condition for meeting. *Inyon*. His electrons have passed to me and mine to him, and we are each changed without acting on each other. Both amber and fur, both spirit and flesh. In Christian terms, we are keepers of each other.

In Buddhist terms, we are karma. If I consult a shaman, he'd say that Kyle is my good fortune.

# Taylor / **Sunflower**

THE DAY OF THE race on the Schuylkill was eights and geese and nervous girls. Rambo's jacket carried the giant *T* for St. Timothy's in gray on her back. Eight oars in unison moved the boat away from the Canoe Club dock. The knock of the blades turning in the oarlocks added a regular beat to the geese honking in the boat wakes.

You were downstream. You were there under the water that flowed from where I stood to wherever your body was. You were somewhere on this river where we sprinted against Penn in '81. I looked for you on the docks that bounced with each girl's steps, in the launches packed with referees, on the riverbanks where cattails turned from brown to gray. I couldn't find you.

There was nothing I could do any more.

The *T* on Rambo's back got smaller, and she turned the boat upstream. Even at this distance, I saw three and four seat were not parallel to the other backs.

Down the ramp, an eight came black and wobbly. The cox'n kept one hand on the bow ball. I waited at the bottom of the ramp. Behind the eight, carried by our rival school, Warrenton, came Crisco, Cris Copeland. Tall like an elm, she paused at the top of the ramp. She looked at the river and took in current and wind and wakes. Her baseball cap was a silhouette against the gray clouds. She didn't look at her crew until her cox'n yelled, "Way enough," and the girls took too many steps with the eight on their shoulders.

Crisco's steps down the ramp were loud on the metal. She said, "Back two steps." The girls stepped back. Crisco walked under the shell, put hands on each gunwale. Her cox'n gave the commands to lift, and the boat rose up over their heads. Crisco couldn't extend her arms fully or she would lift the boat out of reach of the girls. She was six foot, two inches, and one of the strongest women on the National Team. We had rowed together for a season, she at six seat, me at five. For a season, I read her back.

At the start of a race, her back was short sentences and fear, a child in the face of a father's rage. In the middle 1,000 meters, her back was graffiti and living on the street, straight As in high school. In the last 500 meters, her back beat the songs played in every lesbian bar, "Girls Just Want to Have Fun." Nothing stopped that back.

Crisco watched her crew get their oars, take off windshirts, and toss them on the dock. I walked up behind her, and with both hands, tugged her sweats down. They dropped a couple of inches and stuck. She spun around.

"Hey, Crisco," I said. She spun around partway, enough to lean down and wrap one arm around my waist. With one swift motion, she flipped me upside down. In front of her girls and everyone else on the dock, Crisco picked me up like a salt shaker and shook me upside down.

My feet in the air, my hands hitting the dock, my head came close to wet wood. I smelled rot.

"Alta," she said, "how's the view, you rascal?"

"Crisco," I said. The blood pooled in my forehead. "Don't make me hurt you."

"Oh yeah, like you could."

"Ladies," the dockmaster said, "don't do that." A man with a Henley Royal cap, blue jacket, clipboard, and bullhorn, looked down his glasses at us.

Crisco shifted me to her right hip, then bent her waist enough for me to get my feet and hands on the dock. My butt was in the air, but then I folded into a kneeling position before her, sat back on my sneakers, and laughed. Crisco's big buttery face, with her wide cheeks, broad forehead, and blue eyes, was summer in the middle of October.

"Coach Co," her cox'n said, "we're ready." The girl came to Crisco's waist and looked more like a blueberry with all the clothes she wore. The girls sitting in the rowing shell were sunflowers in October turning to Crisco.

"Okay, Wolverines," Crisco said, "this is it. Stay long. Stay connected. For heaven's sake, stay in front of St. Timothy's." The girls looked from their coach to me, obvious in my maroon and gray windshirt.

Since they had won last year, and St. Tim's hadn't, our start time was after theirs. The boats went off every twenty seconds, and the goal was to pass as many boats as possible. I had coached my girls to catch the Wolverines.

"Okay, Melanie," Crisco said, "they're all yours."

From the end of the dock Crisco watched her crew head up the race course. I joined her there, and side by side we stood over the dark water, rising and falling when wakes washed through. The river was girl-voices over PA systems, geese, and launch motors. Without turning, Crisco put her arm around me and pulled me into her side.

"It must be hard for you to be here," she said, "on this river."

"Kind of," I said.

Only Alex and I had talked about you. Only rowers knew what it was like to lose someone whose back you knew. I couldn't talk about you to someone who knew and still coach a race on this river.

"Thanks," I said. "Your girls look good." I stepped away from her arm.

"We lost a lot of seniors, a building year." She looked down at me and winked.

"I better get to the start. See you later?"

"Maybe I'll see you coming next time," she said. "Come to the bar tonight."

"What bar?"

"Sneakers. It's Third and Market." She turned and faced me, put her hands on her hips. She was too bright and too strong on a cloudy day on the Schuylkill.

"Heads up," a cox'n called.

"Ladies," the dockmaster said again, "please get out of the way." His clipboard was at his side, and his glasses slipped farther down his nose.

"Crisco, I'll see you tonight."

"Taylor," she said, "may your crew eat our wake."

My bike was on its side on the lawn. No locks, no helmet, bikes were all over the grass by the bike path. Coaches rode along the river, one hand on the handlebars, one hand on stopwatches, timing the strokes per minute of their crews.

On the other side of the Strawberry Mansion Bridge, I spotted our maroon and gray blades. The girls were under-stroking a crew they were passing. The chop on the river was a cross wind, and starboard side was down. Rambo yelled, but all I could hear was the low tone of her voice.

In two strokes they pulled even with the other boat. That crew was breaking apart. They were an accordion, two seats moving forward, six seats moving back. St. Tim's was moving through them. The silhouettes of the two crews were nearly the same, except our crew was fluid, not broken, and then Crystal at bow, her thick shoulders and bushy hair, showed St. Tim's gaining. The bow of the boat surged and receded, surged and receded, and with each surge they gained a few inches. Soon, Tiffany and Jenny and Carla were ahead of the other crew. Carla's big stroke, her focus, moving the boat.

This was the moment that would change them. Right here, right now. After this moment when their past pain melted away, this moment of rolling oars, sliding seats, and one voice calling, when their race and SAT scores and social status made no difference, nothing would be the same. This moment plugged them into the essence of service, into a love that lasted forever. Or the belief that this love would last forever.

I pressed the watch at Buttons' stroke and pressed again when Crystal's went in. Their stroke was a thirty-one, a little low, but they moved. The starboard blades splashed, and Crystal's blade dug into dark water. Even still, they opened water on the other crew. Another boat was twenty ahead, and Rambo was sure to have it in her sights. She'd take each one.

The last race you and I rowed on this river we were supposed to win. At the start you took us off at a forty. In the first ten strokes, we were half a length ahead. At the settle, when crews shift from explosive pace and position to race pace, we were a length up on the other six boats. That was a different kind of race, a sprint, not a head race like this one. It hurt in a different way.

We didn't win. Despite the announcer at the grandstand saying, "If they row like this, they'll be unstoppable." Despite your words to our cox, Leslie, "Keep going." The pain in your voice pushed the balls of my feet away from me so hard that I almost split in two. Despite each stroke that I willed my blade into water. Each stroke your blade kept going. I kept going.

But six seat stopped. Her name was Nancy. Each catch felt like shoveling mud when she stopped. Her hernia got clipped between muscles. Her winter training of barbells and squats now turned us to straw. Straw oars moving mud.

At the finish line, she doubled over, and it took awhile to get referees to notice. She was loaded into their launch and into an ambulance on shore. Surgery that night. We lost.

For 2,000 meters, the whole way back to the Canoe Club, I cried. You didn't. After loading the boat on the rack, stacking the oars, I reached for you, and you walked past me. You said, "Not now." It turned into not ever.

A FEW HOURS AFTER the race, after loading the St. Timothy boats, the award ceremony, the knock was tinny on the beige metal door. My hotel room smelled like Lysol, a pine veneer over smoke or dogs or vomit. St. Timothy's, a school for families owning farms, for sons of Du Ponts, didn't spend much for off-campus accommodations. The rowers were returning to campus with their trophy in hand. I was staying in Philadelphia one more night on my dime.

"Just a minute," I said.

All nine of the crew on the dock, getting their medals and flashy trophy. Today they won the Head of the Schuylkill. In their eyes was sunrise and graduation and chocolate sundaes. They hugged and hugged and screamed and hugged. And I watched the ceremony from the riverbank; I was an enormous river rushing downstream.

The door to my hotel room opened, and Carla stood, fresh-washed, her curls stretched out and wet. She looked up and grinned, a little whistle in her look when she saw me. My loose jeans, blue and black flannel shirt, and my hair up were not the St. Timothy's dress code. Off-duty meant pants with seams and clothes bought somewhere besides L.L.Bean.

"Carla," I said, "why aren't you on the van?"

"They're waiting," she said. "You left kind of fast after we loaded the boats."

The door still open, I took up the doorframe, crossed my arms. "I just wanted to get back to the hotel."

"Got a date?" she said. "Oh, you're doing that cute thing, like a fly does when you touch it. Back up, shake your head."

"Don't start."

"Inquiring minds want to know."

I don't want her to add up the way I don't touch students, the quick exit today, no guys ever calling or dropping by on the weekends.

"None of your business."

"Then it is a date."

My hand started to close the door. She stepped closer to

block it.

"Wait," she said, "you should know. Just listen, please." In her voice there was child and woman and teammate.

I kept the door part closed, part open. "What?" I said.

"We won for Sarah," she said.

My hand dropped. The name in the doorway. The name out loud. Explosions went off inside me, and my eyes went crazy, a thousand places, no place the same, and then, I charged her, my hands pushed her shoulders, backing her into the hall, my face hot, and my voice. She flattened against the wall, and I didn't know what I would do next. Every inside part of me wanted out.

"Fuck you, Carla."

The hall echoed, even with carpet and all the doors closed. My hands gripped on her shoulders, her shoulders pinned to the wall.

"Miss Alta, I'm serious."

"Quit messing with me." I was eyes. I was voice.

"Rambo called a power-ten for Sarah. I swear. The boat picked up. We won because of her." Her words were little. Her eyes in my eyes, her shoulders in my hands, her back against the wall, Carla was caught and pleading and girl.

She looked at one of my eyes and then the other to see what I was going to do. I looked at her eyes to see if she were playing with me. A breath went in, and my shoulders went down. I pushed away from her shoulders and stepped back.

My hand on my forehead, my other hand on the wall.

"And that's when we really moved on Warrenton," she said.

My steps into the room turned me from storm to rain. My shoulders curled in.

"We all know, you know?" She took a step into the room. "We pulled for you and her."

The words had to stop. I turned around. Her eyes were dark brown, like the cornfield in rain. We stood there like that. No words. The two of us.

"Thank you, Carla," I said. The words were quiet, almost

shy, like we were meeting for the first time. And I opened my arms.

She walked right into my arms, and I wrapped around her, and in that moment, all the hugs I hadn't had moved into my arms. I didn't let go. She leaned into me, and I felt her hips against my hips, her hair soft on my cheek. She was warm. She was really warm. And I wanted to hold her.

THE CABBIE DIDN'T SAY much when I told him where I wanted to go, "North Third, between Market and Chestnut."

He said, "You won't stay." His bushy eyebrows took up most of the rearview mirror.

"Why's that?"

"Only dykes and gangbangers on that block." He hacked up a wad of spit from his throat, but he couldn't spit in his car. He swallowed.

There was a heat that came up my neck, a hot place in my throat that pushed words out. "I'll fit right in."

And that was all we said to each other until we arrived. It took the ride over potholes on the Philadelphia streets for my face and neck to cool. I paid the fare and not much tip.

"Sneakers" was in pink neon on a black sign, flat against the front of an old rowhouse. The streetlight was down the block a ways, and the shadows of stairs and cars reached across the sidewalk.

Up the stairs to Sneakers were women leaning against the railing. Their leather jackets and jeans blurred their shapes. At the top of the steps someone sat on a stool to the side of the entrance. The rim of a captain's cap was the pink of the Sneakers sign. The person had leather pants and a leather jacket and chains hanging low off the leather belt. Standing up, the bouncer was taller than me.

"ID?" the tall one said. The voice was low like a truck on a street.

"Excuse me?"

"Your ID and five bucks."

The door opened at the same moment I handed the bouncer my driver's license. Through the open door, the beat of Donna Summer was fast. The first woman out was bleached blond with hair cut so short it stuck straight up. Another woman's hand was down the back of the blond woman's pants. They laughed and bumped when the blond woman paused by the bouncer.

"See you, Janie," she said, "gotta get some shut eye." She winked.

Janie, the bouncer, turned toward the pair. "You gals have fun. Be careful."

The blond gal stopped again. Her eyes moved over me like a rake and scraped every inch. "That's a cute one. No charge."

"Sure thing, boss," she said and watched the two down the steps. She turned back to me. The five dollars in my hand went back in my pocket. My jeans fell on my hips just right, and for the first time since starting my new job, I felt dressed just right. "Stamp your hand."

A pink triangle stamped on my right wrist, big like a brand.

"Step right in, honey," Janie said. "They don't bite unless you ask them to." Her big hand was loud on my shoulder.

Sneakers inside was cigarette butts, neatsfoot oil, and wine coolers. Smoke hung in the air about five feet off the floor. The entire bar was two rooms, a large one with most of it a dance floor complete with disco ball and revolving light turning the dancers different colors. Women all butched out in black and flannel didn't notice their skin turning red, blue, pink, purple as the colored lens turned clockwise. There were tables with women, leaning toward each other, and tables with nothing but bottles, glasses, and ashtrays stacked. Women sat on women's laps. Some were bundles of bodies against the walls. Some shouted into each other's ears, and some said nothing and stared at the women doing the bump and hustle on the dance floor.

On one side there was a bar with a mirror the length of the room, and women were three deep. Plenty of women looked in the mirror while they waited; everyone checked out who was there, with whom. In a side room there were pool tables with women who looked like Janie chalking their cue sticks and bending over the green pool table tops to line shots up.

"Taylor," I heard behind me. Two arms reached under my arms and around my waist. Crisco heaved me up and down.

"Saw you coming this time," she said and held me off my feet.

"Crisco," I said, "you can put me down now." This morning, when Crisco turned me upside down, I smelled the rot of the dock with your body somewhere in the river. I wouldn't look for you here, in a dyke bar in Philadelphia. In the bar I smelled wet ashtrays and spilled liquor going rank, and the sweat of women wanting not to be alone. The women nearby turned and smiled and raised their glasses to us.

She let me down and held me still. "You're nothing but skin and bones, Alta."

I leaned back into Crisco. Her arms loosened enough that I could breathe, and we stood pressed against each other taking long, slow breaths. Her arms were not Mark's arms holding me before I stepped into the funeral with you not in the coffin. Hers were not Carla playing with me. Crisco's arms were holding me so I could hold myself up.

"There you go," she said. Her cheek was soft on my cheek. My arms reached behind her back and pressed her closer to me. I felt her thighs press against the backs of my legs.

The DJ changed the song to the BeeGees' "Stayin' Alive," and women jumped up from the tables. Crisco and I cleared a place for us to sit.

"I'm glad you came," Crisco said. "Want a beer?" She stood up. Her turtleneck was tight around her shoulders, tight around her biceps, tucked in at the waist.

"Long Island Iced Tea," I said.

She stopped moving toward the bar. She turned toward me. "Coming right up."

All around me were tables with cities of bottles and glasses. The few women not on the dance floor were quiet by the wall, and I was the only one in a seat in the middle of the tables. The dance floor was packed. Women screamed the lyrics, swinging their hair with sweat dripping, and bumped their hips into the butts of women in front of them.

To party this hard was rowing at race pace, no air, instinct kicking in. And to dykes at Sneakers, the dance was a time they moved with their own kind, hit a rhythm they could keep. Loneliness was the bass line, and they danced to it. Except for rowing, nothing in my background prepared me for this movement out of body. This loneliness was its own kind.

What I knew about parties was invitations my mother wrote by hand. Each season she threw one party, mostly for teachers from my siblings' schools, and for her own brothers and sisters, and sometimes our priest, Father M; nearly everyone in the New England town came to our house. They came with matching pantsuits and jackets, with purses matching blouses, kerchiefs matching ties. They drank dark drinks that my older sister and I brought on silver trays. Mother also hired help who wore white uniforms and said, "Yes, ma'am," and "Yes, sir," to people half their age.

By the end of those parties, the tables in our living room were little cities, full of empty glasses, glasses with a cube or two, glasses with red lipstick on rims. By the end, my mother and father were fighting.

One time ended up like a city demolished.

"You shouldn't have invited him," my mother said. She was sitting in the lime green armchair. Her legs were crossed, and her arms were crossed, a cigarette in one hand. My mother loved her burgundy jacket with the wide lapels and shoulder pads. The fashion was out of old movies, like Lauren Bacall, and her waist tapered in a straight skirt. My father was standing up, facing her. His gray suit was pressed so creases ran up his legs, and his leather shoes were polished. My sister and I were across the room on the couch.

"You invited the Catholic one," he said. His forehead was getting red. His forehead was getting red in the places where he didn't have hair.

"That's right," she said. "I invited the real priest." She put the cigarette between her red, red lips. She took a puff, and the end of the cigarette was a dare.

"Forget it," he said. He looked down at the oak floor.

"Forget what? Forget that you're not Catholic?" She uncrossed her legs, leaned forward.

"Quaker," he said. "You knew that from the start." The top of his forehead was red.

"Well, it's not good enough." She twisted toward the end table by her side and crushed her cigarette in the ashtray.

"Never have been," he said. My father didn't look angry any more. My father was a boy alone.

"Oh, great," she said, "poor, pitiful you."

My mother looked at my father's pants, not at him. Then she smacked her lips like she was thirsty. She tried to get up. Stretching one arm to the armrest and trying to push off, she slipped. Her hand was a crushing ball on a glass city. Water and glass and ice flew off the table. The floor was shiny with wet and pieces, and some kept going on the floor, bounced off the wall, under furniture.

Two tall glasses were all that was left on the table. Mother stood up and looked at them. The top of her body swayed side to side a little. Then she drew back her hand like a golf club, twisted, and smacked them off. The tall glasses popped against the sideboard. Everything was loud, but my father. My mother turned her big shoulders with the shoulder pads toward my father, and smiled.

"Here you go," Crisco said. She put her face in front of me, her face not angry or drunk. Her smile was invitation and breath.

"Thanks." The cocktail glass filled my hand. The drink was so strong my eyes watered. The music was so loud that we had to face each other, pull our seats close, and put our lips to each other's ears.

"How's teaching?" Crisco said. She smelled of soap.

"Harder than I thought."

"Like how?" She pulled back to look at me. Her wide face was freckles across the bridge of her nose.

"Like how to reach them."

"How can you?" She pressed my cheek with her cheek but then took it away.

"What?" My cheek where hers touched was moist.

Crisco grabbed my chair and dragged it, with me in it, as close as it could go. My knees pressed between her legs. She took my shoulders in her hands, and pulled me toward her. My skin got hot like she was going to kiss me. But she turned her head to the side to shout into my ear.

"How can you reach them when you're so far away?" She pressed my shoulders with her hands, slid her hands toward my neck, and squeezed my delts. She shook me back and forth a little.

I nodded, put my hands on her thighs. My palms were spread across her muscles.

A slow song came on. Cris Williamson. The dance floor cleared. Some women hissed. No one got up to dance. Crisco and I sat and listened. One of my hands stayed on her thigh, and she held the armrest of my chair.

The waitress came around with a small tray raised above her shoulder. Her jeans were ripped, and her pink tank top showed tight muscles.

"Another round for the rowers?" She looked at Crisco.

"Sure, M.J.," Crisco said.

I sat back in my chair, raised my eyebrows, and smiled at Crisco.

"What?" she said. "What?"

"Does Traski know about this place?" The U.S. rowing coach, Carl Traski, would try anything to break a rower's will. If he found out about Crisco, in every practice he'd tear her down.

"He's too busy sleeping with the girls." Crisco played tough. Years on the streets of Chicago required smarts and se-crets: keeping herself hidden was as easy as breathing.

Soon M.J. brought the second drink. Between rounds we

danced. We jumped when Van Halen told us. Crisco danced like a teenage boy, stiff shoulders and lead hips. She raised her arms above her head, and her shirt wrapped around her triceps. There was nothing like her smile, bigger than the disco ball, bigger than the dance floor.

The next time a slow song came on we stepped into each other. There was nothing soft about Crisco: Her breasts were all pec muscle, her arms were all biceps, and her stomach was a flat plane. In her arms I felt safer than open water in a sprint race. In her arms the race was over. And for the first time since you disappeared in the Schuylkill, I didn't wonder where you were.

Margie Adam sang her sweet, slow song, and Crisco's shoulder fit under my neck. She leaned back enough to talk into my ear.

"Taylor, you know Sarah loved you." Her cheek gave heat to the side of my neck.

"Sure."

"No, she really loved you." Crisco's lips moved air on my ear.

"She really loved Mark, remember?"

"Yeah, but she was in love with you," Crisco tightened her arms around me, like someone might do before the doctor gave a shot.

"No, she wasn't, Crisco. She was like my mom, said I was going to hell."

"Maybe," she said, "but she couldn't help loving you." Crisco pressed her cheek against my cheek. Our skin was wet. Our skin was neither mine nor hers. What Crisco said reached into that forever place, the one that had prayers and mountains in Massachusetts. Sarah in love with me was nothing I could touch, but the words made that place in my chest crack a little more open. Forever was no longer a place any more. In Crisco's arms I knew forever could never be again. With Sarah gone, forever was the crack that kept opening.

After Margie Adam finished, Crisco kept her arm around my shoulders and walked me off the dance floor. I almost missed the step down to the sticky linoleum, and her hand guided me around the tables with all the glasses and beer bottles.

"Grab your coat," she said, her face so close to my face. My face did the getting-hot thing in case her lips came closer. Crisco lived in another part of town, and I lived an hour away. We'd have to swing by the hotel and get my stuff on the way. But with women's faces spinning and glasses blurring and a rower's arm around me, I'd do anything.

Janie's hand was hard on Crisco's back. "Be safe," she said to the two of us. I waved to the women bunched in the shadows and waved to the streetlight down the street.

Inside Crisco's blue Datsun hatchback, there were sandwich wrappers, pop cans, and *U.S. Rowing* magazines. There was condensation on the inside of the windows and mold around the edges. This was the car that got us to practice before dawn every day. Never once did I think we'd sit in the dark outside of a lesbian bar. Never had I thought I'd want the dark in Crisco's eyes.

"Nice to see Joni again," I said. Joni Mitchell Blue was Crisco's car.

"She's glad to see you too, Taylor Alta, but she thinks you're skinny." She turned her sunflower face to me. Her hands came around my ears, wrapped around my head, palms holding my cheeks. She pulled me within inches of her face. I closed my eyes, waiting for soft lips.

"Gotta go." She let go of my head. My eyes opened. "Got to get you a cheesesteak, real one, fatten you up. That's what we're going to do." She turned toward the steering wheel and started the car.

My body was still leaning forward, leaning on the stick shift. My lips got cold. Maybe she didn't notice my face right there, waiting.

I said to the windshield, "Complete with Cheez Whiz?"

"The works. Your body's got to be big enough to hold that big spirit of yours." Her hand left the steering wheel, and she locked it on my thigh. A shock pitched my body forward.

"You call this muscle a quad? Good God, girl. What's happened?" Her smile was hanging off her face, so big. I tried to watch where we were going since she was looking more at me. I figured out we had gotten to west Philly. In front of Marty's Steaks, we found a parking spot.

As soon as I opened the door, I could smell the onions, the grease. The booze from the bar and not much food made the lights too bright, the counter far away. My stomach tightened. It had been awhile. When my crews raced, I forgot to eat. When I had too much to do, I forgot to eat. Over the past six weeks, I lost twenty pounds, and my clothes that I had bought to teach at St. Tim's fit like rice sacks.

"We have arrived," Crisco said, "at the place of your redemption. See and believe, the best cheesesteak in all Philly." Crisco was a loud preacher when we walked in the door, the type of loud that doesn't seem loud when you're drinking. The single man at the counter and the couple in the booth turned around.

We ordered two, and my stomach knotted with hunger. We shuffled down the chrome counter. Within minutes, the server in a black T-shirt slid a steaming plate onto each of our trays. The steak was piled high with onions and cheese over an Amaroso's roll. The steam rose into my nose, and Crisco kept one hand on me, one hand on her tray.

*"Mangia, mangia,"* Crisco said in impossible Italian when we sat in our booth. Everybody in Philly spoke like Sylvester Stallone and charged up the museum steps.

As the steak slid out of the roll and juice ran down my hands, as the roll gave out and the cheese pooled on my plate, Crisco talked to me about spirit, about the way that the body acts as a vessel, about the importance of honoring the spirit by honoring the body. She said it didn't matter what religion I was, or my mother was, or Sarah was. She said I had to eat and keep my body big enough. She gave me the rest of her cheesesteak after I finished mine.

"Just a second," she said, and she went back to the counter.

In a few minutes, she came back to the booth and grabbed her jacket, and with a milkshake in hand, she led me back to her car. "This will keep you while we drive to Delaware."

"You're kidding. You're not driving to Delaware tonight." The cheesesteaks were landing in my stomach.

"You're going to need this coating. And I need to know where you live." She opened the passenger door for me.

"What about practice?" Traski expected the team at 6 a.m. Crisco's coaching was later in the day.

"What about it? I'll get back in time."

"Ah yes, respecting the vessel," I said.

"Shut up. Drink your shake."

# Song / **Particles in Turbulence**

"THIS SEAT TAKEN?"

The stack of lab books takes up the space next to me at the counter. Marsh Road Diner is hopping. Once a month Sam Omura and I meet in Wilmington, vectors from where we live, his short, mine long, no isosceles. Sam knows vectors, electrical engineering, now working on secret something for CIA space labs, satellite surveillance for the Cold War.

"Sam! Sorry about that."

"You're a dull boy, Song." Still lean and short, his dark hair with no signs of gray, he bellies up to the counter, King of Smart Guys, PhD from Stanford, grad student who taught me when I did undergrad. Nobody taught vectors the way he did. With fifteen sharks for students in the class, he turned out the lab lights, turned on lasers, cut the competitive crap out of the class. Sharks forgot our GPAs, GREs, and pedigrees. Nothing like this teacher.

We shake hands once I move the lab books from the Misfits

of Science.

"How's Sheila?" Start with the family, start soft, get harder.

"Still inventing stuff," he says. He turns his head to me, and his dark eyes, with their bushy eyebrows, are bright. He and Sheila have been together ten years, and she's turned ones and zeroes into codes that make machines calculate almost faster than humans can.

"My two favorite scientists," our waitress says with a coffee thermos in her hand.

Sam can never resist. "Where have you been all my life, Nancy?"

"Waiting for you, doll." She turns over the mugs and pours coffee. "What'll you have?" She never writes our orders down. After we call out the same things we order every time, we shake our heads at the news we hadn't talked about since last month.

"Two hundred sixty-nine people, gone."

"Anything you can tell me about that? I know you're not supposed to."

"CIA's not involved." He never likes to talk about where he works. His lab does contracts. "But I can tell you it looks like a colossal mistake. The jetliner went 300 miles off course." He shakes his head, whistles under his breath at the stupidity.

"Any reason?"

"Nobody knows as of yet. We had surveillance in the air, but not nearby."

Behind the counter the waitresses dodge each other, post the orders for the cooks, grab dishes after the cooks ring the bells, slosh coffee into cups.

"Speaking of unknowable, is Dorothy White still kicking around that place?" Sam hasn't been back to Tim-Tim's since he graduated. His family worked the fields near the school, came back after the prison camps during the war. Even though Sam missed years of formal education, he scored the highest of all kids in Delaware on the aptitude tests, and the Du Ponts wanted him in, felt guilty for the imprisonment. Sam was the first Japanese American at Tim-Tim's and he blew the doors off the place, won every prize in science and music, lettered in cross-country, basketball, and tennis. Slight in build, mighty in spirit.

"Queen Busybody? Sure."

"Need anything?" Sam drinks about half his mug of coffee in one gulp.

"You mean, in the labs?"

"No, in the dining hall."

From beakers to Bunsen burners to microscopes to the huge shiny fume hood, Sam kept Tim-Tim's kids in science. The Du Ponts built the lab but didn't make it work. Sam made sure Misfits of Science could at least try the tools. On the giving scale of alumni, Sam is at the top, always setting records.

Nancy places the oval plates in front of us, pancakes and omelets so big they hang over the sides. Before I can unwrap my silverware, Sam stabs one of my sausages and pops it in his mouth.

"Thanks. Sheila doesn't like me eating pork."

"Help yourself," I say. "We could use a thing or two."

"Send me a list." His fork is busy cutting his omelet into pieces, each piece a square. The once-floppy omelet is now an electrical panel perfectly charted.

"Say, Sam, I got a live one this year." By the time I clear the butter off the paper divider, pour syrup, he's eaten his way through half the omelet. The guy never gains weight. No entropy, always motion. "Hungry?"

"Always. What kind of live one?"

"The kind of kid that makes you want to bow every time you walk in the classroom."

Sam sets down his fork. "You don't do that, right?"

"Of course not. For instance, I'm doing particles in turbulence, and I set it up with two kids up front of the lab. Tell them to raise one arm and touch the other kid. They don't want to. Too bad. I make them.

"I ask them how big is the force of gravity? I make them repeat after me, '*A product of the masses of both, inversely proportional to the square of the distance between them.'* Basically, not much. After I explain, the Second Formers at the front of the room about gag.

"Let me back up. Last week, Kyle is his name, all he says is 'Oh no, Mr. Bill.' You know that Saturday Night Live show? Down in study hall, I see him with his head plastered to the desk. I say, 'Hey, Kyle, getting your work done?' and he says, 'Oh no, Mr. Bill' really loud. At dinner, I hear he takes those boiled-to-death beans we eat. Remember those?"

"I still can't eat beans," Sam says.

"Well, he cuts one at a time, picks up the halves, and you know what he says.

"But even when he's jumping off chairs and making noises, he's watching. I see him. Into any room, he bumps, bounces, makes a grand entrance, but then sits in the back. With so much show, he's invisible.

"In the class last week I get the Second Formers dropping cones of paper off their desks. You know how that goes. Some fall smooth. Some tumble. Then, we add tiny weights. The cones go crazy. Kids love it. I give them paper and scissors, and they cut cones out of different shapes, like snow cones and pizza pies. Only a few go Conehead on me, wearing them on their heads, talking monotone. Stupid TV."

"I like where you're going with that," Sam says. The Prince. The teacher for all teachers.

"I try to talk unstable equilibrium, but they get too busy winging the cones upside down. So, I ask what it takes for the cones to find their orientation.

"We talk gravitational pull. We talk aerodynamic force. So then I dump a bag of leaves on the lab table. 'Have at it,' I say. 'Make these leaves fall smooth.' They look at me like I'm stupid."

"They have a point." Sam jabs me with his elbow.

"Thanks." I know he knows what I'm talking about. "Of course they can make a leaf fall. The whole lab turns into a leaf pile, kids dropping leaves on each other, stuffing up shirts. One or two try to get the forces to match.

"'Tell me about the shape of the leaf,' I say.

"Three kids talk at once, 'Pointy,' 'irregular,' 'skinny.'

"'Right,' I say. 'Edges, ridges, stems. Too many variables.' Their faces look like a Rubik's Cube."

"I love that look," Sam says.

"But it's this kid, Kyle, who says, 'No two leaves are alike.'

"And I say, 'So?'

"And he says, 'Density,' 'weight,' 'surface tension.' How does he know this stuff? And because he gets it, they get it, that the slightest variation will destabilize the equilibrium = turbulence, and there is no way for scientists to predict how or where a leaf will fall. Smart. He's the smartest kid I've ever seen."

"But they don't like it," Sam says, "where science ends."

"Hate it."

"Yeah, everybody wants science to explain every single thing."

"It can't."

"Not now."

"Not ever."

On that note, we pay our bills, leave the money on the counter with extra big tips for Nancy. The stack of lab books is on the floor between my stool and the one next to me. I spin around, bend down to pick up the books. When I turn, Sam is standing facing me. Behind him in one of the booths by the windows, I see two kids, maybe six and seven years old. They look at me, and their hands shoot up to their eyes. They tug their eyelids, turn to each other, and smile a fake smile, talk something chinkish. I hear, "Ahhhh, so."

When I straighten up, look at Sam, he starts to turn around to look where I'm looking, but the kids pull their hands down, look out the window. What Sam sees is two boys looking out the window.

Slight variation of that picture, great turbulence. What do these boys know of one man Japanese, one man Korean? They see Chinese, Mr. Chan with his bicycle legs, the two of us inside when Kim played in the pool. He made me say *literal, slanted, let go,* always the Ls. Good men like Sam and Mr. Chan showed me equilibrium.

With so many variables, my mind spins. Equilibrium lost. Without talking to the little white boys, I walk out with Sam, walk out with the fine teacher, the one who helps restore equilibrium by talking teaching, by affirming Kyle is unusual, *inyon,* gift.

# Taylor / **White on Black**

SUNDAY AFTER WINNING THE Schuylkill and dancing to Donna Summer and too much cheesesteak was quiet. Papers stacked around my living room kept me indoors. For hours I graded and prepped classes, and no matter how many student reports I read on South Africa, Carla's body in the doorway returned, her calling a power-ten for Sarah, on the river where Sarah still was. Since the moment I met Carla on the dock when the water and fog were the same thing, Carla was two things at once. Her smile, her curls, the way her words crawled into me, she was the type of cold that wakes your senses, the type of cold that shuts your senses down.

New teacher with three different classes to teach, I arrived most mornings early to my classroom. Monday morning the halls were gray walls and linoleum, but this Monday voices came from Geography. The one talking was soft and curled, and nothing was the other person. Carla was telling that person about her race.

"When she saw Warrenton, Rambo went ballistic. She called tens like crazy.

"'In two,' Rambo said, 'pick it up. Power ten for Buttons. One, two. On this one.'

"What does it feel like? Your legs are already rubber, and you can't breathe. So then she wants you to pull harder. Like you could. But you do because the others are pulling harder. I felt like puking my guts out. She went down the boat, ten for me, for Crystal, on down. Each ten the boat would go ahead. When we got tired, the boat slammed down to starboard. We dipped at the catch, like lurched. Caught my knuckles. See? Doesn't hurt much.

"Rambo was like a hornet. She'd see an eight ahead of us, and talk faster, louder, more intense. The way her hands held the wood steering things, she banged them on the sides. Scared the crap out of me.

"Rambo, with the headstrap for the microphone, and the mouthpiece, and the way she leaned into the middle of the boat, she looked like a hornet, a fucking hornet.

"About a half a mile to go, Rambo said, 'Okay, Saints, there's the boat we've been training for.'

"Then, she didn't say anything else. The oars turning in the oarlocks were boom, boom, boom.

"'Warrenton is a few boat lengths ahead. We can take them.' She talked soft to us.

"'Let's do it, Saints. You're at a thirty-one. Take the rating up two in two. One, two. On this one.' She shouted big. And in two strokes, all of us moved quicker up the slides. We gave her two in two.

"'We're gaining,' she screamed. She could smell them. She wanted that boat. She had already called a ten for bow.

"'One more ten,' I said. Seven seat isn't supposed to say anything. But I did anyway.

"'For Sarah,' I said. It came out loud. Rambo's eyes like stingers. Ms. Alta never said Sarah's name out loud, but we read the papers. We knew. That's when Rambo really looked like a big hornet, like she had a triangle of eyes between her eyes.

"'We're taking a ten,' she said, 'for Sarah. In two. One, two. On this one.'

"And I swear to God, the boat lifted out of the water. It rose up out of the water and took off. We blew through Warrenton. We won.

"You should have seen it, Kyle. We fucking won. Rowing is awesome, something worth living for, you know? That and our geese, you know?"

Kyle and Carla. In the whole school, in all the classes, these two were a perfect match. Carla the confessor, Kyle the high priest. Perfect.

The light in the classroom was gray. A map of Africa was chalk on the board. No maps pulled down from the rolls of maps. The map drawn on the chalkboard was white on dark, shaped like an ice cream cone. Under the table where I usually sit at the front of the class there were cardboard shoe boxes, jewelry boxes, cereal boxes. There were plastic bags and paper bags, and papers pooled around the chair. Carla and Kyle slumped in chairs, the room was more campground than classroom.

"Hi, you two," I said.

Kyle jumped. Gray sweatshirt and sweatpants, his hair greasy and stuck to his head, he turned a circle, picked up books and papers, ran one hand through that hair.

"Gotta go," he said. "Shower, shave."

"Relax, Kyle," Carla said. "It's just Ms. Alta." Carla rested her chin on her fist, her elbow on the table. She waved at me with her other hand, half the hand, up, down, like a puppet.

"Will-report-for-duty-at-designated-time. Zip. Ping!" He picked up more papers and stuffed his arms. At full speed, he was a stuffed bookbag-missile aimed right for me. I sidestepped the missile. Class wasn't for another fifteen minutes.

"What was that?"

"A little-little," Carla said. "He's terrific, all gray. That's the only way to go. He sees everything, and nobody sees him. A gray moth. You know, darker moths survive in cities better because they blend in with soot on things. He's perfect for this place."

"Because no one sees him?"

"Because he can hide."

"He sure sticks out."

"That's the beauty of it," Carla said. She crossed her arms. We kept our distance.

"Meaning?"

"He calls so much attention to himself no one notices. Other times, he's so gray he blends in. Awesome."

"But you see him," I said. The desk where I placed my book-bag was not at the front of the room. Kyle was camped there. My bookbag filled one of the three or four seats between Carla and me.

"Yeah, I know where to look."

"How?"

"My dad taught me."

"I thought your dad was an art dealer," I said and took a seat at the end of the row where Carla and Kyle sat, where Carla still sat.

"Art dealer, peach farmer, #1 asshole," she said.

"Right, you learned bugs from hunting them in the orchards."

"Yup."

"You liked what he hated."

"Apparently," she said. "Don't go all Freud on me."

"Oh, yeah, I forgot to bring my couch."

"You teachers are all alike." Carla was back in the class-room. Her words were curled.

"Like how?"

"You and Song, always wanting to get us to talk about things."

"You talk much to Mr. Song?"

What Kyle had suggested couldn't possibly be true. Since talking to him in the cornfield, something in me pointed toward something more between them. The way that Jack protected me at dinner, keeping the conversation on his end of the table, the way that he was gruff with students, formal and stiff, pointed toward empathy for underdogs. And wanting to know if there was more between them made me coarse. I wanted to know for the pleasure of knowing. I wanted to be on the inside of knowing.

"Not much. He's an ass." Carla looked at the blackboard.

"Watch it."

"Sorry. He's not my cup of tea." She batted her eyes at me. The way she was dismissing him was as good as admitting it. The information tasted like butter on my tongue.

Footsteps in the hall were heavy. Not Second Formers. Maybe teachers on the way to class. Then, Kyle crashed into the classroom. A maroon hood was pulled up over his greasy hair. His chin holding in the binders and papers that stretched his arms full, Kyle bent over the table where Carla and I sat, and dumped the load. Hands free, he pushed back his hood, hopped up and down, grabbed his neck with his hands, pretended to strangle himself, and fell on the floor. His cheek on the carpet, his tongue stuck out. The tie was to the side, the knot pulled too tight. The eyes closed, the mouth open, and the tongue out.

Maybe teachers with experience could tell me what to do. The Second Formers, all sixteen of them, saw Kyle hang himself, jump off stairs, take falls, more than once a day. What to do was something I was supposed to know.

I walked to the side of the room and flipped on the bright fluorescent lights. "Hey, Kyle."

His eyes didn't move. His tongue still out.

"Kyle, you want to do your presentation today, right?"

Carla stood up, stepped over Kyle, and said, "Good luck, punk." She walked out with a backhanded wave.

"Thanks," he said. His head jerked up and slammed into the bottom of the table. He ricocheted back down on the carpet. He was out.

"Ouch," he said.

"Easy, Kyle, how long have you been here?"

"All night."

"You know we're doing Vietnam today?"

He sat up without hitting the table. "But I didn't give my presentation," he said. "I have to give my presentation. Everyone has to know." His tie was still cocked to the side. He spun around on the floor to face me.

"Know what?"

"Uranium," he said. The word came out low and soft and raw.

I took a couple of steps toward him. "What about it?"

"It's the whole reason." His eyes were possum eyes.

"For what?"

"For killing, for apartheid, for everything." His hands flew out from under the table and made big arcs in the air above his head. They stretched out in a Y.

I dropped into a seat at a student's table. "Because of the bomb."

"Duh," he said, "kids today." His hand hit his forehead. He shook his head. A smile was big and fast, a possum smile, then gone. Leaning forward on all fours, he picked himself off the floor, and took the seat at the front of the class.

The fluorescent lights made a hum overhead, and students rushing to class were a racket in the hall. Sitting in the second row of wooden desks, I faced Kyle. A little animal at the front of the class, his feet barely touched the floor, the floor covered with his stuff.

"Okay," I said, "we'll go back to South Africa for today, and then return to Vietnam." I leaned back in the student desk.

"Thanks, Miss Alta," Kyle said.

Maggie and Tommy came in from the hall.

"Zippo's the teacher," Tommy said. He slid his backpack off his shoulder and dragged it on the ground.

Maggie stood inside the door. "Kyle," she said, "what are you doing?"

"Teaching," he said. He brought his tie to the middle. He cupped his chin with one hand and he pointed into the air with the other hand. The Thinker with grease for hair.

"Hey, Kyle," Tommy said, "how many teachers does it take to screw in a lightbulb?" Dragging his book bag, Tommy pushed every desk out of the way to get to his usual seat.

My shoulders twisted around toward Tommy. "Oh, hello," I said.

Tommy's face was a puppet with strings. His jaw untied. "Oh, Miss Alta," he said, "nice to see you."

"Two," Kyle said, "One to do it, and one to write the quiz about it." His hands moved fast, a quick clap for himself.

"Yeah," Maggie said, "that was funny." Maggie knew something was different about Kyle, and she talked to him like he was a hurt bird.

The rest of the students walked in from the hall. All wore the jackets and slacks required in the dress code. All wore them a different way. Some ties were hanging loose from collars. Some skirts were rolled up at the waist and hung more than one inch above the kneecap. Few Second Formers really combed their hair, except Terence Franklin.

Terence stopped at the door. His hair was closely cut, and his part was distinct. The knot in his tie was just the right thickness, the stripes landing just right. His shirt was pressed. He had a stack of books under his left arm.

"This is going to be good," he said.

"As you have noticed," I said, "Kyle is ready to do his presentation."

"About time," David said.

"Oh, great, back to South Africa," Tommy said.

Kyle brought out a sheet of black cloth and spread it like he was making a bed, unfolding the sheet and floating it down on the empty tabletop. Then, he reached under the table and brought out shoe boxes, cereal boxes, and gift boxes. With dirty fingernails he peeled off tape holding the boxes together. Each box opened up, and stuck to the inside were smaller shapes. He lifted each side as if he were lifting a kitten. The Second Formers moved left or right to get a better look.

Inside each box Kyle had built a scene. Inside the biggest

box, he had made skyscrapers and streets, street lights and cars. We could smell the rubber cement. Inside shoe boxes, he had cutouts and painted shadows and plastic trees. With each box he opened, he laid out a world.

Jimmy said, "I want to see."

Maggie said, "Miss Alta, can we come up?"

"Let him finish," I said.

Even the smallest box opened up. One had a shack, a miniature of the houses in the shanty towns, complete with tin roofs. Another was a miniature lake where uranium was leached, with the logo of Nufcor on a shack on its shore.

"It's your show, Kyle," I said. "Want people to come up?" I got out of the table in the second row, and pulled a chair to the side of the room.

Kyle tugged the hair on the back of his head. It was already sticking up. He pulled a wad of papers out of his sweatshirt pouch. They had the rough edges of notebook paper torn out.

"I have to tell you a story first," he said.

Almost all the students had read their reports to the class without looking up. Few had props, and none had boxes that folded out into cities. They read facts and figures easily copied from encyclopedias that Herbert the librarian had brought them. Kyle unrolled the lined paper, tried to smooth it open with his hand.

"Once upon a time," Kyle said, "there lived a little boy in South Africa. His name was Mukutu." Kyle looked at David with his thick glasses. Then, Kyle looked at Tommy.

"He grew up in a township called Soweto with his five brothers and three sisters, his mother, but his father lived in a different place because he worked in a mine." He sat at the table behind his boxes laid out and looked down on his papers only a few times. His feet swung from the chair.

Kyle described the shanty town in which the family lived, told of the food, the water, the work. As he told Mukutu's story, without his metallic voice, without his weird noises, the other students quit looking at each other. They threw no paper balls.

The room was loud like it was when we sang the songs of the African National Congress, but no one was singing. Our room, usually stuffed with sock smell, became dry as a gourd and scented with palm oil. Our room was Kyle's world.

At times in the story, Kyle pointed to one of his boxes. The students leaned to see. His eyes were not animal. His eyes were round and thirteen. He was the center.

Even David said, "Awesome," when Kyle pointed to the box that looked like a lake.

"Uranium," Kyle said, "makes South Africa one of the most important countries in the world." That word, soft and raw, started his speech speeding up. He described the way uranium was discovered in rich slurries of gold mining in the Transvaal. He told how the oil shortage led them to develop the first uranium mine, called Beisa, how the ore was milled, cut with chemicals and turned into lakes, dried out, and then, the enrichment was needed to convert the forms of uranium into fuel, the fission process needed for bombs. Kyle described a nuclear warhead, what it weighs, how big it is, what it takes to blow one up. All of it made his cheeks red.

"And Mukutu knew," Kyle said, "that if a bomb blew up over Cape Town, if the epicenter were right here," Kyle stood up and pointed to the middle of his biggest landscape, "he knew that there would be nothing left. Within an hour, nothing." Kyle bent down, and from inside his backpack he pulled a gavel. It was brown and shiny, like the one Mr. Francosi used to start the debates for the debate team.

Gavel in his right hand, papers in his left, he said, "Mukutu knew that his brothers and sisters, mother and father, didn't have a chance. Everything would be destroyed, shattered, wiped out, melted, eviscerated, gone." Kyle raised the gavel over his head, and before I could say, "Stop," he brought the gavel down on the city he created. He raised and lowered the gavel, and made pieces fly, pieces of plastic and cardboard and little metal cars. I felt the beat of the gavel in my chest. He bashed in the lake. He bashed in the shack. He bashed in streets and shadows and road signs.

The Second Formers cheered. Some yelled, "Oh no, Mr. Bill," and the high pitch of "No" hurt my ears. They filled the room with clapping and voices and whistles, all for Kyle. The Second Form was his. Kyle was the center.

Kyle pounded and pounded the table. Each pound was harder than the last, and his neck was red.

"Shattered," he shouted. "Shattered."

# Song / **Phoenix**

WHAT I DIDN'T TELL Kyle about his falling-brick, falling-body question is G, the Universal Gravitational Constant, $6.672 \times 10^{-11}\ N^2/kg^2$. Newton is amazing. Actually, it was Cavendish.

That Kyle, Mr. Different, there's something different about his different.

After class on the way back to the dorm, the leaves have fallen in turbulence. No scientific way to predict how they fall. The bench by the lake under the birches is free. Good view. The lake is wave drag. Those birch leaves in the sun, they smell like ironing.

No one else could, so I did what I could for Kim: ironed what she used to iron. Shirts, skirts, napkins. It's not like my parents weren't able to iron, or exert the force required. None of that. It was grief. Too much emotion through too small a vessel.

The last year or so, Kim was too weak. Too many episodes. *Thrombotic thrombocytopenic purpura*, such a stupid, rare disease. Purpura, bleeding into her skin. Her blood not making platelets. Her body throwing clots wherever. Her cane tapped on the sidewalk. She was eighty-something, not her real age, twenty-something. I could always find her. Just listened. Mom worked less and less. No painting. Less money. After college, I came home.

Every morning, two flowers in a Coke bottle on the kitchen table. Every morning, Mom and me and coffee. Black.

"How's Kim?" I say.

"In bed." Mom doesn't look up from the dishes she's washing. Last night's burger plate, Dad's beer bottle, the morning's coffee pot already gone. Dad downed his cup, left to join the paint crew. Not only houses any more. Big jobs. Industrial. Face masks and ventilators.

In Korean, she says, "Too much tired," and she puts her hands on the counter, her shoulders rounded beneath her white T-shirt, the one I gave her from Stanford.

"She's amazing," I say, "the way she bounces back."

"Not much now." Mom leans forward on her hands.

Outside the window in front of the sink, agave leaves stick up. A century plant has green buds high in the air, and a jade has grown thick in the fifteen years we've been here. The lawn is nothing but lava rock and cactus.

Not much any more are the evenings my parents spend on the front deck, listening to Elvis, drinking beer, laughing in Korean. We spend our evenings putting pillows under Kim's swollen knees, gently rubbing her skin with all the blood bubbles, taking her to the hospital when her heart rate gets too high.

She shouldn't have died that fall, 1980. Too much blood, nowhere to go. Getting out of the car, her cane. Phone ringing inside the house. Mr. Japanese-Man, her boyfriend, might be calling. She had to get there, had to answer the phone. She tripped, and I didn't catch her. Flat on the sidewalk. Clots, enzymes, autopsy said she threw a clot to her brain. Inherited rare disease, TTP, I could have it, too.

That paisley blue and gold shirt, button-down, with a navy skirt. Lots of pleats. The ironing board is wooden, thin legs that cross. I iron everything on the green dot, red dot, orange dot cover. Unzip the skirt and pull it around the board. Hold the waist with my right hand, fold the one-inch pleat along the crease, put a finger on it, press the steaming iron with my left. With a few minutes free time, I can iron anything. Skirts are cake.

Hot on a fall day. The window over the sink bright with agave leaves, the afternoon sun. Turn the skirt. Fold the pleat, press Kim's outfit. Nose the iron into the seams by the zipper. Smell the steam. Hear the sound of release. Water turning to steam is amazing. At sea level, the temperature that water converts to vapor is 212 degrees Fahrenheit. Move higher in elevation, the temperature needed to boil falls. At 8,000 feet, the boiling point is 198 degrees. Kim loved little facts.

She looked younger than eighty, younger than twenty, lying there in the pleated skirt and paisley shirt. The funeral home smelled of plumeria and jasmine. White flowers. Kim's face so cold, so smooth. No blood bubbles any more. Dark eyebrows, no lines between her eyebrows. No more laughing at stupid jokes. Mom and Dad and I were done with sitting on benches in the hospital, always the pages announced overhead, the doctor's names too loud.

"Mr. Song," someone calls. The lake in front of me, the student behind me. Kyle, I presume.

"Mr. Not-Dressed-for-Dinner," I say. I don't even turn my head.

"Can you show me?" he says. He sits down on the bench next to me, his backpack still on so he's pitched forward. His hand is stuffed with paper, brown package wrap, and colored construction paper, and a few sheets of gift wrap.

"Exactly what, young sir?"

"How to fold," he says. He spreads the paper on the bench between us.

"An airplane?"

"No," he says, "something real, like a bird or dinosaur."

That thing in my chest happens. That Taiko strike to my sternum, my ribs vibrate. Did he see me put the dinosaur in the tree?

"Origami," I say. "It's an art, Mr. Harney. Not just anyone can do it."

"Why not?" He looks at me with small eyes, animal eyes.

"Why do you want to do it?" My ribs are loud with the drumbeat.

His greasy mop of hair, he turns his face away from me. "For Carla," he says.

My ribs can't hold the drumbeat. Carla. My forehead is part of the drum. The waves on the lake are cresting, white caps. The sky holds in the sound. The leaves are falling around us, falling unpredictably.

"The Sixth Former?" I say.

"Sure," he says. "She likes origami. I've seen her collection of bugs and dinosaurs and birds and things." He picks up a piece of the brown package wrap, hands it to me.

"Young man, origami is not for impressing girls."

"Okay, can you just show me?"

I take the brown package wrap. I exhale while the Taiko mallets strike. Young man, big dreams. The mallets soften. To him a Sixth Form girl is the Holy Grail. No pounding in my ribs.

"Do you have a notebook in your backpack?" I say.

And he twists his body to pull the backpack off. He pulls an enormous three-ring binder out, and papers fall as he lifts it. Papers tumble in the wind and land around our feet. The wind picks them up, and we're trying to step on the papers flying around us. We run to ones turning cartwheels on the lawn. I get a foot on one, and another flies off. He stamps on one, and falls forward to catch another. We're playing Twister, on all fours. We move one limb toward the other so we can grab more than one paper at a time. We both are crawling on the ground and we look at each other. Kyle's eyes are child eyes. Papers come up with leaves in our hands, and we rise up off the lawn.

The binder is worn in the creases. On the cover, he's drawn silos, water towers of nuclear power plants. Spiraling lines of the vapor escaping from the towers. Hard, dark lines in pencil, dug in, smudged. Around the towers are bodies, masses of arms and legs and faces melting, piles of bodies, cars upended. His notebook is nuclear holocaust, the point of detonation.

The binder goes on top of the pile of paper he wants to fold. The piece of brown package wrap in my hand goes on top of the drawing on his binder. Each fold I show him, the angles, the different basic patterns. He watches, and his eyes grow bigger than teenage eyes. They get big like a camera lens, like he's recording. And we sit past the warning bell for dinner. And the light on the lake goes purple. We sit on the bench, and I fold, and he folds, and the light from the dorm behind us goes on, and we make cranes.

The part Kyle likes the best is folding down the wings and pulling on the head and tail to expand the body. He likes blowing on the body to fill it out. Enough air to fill enough space. We make real things. Cranes. No gravitational force needed. Cranes spill over the blast zone of his binder. Out of the annihilation, out of the mess of papers, before a lake perfectly calm at night, cranes rise.

# Taylor / **All the Sky Gray**

CAN'T BREATHE. GET AWAY. Phone call from your mom. Your body. Found. Near where your jacket was. Run out my screen door, the slam behind me. Sky gray. Run around the cove where the boathouse is. Run across the lawn between the dorms and the lake, far enough away that no one sees me. No one hears me. Stop. Double over. My hands on my thighs. Can't breathe. Can't stop. Off again. Pumping arms, legs high, lungs burn, no air. Fifty meters, one hundred, into the middle of the cornfield.

Geese take off. Honk. The field explodes. Birds shoot up. The sky isn't gray now. It's tangles, birds going ballistic. My mind runs faster than my legs, and they give out, and I'm down, collapsed like those buildings blown from the inside, collapsing on themselves. That's how I go down. Cornstalks hit my face, and scrape my ear, and my palms try to stop me, but cornstalks poke.

"Miss Alta," somebody yells. Somebody sees me. In the middle of a cornfield with geese crazy, I'm face-planted in cornstalks, and no kidding, somebody sees me.

No way.

I ball up, wrap my arms around my knees and tuck my head in. Maybe I'll blend in, and they'll go away. Maybe they won't see my Tim's windshirt. My arms pull in tight, and I can't keep the cry in any more. It comes out like air leaking, and I rock. The sound is high and little. The sound is like dying.

Somebody reaches me, and knees go on either side of me, and arms go around the ball of me, and I let somebody pull me in. "Ms. Alta," somebody says, and it's Carla, and the high sound in me keeps coming out. I let her rock me, and she's warm. I'm in her arms, and her legs squeeze, and pretty soon the high sound goes low, and my whole body bucks, and she holds on. Carla's wool sweater smells like wet cardboard, it's been out in the cold, and she's kissing my hair, kissing my ear, and I bury my head in her shoulder, and we're warm, and I say, "Sarah."

She says, "Shh, it's okay," and she kisses my shoulder, my back. My head slides down her shoulder, and I brush my face on her chest, and my arms come around her, and we're holding on. My eyes close, and I see Sarah's body all bloated on the shore, under the water, snagged under the surface, and there's wool and Carla's hair in my mouth and the two of us. Warm.

A sound like gagging comes behind us. Over my shoulder I see Kyle. Kyle is here too, and he's gagging behind us, and I turn. Kyle with Carla in the cornfield? Kyle seeing us. Kyle repulsed and gagging at the sight of us.

Kyle is two hands around his neck, his thumbs digging in the front of his neck, his tongue way out. His gagging is a dry cough, hacking, and his eyes roll back, and then he keels over on the corn. His hands are locked on his neck, his elbows high in the air, and his legs kick out. He's totally choking himself.

I'm on my feet and over to him. "Kyle," I say, "Kyle," and I kneel in the mud next to him, grab his arms, and Kyle twists on the ground. I pull back, try to get his hands off his neck, but he twists and his face is getting red, and he makes different sounds, like flat tire sounds, like flap flap, and I'm trying so hard to get his hands off his neck that I pull him toward me in the mud, and I rock back on my knees and stand up, and Kyle comes off the ground. I'm lifting him off the ground, and he won't let go of his neck.

"Kyle," I say, "let go," and he does.

His eyes bug out, and his arms stay in my hands, but the rest of him crashes to the ground. He lands on his knees. And then he's panting like a dog, his tongue out and his head down. His arms are up in my hands, and I'm standing, and it looks like he's almost praying, begging me for something. He looks up at me from far away on the ground. His eyes, looking up into my eyes, hold no disgust for two girls hugging in the mud. His eyes have the geese and carry the sky.

I say, "What's wrong?"

"Everything," Kyle says. "Too much."

"What is, Kyle?" My hands let go of his forearms and take his hands. His shoulders go lower.

"Pain."

"You've got too much pain?"

"Everybody," he says.

And it's the three of us, Carla sitting on the mud, me standing, and Kyle kneeling. The gray sky almost touches us. The geese are settled into the next field. It's the three of us in all the sky gray.

And way too much pain for one little boy.

And Carla starts talking. "Shit, Kyle. You totally scared me."

"Sorry." Kyle slumps back on his feet.

Carla starts talking really fast, like she's a little girl and trying to tell a big person that there's a fire. She tells me how she got to the edge of the cornfield and took a runner's stance, hands on mud, how she said the start commands for a race, '*Êtes-vous prêt? Partez*!' and sprinted into the field, blew right by Kyle, how he blended in like a moth. But then he stood up and scared the shit out of her, how he asked her why she scared the geese, and she said she didn't know why, just wanted to. And he called that "gratuitous stimulation" and went all machine-talk on her.

"'Gra-tu-i-tous-stim-u-la-tion' and moved all choppy like he does," she says. I can really see his head jerking with each syllable. He kneels while she tells the story.

And she keeps talking, says that she told him to cut it out, and he did. She asked him what he meant by the gratuitous thing. And he said that kids in the dorm jump him just for fun, just for the satisfaction. Gratuitous.

Carla is breathless telling this part, and the sky is clear of the geese, gray with clouds so low they keep the sound close.

She says he raised his shirt and there were bruises all over that the boys gave him. They wait till he's asleep, and then they come in his cubicle and jump on his bed. He's sleeping on his stomach, and they pinch him all over. And he says that he doesn't let the kids see it hurts. Mr. Song can't know, or the kids will do him worse. They said so to him. He said he can take it.

And maybe he can take it, this little boy in the brown field. But he shouldn't.

"Show her, Kyle," Carla says. "Show Ms. Alta your legs."

"Will not." His hands press his sweats to his ankles.

"Show her."

"No." With one hand he grabs a handful of cornstalks, tosses it.

"Why not?" Carla's voice goes louder. She leans toward him.

"You're making stuff up," Kyle says. The way he's kneeling makes his head about the same height as Carla's, the way she's sitting in the mud. He's looking at her, and his face is blank the way the sky is blank.

Carla's face is a painting. It's a Warhol, a stencil, a white face against red, then a red face against yellow, then a yellow face against blue. There's a red thing coming from her taking over. It's like the field and the sky and the geese have a film over them. Brown field goes red field. Gray sky goes red sky.

"Fuck you," she says. "I saw them."

Her words land on him, like she pushed him, and he rolls back, his feet coming up, and then he curls up on his side, on the mud in the cornfield.

"Cut it out," I say. I step in front of Carla, my legs blocking her, and I face Kyle, curled up like a potato bug in the field.

His arms go over his head. "You can't be like them," he says. "Go away." He tucks his legs up.

My knee lands in the mud. On one side of me, a little boy lies, holding everything in. On the other side of me, a girl sits with her fists on her knees. Her face flashes red, white, yellow. She is a canvas, flattened. The red hot thing comes out her eyes.

"I'm not like them, Kyle," she says. "I'm not like them." And she's crying. I don't think she ever cries. And inside me two forces pull apart. I know what it means to be torn down, the coaches yelling, picking at every catch, calling us names, demeaning. They toughened us to care less about the body and more about the win. The boys in the dorm, they care nothing about Kyle. They tear him down to feel more about their bodies. If I tell Mr. White and the boys are punished, Kyle will be pummeled. If I don't tell, Kyle will be pummeled. What I know now, I'll keep. I can keep him safe.

"It's turbulence," Kyle says. "They do what they want. You can't stop them."

And it's the three of us, one girl, one boy, and me, the one who is supposed to tend. And geese in the next field. The cold of November is the mud where my knee rests, where Kyle's shoulder curls, where Carla sits. There is no other world than this, me with a body rising after ten weeks in a river, Carla with all the want red in her eyes, and one little boy with pain marking him inside and out.

# Song / **The Mass of the Earth**

CAVENDISH ADDED TO NEWTON = mass of the earth.

Figure out the distance from the center of the earth to the center of a person: $6.38 \times 10^6$ meters. It's all in the relation of two bodies. Cavendish is awesome.

He got G, the universal gravitational constant, and that's what I didn't tell Kyle when he asked about a body falling.

Even in the middle of Einstein's theory of relativity, there's G. And all those pansy social scientists say there's nothing absolute. Here's one. G is always the same. Always. They also throw around terms like "sphere of influence." They make it sound like science. Like gravitational field. Tell me about it. Let's talk Japan during the war. Koreans can tell you lots about spheres of influence.

But G is benign.

Figuring out G gives a person the mass of the world.

The way Cavendish did it was so precise, so patient. He measured the way that metal balls affect each other when suspended from long metal rods, and he helped measure the inverse proportional pull of two objects on each other. Since Newton couldn't figure out the mass of the earth in his time, Cavendish had to go at it a different way, and turn it on its ear, solve for G. Once he got $6.67 \times 10^{-11}Nm^2/kg^2$, he could figure that the mass of the earth was

$$M_e = \frac{9.81 \times (6.38 \times 10^6)^2}{6.67 \times 10^{-11}}$$

That's the mass on Alta's shoulders.

It's in the news. *Body surfaces a mile and a half downstream from Boathouse Row, identified as female in her twenties, presumed the rowing coach from the prep school who drowned ten weeks ago in a rowing accident on the Schuylkill.* The media have a way of putting things. Body. Presumed. Prep school. Not Alta's friend. Not someone's daughter. Not Sarah.

My sister's name, Kim, 金, means gold. My father, the chemist, was also Mr. Historian, proud of the biggest clan in Korea, bragged about our heritage through Kim. But when she died, from an inherited disease, he didn't want anything in the papers, only the short obit I wrote. I'm no Hemingway, but in the paper, she was our sister and daughter, our gold.

Rower Girl Alta lives in an apartment attached to the girls' dorm. The day the news breaks, I go to check on her. Not that she knows I exist. Before I go, I fold a rowing shell. Give me a big piece of paper, and I can make anything. Oars are tricky.

The distance between her dorm and my dorm, maybe fifty meters. Down the hall to her apartment, one open door blasts Grateful Dead, and another blasts Earth, Wind & Fire, and another Talking Heads. Pitiful music afflicts both sexes. There's music coming from Ms. Alta's place as well. God-awful. Christopher Cross. King of the Sappy.

Knocking pushes the door open, and King Sappy's song slams me. "Sailing, sailing" are the only words I catch. It must be their song. A song about skin drag, the tension of a body across water. Rowers are predictable.

The living room is girl bodies. Ms. Alta is the queen sitting in an overstuffed armchair, and two Fifth Formers sit on the armrests. Fourth Formers and Third Formers sit cross-legged on the floor, leaning back on knees. Her rowing team is here, the one Second Form girl, Maggie Anderson, and the girls assigned to her dinner table.

And Carla.

The curls fall in Carla's eyes, and she uses that hand, fingers straight out, wrist flat in line with the elbow, the mannequin move, to sweep the curls out of her face. Her high-tops, untied, are parked in front of her. She's leaning on her elbows, elbows on her knees, toward Alta. Inverse square formula applies to the attraction two bodies exert.

"Mr. Song," Alta says. She tries to push off from the chair, but kids are at her feet, kids on her armrest. She's stuck under the weight of the world.

"Ms. Alta, you're busy," I say across the room, over Christopher Sappy on the record player. The girls on the floor and the girls on the armrests look at each other. The rumor mill fires up. Few men go into the girls' dorms. No boys. No girls in boys' dorms. Usually.

"No, please, have a seat," she says, and that's when Carla turns to me, her shoulders turning with her chin. That's when Alta stands up. So I hold out the paper shell.

About fourteen inches long, the ends pointy. I made it from brown origami paper with leaf prints in a darker brown. The hull is rounded like a real rowing shell. But the oars look like legs. Another stupid bug. A centipede. That's the way Carla will see it. How simple. Anyone can make a centipede. Adolescent boy in the middle of Tim-Tim girls, my gift is a stupid piece of paper.

Ms. Rower meets me in the middle. "That's an eight," she says. "How did you do that?"

The fourteen-inch paper is small in her hands. Her eyes are level with the shell. The creases and the folds have names.

"Practice," I say.

"It's beautiful. It must've taken forever."

"Give me a big piece of paper and twenty minutes, no problem." This line almost stops my throat. I've used it so often. Carla knows. Carla's looking at me, Ms. Testament to My Indiscretion. She is static electricity.

Alta tips the shell one way to look in, tips it another. Her blue eyes are gray, and the eyelids are puffy. She's not here, not in this living room packed with Tim-Tim girls. She's not on this beige carpet, and she's not six feet tall. She's on the lake, feeling the drag of the eight on the surface of the water, timing her body to match her friend's body. Floating in the Schuylkill.

After Kim died, I wasn't a lot of places. The grocery store. The kitchen. The classroom. Sure, I cooked meals, and I graded lab books, but really, I was sitting on Kim's bed, reading to her the latest *Doonesbury* and *Bloom County*, taking her temperature.

No science can explain grief.

"Won't you sit?" Ms. Rower-Girl has manners, white girl, old money. Every place to sit is taken by one or two girls. A Little Miss Manners gets up from a chair, and I sit in the mass of bodies. The girls on the armrests where Alta was sitting are still looking at each other, talking without talking.

Rambo, by the brown dresser, gets up to change the record. Bye-bye, King Sappy. Grateful Dead. Carla's music. She puts on "The Wheel," and she cranks up the volume. Dorms are dens of hearing loss.

Carla doesn't sit down. She turns toward Alta and me. We're on one side of the living room. And she closes her eyes, and her body goes liquid. Like amber, electricity. Things that change substance. The way she moves, her jerky motions smooth out. She follows the form of the music. Her shoulders curl closed and open, and her hips and shoulders and knees turn little circles. The curves of her body catch her loose clothing, suggest the waves that bodies can make when skin drags across skin.

The other girls in the room aren't looking at each other. Their faces are spotlights. They stare. Conveyers of Negative Ions. I stare.

Carla dances in a room full of girls, and one coach stuffed with grief, and one guy stuffed with guilt. We are caught in her gravitational field. The two adults in the room have the greatest mass, and thus, we are attracted more. My greater emotional mass generating attraction has an inverse effect on my resistance.

Sure, it's science. Carla exerts her sphere of influence, and we are caught in the sphere. But each of us has a sphere. Therefore, Alta and I exert ours on her, ours on each other. All objects with mass will pull toward each other with gravitational force.

Imagine the pull if a person carries the weight of the earth.

EVENINGS IN STUDY HALL, forces acting upon inertia are revealed. Most students believe that inertia is the resistance to change. Wrong. Or it's doing nothing. Wrong again. It's the resistance an object has to a change in its state of motion. Inertia is potential, and it relies on tension.

So, if Donny Zurkus, King of the All-Nighter, keeps his head on his open textbook, drools on the page, and keeps sleeping, that's not inertia. That's study hall.

So, if all goes well, I can blast through ten lab books in the hour. Since Kyle's here, who knows. Study hall's for the kings and queens of wayward acts or mediocre minds. Every time Kyle's here, he asks me to fold bugs and buildings and gifts. He asks about inertia, skin drag, and vectors. He's here a lot.

Ever since we folded cranes, he's folded simpler things and pretended not to be folding. Not usually the Sneaky King. Strolling through the desks, I read late homework for Algebra and Geography, French and Social Science. When Mediocre Minds try to hide their procrastinating habits, they slide homework over the top, bring pencils to their mouths, and say, "Hmmmm."

"As if," Carla would say.

On one of my tours of the procrastinators, when I saw an origami box with "You're the best rower. Donny Zurkus" on Kyle's desk, he didn't pull a paper across it. Not subtle. So obvious he goes invisible.

The second one was a bat, the mammalian kind. Kindergarten kids can make bats. Inside the wings, it read, "You're number one" on one wing, and "in my cave" on the other. And "Donny Zurkus" was down the belly, all caps. Kyle was playing a dangerous game.

The third one was a bluebird. On a scale of one, easy, and ten, tough-to-make, it's a two. Nice folds, though. No do-overs. Striking blue paper. Inside it said, "Meet me before dinner in the cornfield. Donny." Since dinner happens before study hall, this note was to be given the following day. The boy was planning. He was so engrossed in his planning, he didn't see me pass behind him.

Here inertia was motion, the tendency to stay in motion. Kyle was Newton's First Law by setting something in motion at a certain velocity. Newton was amazing. If there were no drag or other force acting, what Kyle starts would continue forever. Surely Zurkus will stop whatever it is.

In any way I can, I will resist resistance to this object in motion. Kyle will complete what he has set in motion. He will beat Bad-Boy Zurkus on his own. Completion of his plan by his own hand will teach him more than anything I can help him achieve.

# Taylor / **Rokkaku**

Y<small>OU'RE NOT IN THE</small> fog on the lake, not in the beat of the music in the lesbian bar, not in the honey smell when the bay doors of the boathouse open. Last weekend you were buried in the mountains in Colorado. That's where you are. Rand McNally maps are not so simple any more. Not looking for you any more leaves me with a watermark, like a rowing shell kept out of the water, a gray line along the hull, a mark that won't go away.

It's Kyle I'm looking for now. Ever since the choking episode in the field, he's been hard to keep an eye on.

After the 300 kids in the school went to UD, Wilmington, to see *"Master Harold" . . . and the Boys*, I made my Geography class make kites. They thought I was nuts. But then, with spools of string and balsa wood and paper and glue all over the tables in the classroom, with Second Formers sticky with concentration, they got quiet. Folding and gluing and tying tails was the world made simple.

After twenty minutes the dozen of us ran into the cold sunny day, the air like tight clothes around us, and despite their St.

Timothy's coats and ties and skirts and blazers, they ran over the lawns in front of the buildings, those prep school buildings with stone blocks this way and stone blocks that way. The Second Formers were kids laughing and yelling to each other. They were thirteen-year-olds, adolescents, wild things allowed to be wild.

The teaching objective was to lift their faces to the sky like in the play. They lifted their voices and ran together. Even Kyle was one of them. Maybe the objective was to make me look up. It's been awhile. But like everything else this year, something happened instead.

His kite was fold after fold in a design unlike anything. Everyone else made the Charlie Brown kite, the long cross of balsa wood, the newspaper folds at the corners, the little tail off the pointy end. Before we came outside, Kyle made no machine noises from his seat in the back row, simply added another spar across the spine. He took two pieces of newspaper, and folded the corners back, and made a hexagon a little longer than wide. He called it a "Rok," said it was Japanese, a master fighter. On the underside, he painted tie-dye colors of purple and red and yellow, and in the middle with thick black markers, he made a peace sign.

The other kids acted strange. They didn't call him Zippy or weird or teacher's pet. They watched Kyle bring his big, bright kite out on the lawn. They looked at the kite with a different shape, and they didn't say a thing.

Maggie was the first to launch hers. She put her Charlie Brown kite on the ground and walked twenty feet, then turned to face it. She called to herself, "One, two, three," and on three, she yanked the kite up in front of her, ran backwards a few steps, and fell hard on her rear, her legs rising up, the kite crashing on the ground.

"Smooth move, Ex-Lax," Tommy Underwood said.

"As if you could do it, dweeb," Maggie said. Her legs were in a V in front of her.

"Okay, okay," Tommy said. "Piece of cake."

His kite was orange, so soaked with paint that the entire Geography class might not get it off the ground. His dad went to Princeton, and many of Tommy's notebooks and sweatshirts were orange and black. With one hand, he held the kite over his head, and before he even started to run, he roared like the Princeton tiger. It was a few steps before he threw the kite into the air, a little too hard, the kite too heavy, crashing in front of Tommy with a crack.

Still on the ground, Maggie said, "Psych."

Kyle was quiet, standing in the middle of the lawn, the Second Formers crashing their kites around him. Then, Terence set down his own kite, made from newsprint and no colors, walked over to where Kyle stood with the Peace Rok, a bright slab of color, resting on the tops of his high-tops.

Terence said, "Hey, Kyle, let's try it, running, with yours."

Kyle looked at the spool of string in his hands, and nodded, and didn't look up at Terence, the first boy to team with him in ten weeks of class. Kyle's lips were a little curved, a smile he tried not to let into his cheeks. Terence took the Rok and walked about forty feet away.

"Ready?" Terence said. One hand was on the long side of the Rok held over his head, and the other hand was where the strings came together from the four points attached to the kite.

"Ready," Kyle said.

"Okay, on three. One, two, three." And both boys ran together against the wind, across the lawn, lined with maples bare in the cold. They ran, attached by string, until Terence released the Rok, like releasing a dove, letting it fly above him. Kyle stopped and held the string.

For a moment the world was a kite going up and a dozen people on a lawn. For a moment, the maple limbs were not the only things reaching into the sky. The thirteen-year-olds were quiet and watched the kite.

Then they exploded with "Woo-hoo!" "Up, up, and away!" and "Awesome, Kyle." The kite kept going up and up. A couple boys did high-fives. Kyle's kite was the only one to fly.

Kyle fed the kite. He let it rise. It rose to the tree tops. It rose higher.

And we looked up. Maggie, the one girl in class, and I, and all the boys raised our eyes. It felt good to see the sky and branches without leaves and the sun in the fading light of November, near December.

But I didn't see Donny coming.

He came really fast, his arms out in front and pumping. He came for one reason.

"Son of a bitch," Donny said. His hands out in front of him, his forearms plowed into Kyle.

At five feet ten inches, Donny outweighed Kyle by a good fifty pounds, and even if Kyle hadn't been looking up above the trees at his Peace Rok, he would've flown through the air. Kyle rolled, but kept his hand gripping the string. His body was a spindle spinning. He wasn't hurt. But no matter how careful he was, the string tugged the kite. The Rok dove and rose, made drunken loops, plunged toward the maples. His classmates covered their eyes.

Kyle down on the ground, his kite diving, I ran. My voice wasn't going to stop Donny, but from thirty feet away, I said, "Donny Zurkus, stop." Donny took three steps to where Kyle landed, and he rammed his knee into Kyle's stomach. His elbow cocked up, his fist at the end of it, I grabbed his shoulders and jerked him back. Donny went down on his side. Kyle twisted away and stayed on the ground, held the string, kept his eyes on the kite. Donny spun around on all fours like a cat attacking.

"Stop it," I said.

Donny went still, the still of muscles taut, the type of still that's ringing. "He's totally dead," he said.

"What?"

"I'm going to kill him."

"Kyle?"

"Totally."

The Second Formers gathered around the three of us, their kites in heaps on the lawn. The three of us, Kyle on the ground, holding on to his kite, still flying. Donny kneeling on the ground, sitting back on his heels, and me standing above the boys.

"Why?"

"He knows." Donny looked down at Kyle. His greasy hair sticking straight up, Kyle still held his kite, still watched it. The line was almost all let out, and the kite a speck in the sky.

"Okay, let's go. Both of you go see Mr. White."

Donny swung his arms out from his sides and spun like a corkscrew. "Why?" Donny said. "He's the one who did something." His voice was not the menacing voice in English class. It was smaller. It let in the picture of him as a boy. He was not the muscular teenager, pinned by a desk.

"We'll see," I said. "Just meet me there at the warning bell for dinner. Now, get to your class." Donny turned toward the main building.

"Okay, everybody. Get your kites and head back to class. We'll be right there." The Second Formers turned away from us and shook their heads, scattered across the close-cut lawn to collect their kites.

Kyle was winding the string. He started his noises. "Zzzzz," he said. Like the string was a fishing line, and he was reeling. Whole breaths were Zs. One after another.

"Kyle," I said. But he kept making his Z noises. "Meet at White's."

Kyle had no response to being sent to the headmaster's, no response to Donny. He wound the string of the kite into a ball, kept wrapping the string, reeling in the Rok. Terence stopped before heading into the building. He stood behind Kyle and said nothing. He turned to face me. His eyes were dark when the sky was fall bright. His eyes looked to see if I knew what would happen next, but I didn't know. In the breeze of that afternoon, an afternoon of kites and friends making kites fly, Terence showed me with his eyes that he didn't need me to know.

All the other Second Formers had Charlie Brown kites, now pieces. All the others went back in the building of stone blocks this way and stone blocks that way. Kyle never came in. He didn't come to the meeting at the headmaster's office at the warning bell for dinner. I checked the table he was assigned for dinner, and he wasn't there.

The next day, Kyle's kite, caught in the maple limbs reaching into the sky, made a flapping sound. Without leaves any more, the maples made no sound. With a kite torn and caught in the limbs, the maples beat the blue sky.

# Song / **Study Hall**

BESIDES LAB BOOKS TO grade during study hall, I have to prepare. Big time. Mr. Forward-Thinking White wants me to prepare the students to see *The Day After*, some hyped-up Cold War movie about the day after nuclear holocaust. Made for TV. Great timing after accusations of meddling in air space, after a Korean jetliner was obliterated in a test of nerves. I'm supposed to teach the physics of nuclear energy and weaponry and, as the headmaster puts it, "nuclear survival."

"As if," Carla would say.

At least White wants discussion. The plan is not to foist the horror upon the innocents, but to expose them and to help them understand. Tomorrow night the whole school is watching the TV movie together. Even Kyle, with the nuclear mushroom cloud on his notebook. The students excited to get out of chapel are Children of Inertia. Others with real fear of real possibilities are Children of the Cold War. Like Kyle.

But tonight Kyle is Mr. Chuckles. I've never seen him so smiley. His hair is slicked down and parted, not sticking in every direction. He has his Tim-Tim's blazer on, and his tie is tied evenly. Brochure Cover Boy. His books are stacked in front of him, instead of scattered around his feet. His notebook, with the nuclear epicenter on the cover, is spread flat across the desk, and he's bent over some white-lined paper. If I'm not mistaken, his fingers are clean. He's digging his pencil into the paper and writing something. Every few words he looks up, laughs like a kid who's discovered snow.

Maybe he's writing a comic strip for Ms. Alta's class. Probably not a Geography assignment. Maybe English. Maybe he's writing a love letter to Carla. Maybe not.

One time reading *Bloom County* to Kim, I got her laughing so hard her IV almost popped out. The comic strip was the one where Opus has amnesia until he finds out that Diane Sawyer married Eddie Murphy.

The nurse who Kim and I called Ms. Weasel came through the curtain to check Kim's temperature, like clockwork, and she said, "Sir, Ms. Song is not to be agitated."

And I said, "Laughter does not agitate. That requires an entirely different motion."

"Mr. Song," Nurse Weasel said. "Try to behave." And she spun on her thick white shoes, slapped the curtain aside, and vanished, although that takes an entirely different motion as well.

We only laughed harder, me in my metal chair next to her bed, Kim holding her stomach and falling back into the stack of pillows on the hospital bed.

Kyle is laughing hard, too. The other students near his desk turn their heads to look at him, but they're used to his noises. One person throws a wad of paper. Kyle knocks it away with one hand. Laughs again. He's all smiles. Mr. Happy-to-Be-Here.

The door hinge to the study hall squeaks even if opened slowly. There's Alta sticking her head in.

"Mr. Song," Alta says. Her neck is long like the rest of her. "May I speak with you?"

I nod.

Without causing friction between my chair and the wood floor, I leave my stack of lab books and make it out the door. She's still in her chapel clothes, skirt, blazer, penny loafers.

"Is Kyle in there?" She crosses her arms.

"As usual."

She smiles a half smile into her cheek. "That's funny," she says, "he missed half my class, an appointment, and dinner." She looks down at her feet. Her body is so muscled she has to tip forward to see over her crossed arms.

"Who knows the mind of a Second Former."

"That's for sure," she says. "But Donny Zurkus is on the war path."

"What for?"

"I'm not sure. Both of them were to meet me at White's before dinner. Only Donny showed up." The fingers of one hand stroke her forehead.

"I can tell you that Mr. Zurkus is asleep in study hall, and Kyle is quite ebullient this evening."

"Kyle?"

"Mr. Smiles. He's writing something and laughing."

"Well," she says, "this Donny thing can wait, I guess. I'll find out when White's free tomorrow morning, and leave you a note tonight for Kyle." Her hand drops from her face. Laws of gravity work for falling objects. There's no law for concern falling away. Alta's face no longer has the emotion it did when she walked in.

"Fine idea."

What I don't say is that I saw Kyle meet Carla in the cornfield before dinner. What I don't say is that Donny could sneak into Kyle's cubby tonight. But it's late in the evening, the lab books are not grading themselves, and what I could say is unscientific.

Rower-Dyke Alta, her skirt and blazer, turns the hall into a cave with her tall walk, her shoulders rotating each step. Optical illusion. But since the beginning of the year, since the faculty cocktail party on the lawn of the main building, she's shorter. A friend's death by river makes any body shrink. No object resists that much gravity.

Back through the squeaky door, I return to my pile of lab books in time for the bell to ring. Study hall turns into racetrack. Masters and Mistresses of Underachievement spring from their desks, grab their books, and sprint out the door. Donny Zurkus stretches one arm high in the air, looks over at Kyle, drops his arm, grabs the book he slobbered on, and takes off.

Not Kyle.

Cover-Boy Kyle has two hands on his desk. Between them is his open notebook, his white lined paper, and the letter or whatever, written in pencil. I swear, he's smiling. His elbows straighten out, his palms press flat on the desk, and he grins at the paper. King of the Contented. No box or bat or bluebird to fold.

"Mr. Harney," I say, "time to go."

"Yes, sir."

"Everything okay?"

"Yes, sir." He's still looking at his paper, not turning around to look at me.

"Let's go, young man."

"Yes, sir."

He slides the paper off the edge of the desk with one hand and picks it up with the other, careful not to wrinkle it. Out of his notebook he pulls an envelope. Then, he folds the paper, makes the creases with the pad of his hand, slides the paper in, licks the envelope, and seals it by patting it down. While I am Mr. Patient, he addresses the envelope, goes back to the notebook, takes stamps out of the inside flap, and puts one on. He presses the stamp in place and pats it and carries the letter like a feather in his hand. The letter is all he looks at as he walks.

He passes by me without looking up.

He doesn't see the door open in front of him, and Donny Zurkus standing there with his minions. Mr. Menace.

"Well, Zippy hasn't left, yet," Donny says.

Kyle looks up, looks at each of the five boys, and his right hand, with the envelope, tries to find his jacket pocket to tuck the letter in. The envelope bobs up and down until it slips into his pocket.

"Mr. Zurkus, get out of the way," I say. Now I know Ms. Alta should've taken Kyle to see White.

"Mr. Song, we're just escorting Kyle back to the dorm. We're his bodyguards, aren't we, Kyle?" Donny's face is a bad commercial, all smiles and cutesy wink. Mr. Ingenuous.

Inside a ring of Fifth Formers, Kyle is small, a ball in a pinball machine. The bigger boys start to pat him, push him, pretend to be a pal. He bounces between the hands. But he's smiling. His smile is soft and big, and his body is loose, swaying between the hands pushing him.

"Enough," I say, "leave him alone."

"Hey, Mikey! He likes it," Donny says, like Kyle is on a box of Life cereal. Even Donny appears a little surprised at the way Kyle's neck sways as his body moves between the boys' hands. Donny looks at me with something small in his eyes. If his eyes were someone else's, the look would be a question, asking for approval. In this moment, Donny shows how young he is.

But five big boys are bouncing one small one between them. My throat opens up, the right space for the right amount of air, and my voice comes out loud. "Donny Zurkus, cut it out."

All the boys step back from Kyle. Kyle's body makes a pendulum motion even though the boys aren't pushing him any more.

"And we thought Zippy was just Alta's pet."

Donny's henchmen smile.

"Mr. Zurkus, you will report to Mr. White in the morning. You will return to your dorm right now. You will remain in your room for the entire evening."

As if I can make Donny stay in his room.

The other boys, lemmings all, turn away. Donny takes a few steps back from Kyle, and he raises one arm, points at Kyle, keeps pointing as he walks backwards. He tilts his head and sights down the length of his arm. He keeps Kyle in his sights until he is about to run into the wall and drops his hand, spins around. With so much show, Mr. Bad Apple acts more middle school than applying to colleges.

Kyle doesn't say anything. Stands there. He sticks his hand in the pocket of his jacket.

"Got to go, Mr. Song. Off to off myself," Kyle says. Study hall often ends this way with Kyle making a joke about his demise. A body in motion. His hand in the air, he waves it like a royal wave down the hall. As if he is king for a moment. The hall is bigger with Kyle walking down, the brown linoleum floor more shiny. Like a hospital ward, but shiny.

# Taylor / **Plato's Face**

STRANGE DETAILS STUCK WITH me. Time: 11:40 p.m. A knock at the door like a stick on a trash can. Jack Song stood there with Terence. Jack Song was jeans and a T-shirt in the cold, and Terence was plaid bathrobe and matching slippers. Jack's big hand, white on Terence's dark neck.

Jack's sentences were words like "Excuse me," "terrible," and "asked to speak with you."

Something in me was ringing, like that tin can hit by a stick.

"Come in," I said. My robe thin in the cold of them passing, and Jack Song's hand on Terence.

They bent down at the same rate, both the same way, to sit.

Terence looked straight ahead, not at me, at nothing. His eyes were wide open, like windows without curtains.

"We didn't know. My friend. Flies. How we knew. Dead. We ran." Each word was flat like he had to discover each word before he said it, and what he discovered was the shell of the word. The ringing in me had a hole in the center; the sound was circular and echoed.

Jack Song kept his hand on Terence. Jack Song affectionate.

"And Tommy, he froze. On the corner, went stiff, slammed the wall. We kept running." Terence looked up into Jack's eyes, then turned to look at mine. Terence's eyes were windows with no light getting through.

Next to Terence, Jack was gone. His face was the image of a face, not the thing itself. The ringing in me turned to clicking, the stick on the can, now a clapper on a broken bell, the sound dry.

11:50 p.m.: Jack Song left Terence with me. Terence quit talking altogether. His eyes were windows with no light.

12:10 a.m.: The headmaster called.

"Is it true?" I said to Mr. White.

"Regrettably. Alex Jeffers went with Kyle in the ambulance. The family's on the way." White's voice sounded like a radio announcer at a sporting event. His voice was wrong.

"Is Kyle okay?"

"Don't know. In the meantime, please keep Terence with you."

"Anything else?"

"Yes, you must watch for contagion."

Bumps on skin? Quarantines? I had no idea.

"Yes, sir," I said.

12:15 a.m.: A glass of milk. Terence swallowed hard, looked down after each gulp. He moved off the couch long enough for me to unfold it into a bed, put sheets and blankets on. The covers up to his neck made his head small, and his fingers curled around the ends. He looked up at the ceiling. The tight curls on his forehead were soft.

Terence staring at the ceiling, me sitting on the edge of the fold-out couch, the world was my refrigerator turning off, the click of the clock flipping numbers, and a Canada goose flying over. A lone goose, one cry, two tones, one breaking into the other, over and over, long and raw in the night quiet.

# Song / **Vacuum**

THERE IS NO SCIENCE for this.

# Taylor / **Contagion**

12:30 A.M. CARLA IS curls and wool sweater and push. With the door open a little, she walks past me and lets out loud words.

"I don't fucking believe it."

"Quiet. Terence is asleep."

She keeps walking until she sees the pull-out couch, then turns her stiff way and walks straight back to me, doesn't stop. Her arms inside my arms, her face turns into my neck, her body presses flat against mine.

"What're we going to do?" she asks into my neck, like we do things together.

Her arms around me. My arms wrap around her back. I pull her into me. Sarah gone and now Kyle. I am sinking.

We are standing there, in the middle of my hall, and Carla's arms tight, her head on my shoulder, her breath, and the walls are wavy, the floor soft. We rock back and forth, and the goose overhead in the night sky is loud. It cracks the sky open.

"What about lights-out?" I say. My head backs away from her, and my hands go to her upper arms. Her eyes move from one of my eyes to the other, and we are still too close. The floor is still soft.

"Whatever," she says and bends her head down. My arms straighten out, hold her away. "Nobody'll know I'm not in the dorm. Screw it." She bends from her waist and leans her forehead on my sternum.

She says, "He's gone, Taylor, he's gone." Since when does she call me Taylor?

"Maybe not."

"He's dead."

"Says who?" The question feels young in my mouth.

"Mr. Song and Mr. Jeffers. They tried to save him."

The only room where we can talk and not wake up Terence is my bedroom. "In here," I say.

There's no place to sit but on the bed. "Have a seat." I point to it, the covers pulled back from the first time I answered the door. The light on the bedside table makes everything in the room half light. I sit on the floor, my back against the wall.

Carla sits on the edge of the bed, her boots dark on the beige carpet. She tucks her arms around her middle, and her back and shoulders curl around her arms.

"Tell me," I say.

She rocks forward. Maybe Carla is the wrong person to tell me. And it is the curl of Carla's body around something sore, some hole in her, that makes me think I don't want to know. Maybe I don't want to hear.

After a little while, after the wind clicks branches together on the maple outside, Carla says, "There's no way. No fucking way. I just saw him. He was just there, in the cornfield. We talked. He can't. No way." She says it like she can change what happened.

Maybe this is White's warning. Maybe the way things spread is the bad thing. Maybe what I hear isn't true. Kyle. Zippy. Zippo, the students called him.

Carla says, "Around eleven, maybe, Rambo crashes through my door. Her eyes are totally popping out of her head. She says, 'Kyle's dead.'

"'Shut up.' But I know Rambo's no drama queen.

"'Serious,' Rambo says, totally serious. Standing in front of me, she's panting, big time, with her eyes all bug-eyed. She says, 'Donny Zurkus killed him. Somebody said so.' And I don't believe her. So, I tell her somebody's wrong. Kids don't kill kids here.

"Rambo stops pacing around the room, and her arms go up on her hips.

"I say, 'What the fuck?'

"And Rambo says, 'The Second Formers were playing in the little common area by the cubbies, and they're wrestling, all of them, like Tommy and Terence and the other little guys, and they see Kyle hanging from the rafters, but he always pretends, so they didn't, they don't, you know, think.'

"'So, a couple of them fell through his curtain, and bumped him, and he was all stiff and blue. They thought he was still kidding until they saw flies, like, around his eyes. They thought Donny Zurkus made Kyle jump off a chair, or something.'

"Kids don't kill kids at St. Tim's. 'Donny didn't,' I say, 'kill him.'

"'How do you know?' Rambo says.

"'No way Donny Zurkus did it,' I say, and Rambo gets tired of me saying the same thing. And inside I feel this molten thing happen. In my throat and going up. My throat fills and the back of my mouth, and pretty soon my eyes rip open. Tears shoot out.

"And Rambo says, 'I'm sorry, Carla.' And I almost slug her."

Carla looks at me like I'm a life ring. But I am way off shore in an ocean with winds rising, and there are peaks of dark waves between us. Carla tells me everyone thinks Donny Zurkus killed Kyle.

"Murder at Prep School" in three-inch letters will top the papers in the morning. Tomorrow the media will drive the black driveway through maples, and there will be TV trucks and lights and reporters with fake concern.

In my bedroom there is only half light and half sound and two people across a room. In a room with no words, I keep seeing Kyle. Kyle at the back of the classroom. Kyle raising a mallet to smash his city at the epicenter of a nuclear blast. Kyle running with Terence to launch his kite.

Carla looks up and shakes her head. "You know what's weird?"

I don't know where she's going.

"All I can think about is Kyle's hair, the way it sticks out."

Kyle with his greasy hair, like pickup sticks. The gray sweatpants. Weird sounds. Poor personal hygiene. Inappropriate behavior. Erratic moods.

The signs were there.

He said he would do it.

I should have done something.

The ways Kyle pretended to commit suicide are images swinging in me. Kyle grabbing his tie, Kyle in the corn field, Kyle kidding. He wasn't kidding any more, and this true thing presses against my neck.

Carla clenches her fist and opens it, hits her forehead with her palm, hits it again and again. She says nothing, shakes her head, hits her head. Different signs from a girl smart enough to know them.

If we were anywhere but St. Timothy's, I'd reach for Carla, pull her down on this floor, and wrap my arms and legs around her. Her curls would get in my face, her head under my chin, and we'd lie here and watch the light come up in the window. But we're at a boarding school, and even though I'm only four years older than she is, I'm the teacher. Teachers don't watch the sunrise with students in their arms.

And besides, there's Kyle. There's Terence. There's a goose cracking the night open.

"Everybody's wrong, you know," Carla says. She looks at me with the left side of her face lit up and the right side of her face dark. The left eye is a flare, spitting sparks out.

"You mean, Donny?"

"No, everything." Her lips come together, and her nose wrinkles like she might spit. "Kyle killed himself."

"How do you know?"

"I know." She turns away from the light.

"But how do you know?" The way Carla isn't looking at me feels like cells dividing, like something bacterial, spreading.

"There was no reason for him not to." She turns her head to face me, her face a half face.

"There's always a reason to live," I say. The words are flat like something in a brochure, words Mr. White wants me to say.

"Like what?" she says.

There is no life ring for me to hold. There is no life ring for me to throw.

"Kyle's better off. He did the right thing," Carla says.

We're sitting a few feet apart, but there's an ocean between us. Whitecaps keep me from seeing her all the time. We're both floating, but she rises into view, and then disappears.

"First of all, we don't know that Kyle committed suicide." I'm rising. She's falling. "And even if he did, how could that be the right thing?" I say.

"It's right for him."

"What's right for him doesn't make it right." All the muscles in my arms are tight, my hands flat on the floor. "It's not that simple."

"He didn't murder anyone." Carla tips her mannequin-head to the right, trying to see her way to a type of logic I can't follow. Maybe she's trying to look at right and wrong. Maybe she's trying to figure out Donny. Surely this is wrong.

"Yes, he did." My chin rises up a little. I tumble down the face of a wave into the bottom of the swell she creates.

"Well, it was self-defense. Really, it was. He defended himself against other boys. Against Donny."

Carla has a point.

"Self-defense by killing yourself?" My voice goes high. At the crest of a wave, I see whitecaps all around me. We have no lifeboat, no shoreline, nothing but our bodies in all the waves breaking.

"He was just carrying out his means of survival, you know,

the survival of the fittest, laissez-faire, Adam Smith, and all that." Carla's smile is curl. She's enjoying the crashing, the submersion in water, the splash.

I swallow, drop my head down, tuck my chin in. Then, I look right at her. "Carla, he didn't survive. If he's dead, he wasn't the fittest."

A laugh almost leaks out of her. Carla raises one hand to ward off the thought.

"Well, it's lucky then." She pushes her hair behind her ear. "Then he won't be disappointed when his dreams don't come true. He saved himself from pain," she says. "Smart."

My hands rise up to my forehead. My elbows on my knees. The way I turn my head back and forth, I try to wipe my thoughts on my hands, back and forth, my forehead on my palms. "Tell me you're not serious."

"I'm dead serious," she says, and she doesn't flinch at "dead."

"You would never kill yourself, right?"

Each time she turns the logic around, the waves hit. Carla rises, and I sink. Each time she disappears, a piece of me bangs against my skin from the inside, trying to get out.

"Sure I would," she says.

The feeling I had when she came in the door is still the supple floor, the soft walls. Sarah gone, and now Kyle, and I am breathing shallow. Something has to hold. Something has to keep me from sinking.

Both hands push off from the carpet, and I'm up, and one step to the bed, and my two hands go to her shoulders, the shoulders still curled around an ache in her. I go beside her, curl her inside my arms, draw her into my chest. Her weight topples on me, her head under my chin, her curls soft on my neck.

Back and forth, I rock her. Back and forth until my abs ache. The world is this bedroom, no noise from Terence in the living room, no movement outside. But there's that one goose, loud in the night, two notes rolling into one, above the trees, crossing over campus, the lake, over Delaware. It breaks the sky open.

With her breathing, I breathe. No drowning any more. Not one more drowning. Her head folds into my chest. She rubs her forehead on my shoulder. Her arms around my waist, we're warm. My chin brushes her curls, her neck white and wet. My mouth opens, to let the hot out of my body, and my lips press against her neck. I kiss her neck.

And her mannequin arms shoot into the air, like someone sinking and trying to find the surface. She gets off the bed, turns around and faces me.

Holy shit.

Holy shit, I kissed a student.

Her eyes are big, and the ocean is there, too. She backs up a step, backs against the closet door, and slides to the floor. All I hear is the rush of her clothes on the wood. Her knees bend in front of her, her legs at funny angles, her lips make a smile that is more secret than happy.

# Song / **Suction**

KNOTS TOO TIGHT. NO space, so, no air. No way to breathe. No breath.

Second Formers' yelling comes with lights out, a regular routine each night for the youngest boys in the dorm. But tonight the yells are screams. Hurt coyotes. Coyotes all over San Diego hills when I grew up. Now a crash. And then they're on my door, boys banging.

They're coyotes, eyes too big for their sockets, voices too big for mouths.

"Kyle" and "Come on" are some of the words I make out. They start running back the way they came. Running back, they're quiet. My sneakers, their bare feet on linoleum. Suction on the floor. We're a herd. We fall in step, recruits, basic training, brothers. Every door is filled with boys looking. We pass Tommy Underwood lying against the wall. Tommy lies rigid, flat out. A boy kneels by him.

"He's okay," the boy says.

I'm ahead of the Second Formers, and they say, "Kyle." And turning the corner to the common area, I see the curtains, the dirty canvas drapes, the insane treatment of Second Formers, animals in stalls, stalls with bed, and so many of us moving so much air, the curtains move into the hall a little, let a space open behind them, let me see the foot of Kyle's bed. Before I slow down, I see the tie, the Tim-Tim's maroon-and-gray stripes around the beam, the other tie knotted to the end. The tie around Kyle's throat digging in, the chair on its side, the tongue, the blue.

And behind me, heavy steps, Alex Jeffers.

"Jesus," he says, "I'll lift him. Get the knot."

# Taylor / **The Switch**

"YOU KNOW YOU WOULDN'T miss me," Carla says. She's on the floor, and the dresser, the clothes off their hangers, the comb are things I look at, have to look at. She keeps going.

"You wouldn't," she says.

From some other planet, I look at her. "Carla, what are you talking about?"

"You know, like if I were out of here." She waves her arm like an umpire calling someone out who slid into home base.

"Stop talking like that." I say the words. That's all.

Carla starts to laugh, a laugh that is old like a hollow tree. "I'm right. No one would notice. How funny is that." She presses her palms on her legs and stretches. "But you know who really wouldn't miss me even if he were alive?"

I shake my head.

"My dad." Her eyes wince in the corners. "My dad wouldn't miss me." The idea hurts her, but she throws it at me anyway.

"How do you mean?"

"Ever since I was old enough for school, he sent me away, to places far enough that he couldn't see me during the week, or he sent me to boarding schools. It's like I wouldn't see him for days since he spent so much time with his artists, and then, on weekends, just the two of us, we'd walk down the rows of peach trees. He'd tell me how much he loved me. But I'd end up alone by the end."

"What about your brother?"

"Sure, there's Doug. Druggie, jail, the whole thing. He's gone. We don't talk about him."

"I'm so sorry. Why did your dad send you away?"

"He loved me, too much, more than my brother," she says. There is no curl in her words.

"Like how?" I say. How I say things sometimes is how she says things, young.

"Don't know."

"Giving you things?"

"No."

"Holding on to you?"

"Kind of," she says.

Whenever I try to get her to talk about her family, she changes the subject. This time, with Kyle and the sunrise in my apartment, she answers.

"What's your dad like?" she says. Here's the subject change, the switch of tracks. She's back to the curl in her words.

"Doesn't matter," I say. It comes out more curtly than I meant.

My bedroom is the breeze outside, the growing morning, the fridge in the kitchen turning on.

"Nobody'd miss me," she says.

My lips go tight. Her type of smart is the chessboard kind, each move carefully tabulated, angled. I don't want to be a sacrificed piece. But she looks left and right as if she's looking for a way through the floor. I don't know how to move the pieces so we're king to king.

"Sure they would," I say, but the words sound like a brochure by Mr. White's phone.

"No," she says. "The only person who'd miss me is Kyle."

She's shaking and her jaw gets tight.

That one hits me. My eyes squint. My lips stay tight and thin. There's nothing but us in this room, nobody else in this world that's tipping one way and then the other.

"I'd miss you," I say.

She looks up. "Really?"

Her excitement came too quickly. I'm being played, and the game is more than a match in this room. There's her life. There's my job. There's a goose crying out in the night sky.

"You're just saying that because you think I'll kill myself."

Right now I'll say anything to keep another person living.

"Carla, I care about you," I say. And I do. Maybe too much.

"You do not. If you cared about me, you'd keep away from me."

"Meaning?"

"People hurt what they love."

"Wrong," I say, "people protect what they love." My feet over the edge of the bed, I lean forward, looking down at her on the floor.

"Like you loved Kyle," she says. "Nice job."

My head turns toward my shoulder, away from her. That was low.

"Nice, Carla" is all I say.

And we sit in my room for awhile, the sun coming up outside. Breakfast will be ready soon, and we'll have classes, and everyone will be normal and "Fine, thank you" and worried about college. And we'll forget tonight, and Kyle, and Donny Zurkus will get his name cleared, and St. Tim's will make the top ten boarding schools.

"This isn't worth it," she says. With her elbows at angles, she gets up from the floor. Her head gets taller than my head in the room since I'm sitting on the bed, leaning my back against the wall, my legs flat in front of me.

"Where you going?"

"What do you care?" The curl to her words is sharp.

"Promise me you're not going to do anything stupid." I'm

standing up, too, taller than her tall. One of my hands reaches toward her, but she steps away.

"I'm going to breakfast. Later, Ms. Alta."

And she gives me a little salute with two fingers touching an imaginary cap.

"Come back after breakfast, okay?" I say.

Out of my bedroom, she's already reaching for the outside door.

# Song / **Happy**

It's 5 a.m., and finally the boys are sleeping. Bodies can only take so much. Witness Tommy Underwood, only hours ago when it happened, his muscles froze when he was running with the others to get me. His flight mechanism overwhelmed by adrenalin, by shock. Every muscle in his body flooded, and his body went rigid. He slammed against the wall. Temporarily paralyzed. Too much moving through vessels too open.

There are two boys asleep on my pull-out couch, and other Second Formers are sleeping in older boys' rooms. They can't go back to their cubbies, not yet. The boys in my apartment don't even move when the phone rings.

"Song, this is Alex." He doesn't wait for me to respond. "Kyle's dead. DOA. So much for CPR. I mean, I took the class two weekends ago. The doc said there was nothing I could've done. But we tried, didn't we, Song?" He is talking fast. Big man talking like a boy, a boy whose job was to ride with a dead student in the ambulance to the ER in Wilmington.

What am I supposed to say? Kyle was blue, and there was

Alex putting his enormous mouth over little-boy lips, folding enormous hands and pumping boy lungs. The color of Kyle, his bloodshot eyes, I knew there was nothing we could do, but Alex acted. He tried, and what might have seemed foolish then proved the measure of him, a man with honor.

"His parents are here. Mom and Dad. It's like they've checked out, zombied, nobody's home." Alex's words trip on themselves. He starts to giggle. "They're gonzo, gorked," and his laughing has high notes, close to crying. A paper bag should go over his mouth to save the man from passing out. Every good man gets overwhelmed.

"What was the cause? Did the doctor say?"

"Cerebral hypoxia, strangulation." He sounds like a report. Gone is Kyle, the boy wonder, the weird genius who made animal noises. Now he is a report.

"Suicide?"

"Looks like."

"So, they're not going to investigate?"

"No, Kyle did it. You know how he was, Song. Somebody found a note. It was in his pocket, his mother's name on it, even a stamp."

"A note?" Mr. Happy-to-Be-in-Study-Hall?

"His mom had it in her hand when I saw her. An envelope."

My head feels heavy, so heavy I need my other hand to hold it up, my elbow on my desk.

Kyle wrote his mother, all smiles, not caring when Donny and his minions surrounded him, when the boys pushed him. The decision was made by then, and he was happy.

"Song, you still there?" I forget Alex is on the line.

"Still here," I say, but I'm really back in study hall, back with a boy writing his mother. Kyle in his blazer, tie tied right. Kyle with his hair combed. The times he burst out laughing, the other boys ignoring him. The way he kept me waiting to fold the note just right.

"We did what we could, right?" Alex's voice, so high, brings me back to my apartment, my desk, the maroon ink blotter. The phone is hard in my hand. His voice is so much smaller than he is.

"We did all we could, Alex," I say, and I don't say we could've done more.

Alex says he'll be back for breakfast at school, he'll teach today, hold practice. Mr. Tough Guy, macho jock who tried to breathe into a little boy.

He'll fold.

There's nothing left to do but fold.

# Taylor / **Beets**

"MR. WHITE?" I SAID into the phone. "I'm sorry to bother you. This is Taylor Alta." After Carla left for breakfast, thoughts piled up in my bedroom: She might kill herself, what if she tells, and why can't I talk her out of it?

"Yes, Taylor. What can I do for you?" The headmaster's voice was edges.

"A student last night talked a lot about committing suicide." Telling Carla's thoughts to the headmaster was telling secrets, a sin to be confessed.

"And you're concerned for her safety and/or the safety of others?" His words were rehearsed. Maybe he was reading that pamphlet.

"Yes, she could hurt herself."

"You're sure. What you're saying is very big, and we can't take anything lightly."

"I know."

"Everyone is very shaken. Are you okay, Taylor?"

"Not really. But I'm more concerned about Carla."

"Carla Spalding?"

"Yes, she's coming back to my apartment after breakfast." Meeting me at my place sounded dirty. How many Hail Marys would I say? How much would she say?

"I see," he said. "We'll have to act quickly. When she leaves your apartment again, call the school nurse who will pick her up outside the dorm, take her to Wilmington for a psychiatric evaluation." Everything was happening fast. Carla would be pissed. A Hail Mary for wanting her neck, another for kissing her neck. A novena for saving myself.

"And after that?"

"Maybe hospitalization. Maybe not. You're doing the right thing, Taylor. One suicide is enough," he said.

"Too much," I said.

"Indeed." Mr. White hung up.

The receiver weighed forty pounds and landed in the cradle with a bang, like the little window on the confessional slamming shut.

Years ago I made my last confession. At St. Barnabas the confessional always smelled like bad breath. Opening the curtain gave enough light on dark wood and velvet to lead me to the kneeler.

After enough time for me to think of what to say, the window to Father Mortimer opened so fast and so loud I forgot. The shadows through the window showed him crossing himself. The ritual always kicked in.

"In the name of the Father, the Son, and the Holy Ghost, Amen," he said.

"Forgive me, Father, for I have sinned. I have not been to confession in eight months," I said, even though it had been more.

It was ninth grade, and most of the kids were Episcopalians, and didn't have to confess a thing. It was my mother who packed us into the VW van and marched us into the back pew on Saturday afternoons for confession. It was ninth grade, and most of the kids were pushing off the walls of the gym toward the dance floor during Saturday night dances and making out in the bushes outside. Many kids smoked pot, and I made up excuses why I couldn't, like my dad would kill me, or my mom would know, or I had to go to church in the morning. None of the excuses sounded good enough for ninth grade.

Sometimes during the converted-gym dances with disco balls blinking, a few girls were left sitting. There was Mary Maguire, a field hockey player whose thick auburn hair defied the rubber bands she tried to tame it with. Mary cracked jokes in math class, winking at me when the whiskey-breath teacher tried to get us to believe in imaginary numbers. $i = \sqrt{-1}$ could not possibly be real, and recognizing something about adults gave us a secret, something separate from ninth grade, something ours.

One Saturday night Mary Maguire leaned back in the folding metal chair along the gym wall and stretched her long, half-back legs in front of her. And her short skirt ran perpendicular across the line of muscle down her thigh. In me there was something shivery when I looked, something that dropped down my throat, down my stomach, farther down.

That's what I tried to tell Father Mortimer. I knew that something was bad, that girls shouldn't like girls, that I might turn green and grow warts. This metamorphosis I believed to be possible from merely having such thoughts. The change on the outside of me was not complex; it was $x$ causes $y$. The world would be able to tell by one look that I was bad, and being good was the most important thing.

"My child," he said, "have you shared your feelings with your mother?"

A shock wave ran from my elbows to my knees. It was the electric fear of my mother sitting across the breakfast table, her eyebrow rising behind her bug-eye glasses, and it was also the hope that filled my lungs of talking to someone like Father Mortimer. I had saved this secret for him.

"No, Father."

"Good," he said. "Never tell your mother. Feelings for the same sex are expressly forbidden. Further, they are mortal sins and make you immoral. Ask God for forgiveness." His voice was bigger than the bell in the church tower. This wasn't the same priest who came for cocktails, the priest my mother called "Father M."

"But Father M . . ."

"There is no room for you in God's kingdom. Say two rosaries, and do not act on your feelings. For your own sake, child. For the Lord's," he said. "In the name of the Father, the Son, and the Holy Ghost," and he slammed the window.

That's when I knew I was bad.

Bad has a taste and a color. It's crimson, like the velvet in the confessional. And its taste is firm, a little sweet but bitter when it slides down your throat. Like beets.

One time walking away from Sarah's room in college, the bile that rose in my throat was beets. The beginning of our senior year, I didn't go to sleep without walking across campus to her room for a hug good night, Orion guiding me there.

In her dorm room, where stuffed animals crowded the bed and a cross hung above the bookshelf, when we rose and met each other in the middle of the room, held each other and swayed back and forth, one night she said, "You know, I can really understand why you fall for women."

Inside, something sweet and bitter slid down my throat.

This was Sarah, the one who walked out junior year when I confessed my feelings for women. My Sarah whose body I matched in rowing, and otherwise didn't dare notice. Mark's Sarah, who called him every night after our hug.

The swaying stopped.

All I said was "Yeah, right," and backed away. A shock wave stiffened my arms. The fear that all things good could be damned by Father M, and the faint hope that my love could be returned.

"No, really," she said. "I get it."

With Orion holding up the night sky behind me, I ran back to my room, the night the type of cold that breaks twigs from branches. The bitter red bubbled up. I tasted it.

That's what was in my mouth when Mr. White hung up. Beets.

# Song / **What Makes Good Luck**

IT'S VERY OLD. MAYBE Korean. Maybe Chinese. Make origami figures of what the dead person didn't have in life. Send those things with the body into fire, into the next world. You create good luck for the next time.

Young Mr. Harney, King of the Circling Lab Stools, once-twice, always-in-motion. Never was there a student like that student, always watching while being watched. Newton's laws embodied: What is in motion stays in motion unless acted upon, something can only touch and be touched. Kyle was amazing. Was.

In the dorm the older boys must have snuck into his cubby after lights-out or during the day when I wasn't there. The report said he had bruises on his back, on his triceps, on his hamstrings, places concealed by Tim-Tim's clothes. What types of boys pick on the smallest one? What type of school protects the strongest ones?

The best paper I've been saving, the gold leaf on crimson,

the royal blue swans, even the hand-painted cranes dancing, and the hokey stuff that Americans think is super special, the thin paper with Escher drawings, even the cheap brown package wrap. I take it all down to the dining hall. Those faces the same in the stupid Wyeth mural all stare at me with my armload of paper rolls sticking out, walking up to one of the round tables, where nobody's sitting. Bending at the waist, I dump all the paper rolls and scissors and rulers on the table. Young Sirs and Madams of Breakfast stare at me.

There aren't assigned tables at breakfast. It's cafeteria style, and students grab a plastic tray, slide it along chrome rails, and the African American kitchen staff in their white uniforms and hairnets serve fat spoonfuls of grits or oatmeal or eggs. The world is different this morning, but not breakfast. An orange juice glass with ridges for little people with little hands is silly on the orange tray.

A spoon tapping on my juice glass stops the few conversations.

"Ladies and gentlemen," I say to the masses, "good morning. After what happened last night, please join me in a ceremony." All students turn toward me. "I invite you to fold origami cranes. The crane is a symbol of peace, and when someone dies, we place with the body the thing or things that person did not have in life. Mr. Harney did not have peace."

Maggie Anderson raises her hand. Always the good girl.

"Yes, Miss Anderson."

She puts her hand down, looks around before she says, "What's origami?"

"I'll show you. Please, anyone interested."

The chairs skid on the floor. Students around the dining hall walk with slow steps. Maggie Anderson has pouches under her eyes, and her Irish skin is whiter than white. Shoulders are lower. This is shock.

Too much adrenalin in too-open veins, the students have flooded. They are fat with last night's news. They are slow moving. Newton couldn't calculate the total weight they bear. Not Cavendish.

"Take a piece of paper, or cut one from a roll," I say. Students are two-deep to the table. They reach around each other and unfurl the rolls. There aren't enough scissors. Usually students push each other around or make fun. This morning the world is different, and they wait.

"What size?" someone asks.

"Eight by eight," I say. "And then make a crease down the middle to mark the center, and diagonally fold down the right side of the paper toward the front."

I make the folds and hold them up. Some students move to other tables but keep an eye on me. Some kneel and squeeze their arms in between bodies so they can use the table to crease the paper.

In a classroom demonstrating anything, I have to get their attention again and again. This morning in the world that is different, they don't talk. Masters and mistresses of listening, they fold. Without washing hands, without wiping hands on napkins, the students and I fold. We are tables of students bent over, folding paper to bring peace to a student who had none.

My mother and father and I sat at the breakfast table in our house in San Diego the morning after Kim died. The Formica table had shiny specks that caught the sun. The packages of paper were out when I got up, and my mother and I started before my dad got his coffee and sat with us. We didn't talk.

One folds what the dead didn't have. Husband. Coins. Car. House. Diploma. Good job. Blood that didn't clot.

How does one fold these things?

Give me enough time and paper, and I can fold anything.

A piece of royal blue paper with gold-leaf junks, twelve by twelve inches, and I made Kim the house she never had. Windows and doors and two floors. Houses are cake. My father made a chest full of coins. My mother made Kim's boyfriend. A wicker basket filled with origami, and we sent the basket with her body for cremation.

Not so easy are cranes for hands not used to folding. The cranes come out bent and stupid.

Sixth Formers and Second Formers and Third Formers fold. Each student who can make one shows another who struggles. Carla walks in, her way of walking, improbable that her body stays upright, that her rowing is so smooth. Her body and her movements are part of the past, the force of negative equally balanced and repelled by the positive. By nature, since she is the student, she is the positive. By nature, I am the negative. I am the keeper of distance. She goes to another table, stands with her hands on her hips, and knows exactly what to do. Carla doesn't look at me. Not once.

In the letters she folded into envelopes this summer, Carla wrote that she was my chair. Now she's the crane in every kid's hands. What would each kid say to her, the crane in their hands? What would each crane say to Kyle?

When Kyle asked me to teach him to fold, I was a fool. Mr. Crap-on-My-Career, jealous of a Second Former, a boy with a crush on an older girl. Kyle, on top of his notebook, his grubby hands folding boats and bats, we sat on the bench outside, overlooking the lake. I became something besides skin drag. I was teacher. Carla became student, the object of another student's desire, the girl a boy wants to make origami for.

Two nights ago in study hall, Kyle folded the box with the message, "Meet me in the cornfield before dinner. Donny Zurkus." And I went to the cornfield to see who thought Donny Zurkus would appear. Kyle had made a box, a bat, and bluebird. He signed them all "Donny Zurkus," but it was Kyle who came to the cornfield in between fifth period and dinner.

Geese love the cornfield. I do not love geese. Messy birds. Poor flyers. When I got near the cornfield, the sun was low on the horizon, the angle of light not isosceles. The woods made elongated shadows into the fields. Carla was past the shadows.

It made sense. She and the geese are good for each other, awkward in movement, keen sense of surroundings. She walked into the middle of the field right past Kyle. Maybe she's not as keen as the geese.

"Boo!" went Kyle, right behind her. She jumped and yelled, and Kyle clapped. Carla's long arms folding across her front. The look on her face, sure to say, "Back off."

They talked in the field. One girl went to a cornfield to find Donny Zurkus and found Mr. Different instead. She talked with her arms crossed in front of her. He brought out a magnifying glass from his jacket, hunched over, turned circles, and spied the ground. She came to the field and found a weird, little boy who had given origami gifts and had a crush on her.

Two bodies exerting force on each other until imbalance breaks their attraction. Whatever they said to each other, I couldn't tell. He kept in motion the whole time, a moon around Jupiter. But then he broke orbit, bounced up and down. He pulled something besides the magnifying glass out of his coat. He tossed it up in the air, turned about-face, and ran from the field. His hands were up in the air, and he yelled something over and over. Carla stood there. She stood there in the middle of the field. Another person broke orbit from her.

After talking to Carla, Kyle came to study hall, Mr. Happy. After study hall, Kyle went off to off himself. That's what he told me he would do. That's what he did.

When Tommy Underwood and Maggie Anderson finish folding at the dining table, they drop the cranes into the basket in the middle. Grease on their hands from breakfast spot the origami. No matter. From the other tables, other students reach over and drop theirs in the pile. Everyone but Carla. Crimson and blue and yellow and brown cranes spill over the basket in the middle of the table. They make more, and the table fills with cranes, big ones, little ones, bent ones, crisp ones.

The only person missing, the person who makes perfect cranes, is Kyle.

# Taylor / **Breakfast**

IT WAS ALMOST THE end of breakfast time, and Terence hadn't risen. His hands were still curled around the sheet pulled to his neck. His eyes were open and staring at the ceiling.

"Can't I stay here?" he said without looking at me. His words were a surprise and moved up my spine where I stood at the foot of the bed.

"I wish you could," I said.

"Don't make me go back."

"But you have to eat."

"Not now."

"I know, but try. You don't have to go back to your cubby. Go back to the dorm, and ask somebody for clothes, okay? Your pajamas are cute, but school clothes are better."

He tipped his head toward his toes, and his neck got thick. His smile was part boy, part old man, and his eyes were still windows without light.

"I'll meet you in the dining hall." My hand was big over the blanket covering his foot. A few steps down the hall, and the door pressed into place on my way out.

The way into the dining hall was the far end. Students were two-deep around tables by the mural. The dining hall was quieter than it had ever been. The laughs of the kitchen workers and the clatter of dishes loading into the washers broke the quiet. No students cracking up. No students yelling to each other. No talk at all.

Jack Song was at one table, Carla at another. Everyone bent over something. Carla's curls fell down. She didn't see me.

If I went to her right now, I could tell her not to meet me after breakfast. If I called her away from the table, I could tell her it was wrong to kiss her. If she knew how bad I was, she wouldn't meet me after breakfast.

But I didn't go to her.

Outside a window on my end of the dining hall stood a large person with a pink shirt. Outside was a covered walkway of stones going this way and stones going that way.

Alex Jeffers was bent over, holding on to the railing of the stairs, students passing him, not stopping. All six feet, five inches of muscle-bound Alex Jeffers were shaking in that covered hallway outside. One hand across his forehead covering his eyes, his huge hand making his head look like a child's, he was crying. He leaned into the stone wall, one of his feet on a higher step than the other. Students stared as they passed him. Nobody stopped.

This was the man who followed me into the ladies' room at the first faculty party, who held me after Sarah drowned. This was the big man who turned boy rowers into champions, the man who tried to save Kyle.

"Alex," I said. I stopped on a stair above him.

He looked up, and his hand slid from his eyes to his mouth. His big hand couldn't stop the high notes leaking from his mouth. His eyelashes were red rims and water caught thick. Terror was stuck in his eyes.

"Come here," I said, and I stepped into him. He tried to speak, but high notes came out instead. My arms went wide around him, and I held him for all that he had seen, for all he couldn't do. I held him for all I couldn't do. Students passed us and pretended not to see.

I held him to keep from being bad.

# Song / **The Science of Loss**

CARLA AT A SEPARATE table folds paper one way, makes diagonals, folds the bottom points to make a tail. Just so. Ms. Adept. Even two tables over and most of the other students gone, I see her open up the left and right sides, fold down the wings and pull up the head and tail. She learned from me. While students with untrained fingers mangle their cranes, the crimson and gold crane rises from two dimensions to three in her hands. She doesn't toss it in the basket. In her palm the crane is crisp and bright.

She walks out the dining hall door by the creepy-boy mural. The few students left are busy, heads bowed. I catch the door out of the dining hall before it swings shut.

"Wait, Carla."

She stops so fast the forward motion keeps her head moving forward; then it bobs back. No force but the force of her will resists the momentum.

"I don't hear you," she says.

"Fine," I say, "but don't go."

"Because why?"

"Because I saw you with Kyle." Carla straightens her back. The crane rests in her hand, palm up.

"So?"

"So, I'm wondering how you're doing," I say. Two meters behind her, I am the distance from the earth to the moon away.

"Now you wonder?" She spins around. "Now you wonder. Does someone have to die before you talk to me?" Her face is red, and her curls bounce right to left.

"In here," I say and take her shoulder in my hand. She jerks her shoulder away and takes straight-legged steps into the class-room. The chairs scrape the floor. We sit facing each other. Carla crosses her arms across her front. She's the sitting-down version of the standing-up Carla after Kyle said "Boo!" in the cornfield.

"How are you?"

"As if you care," she says. Her fingers through her hair make her curls fall in her eyes.

"I do," I say. Mr. Crap-on-My-Career not thinking about Carla, my only concern has been the force to resist the forward momentum we had. Mr. Empathy. Mr. Mature.

"Sure." Her arms crossed, she falls back against the chair.

"What happened in the cornfield?"

"Did you follow us?"

"Something happened out there."

"Now you're spying on me? Why'd you go there?" She looks at me through her curls. All of her is far away. "Oh, I get it," she says. "You want to know about Kyle."

"Of course. Kyle is, Kyle was one of my concerns." Using the past tense is hard.

"Right," she says. She draws out the one syllable into a long sound, pulls the word with her chin from left to right. "I saw you two together. You liked him." The slump in her body keeps her farther away from me, but her face gets brighter. The optical illusion is the idea of a smile on her face. It builds into a smile. She likes this idea.

"Liked," I say. "Yes, Mr. Harney was unique."

"Is that what you'd call it?" The smile is breaking out on

her face. Its force is motion with no equal or opposite reaction except inside me. The Taiko mallet rises inside me. "Suuu," the drummer exhales. The drum beats on my sternum, beats on my ribs.

"He was brilliant, if different."

"And you like different," she says. She straightens up in the chair. "Did you like him the way you liked me?" In unison the team of Taiko drummers sound the drum so loud the building shakes around me.

"Stop it."

"Stop what? You're the one who likes students." The mallet cracks my sternum; the cracked sternum presses my lungs.

"You know better than that."

"Whatever."

"Stop it, Carla. You like messing with minds too much." My hand rises up like I might bat away a ball she tosses. If only my hand could bat away my transgressions.

"Turn it on me, why don't you?" she says. "Awesome. Good work." Satisfaction on a face is an equilibrium of forces. The strike of the mallet on my ribs has less force. "Blame everything on me. Go ahead."

"Forget I asked," I say. "Forget it." I'm the one now to lean back in my chair.

"I try," she says. "A lot."

Standing up, Carla is a girl, not fully grown, her motion in pieces. Her back leans forward, legs rise, legs straighten, back opens up. The distance between her standing and my sitting is a meter, and she is still a moon away.

She cocks her elbow, twists her wrist, raises her middle finger, bends her arm, flips me the bird, and walks out.

The mallets do not rise to strike the drum in me. Carla's wrong. I care a lot about her. Two masses exert force on each other. The one with greater mass exerts the greater attraction. What I can't explain to Carla is the force that Kyle exerted on her, or on me. Without the mass of him, we are not balanced. What I can't explain is the science of loss, the weight, the density, the draw. There is turbulence in loss, a wild spinning of particles. There is a vacuum that is not an absence. It is full.

How to fold a crane is all I can explain.

# Taylor / **Sand**

"NICE SHIRT." THE WAY Carla closed the door behind her was angles: head forward, chin up, one foot ahead of the other, left arm raised to the front, wrist in line, right arm lowered to the back, the heel of the hand pushing the door, the fingers bent forward.

My shirt had Alex Jeffers' tears in the shape of Rhode Island, the simplified map. I guess, he and I are even. At the beginning of the year I left a spot on his shirt when I cried in his arms.

"Yeah, thanks for pointing it out," I said.

If she were a different student, if we had something different, if today were yesterday, I might have excused myself to change my shirt.

"Any time." She walked past me and swung her arms high and stiff.

In the living room, the pull-out couch was back to a couch. Carla turned on her heels and said, "No Terence?"

"Breakfast."

"Right." Her flop on the couch was a big bounce, and her legs crossed. "You know what I figured out at breakfast?" Her sweats were the same ones she wore all night, and her shirt was untucked under her hoodie. With one hand she pulled back her curls, and they fell down anyway.

"No clue," I said. The armchair, not the couch, was the best place to sit. No longer did I feel the walls go wavy, but there was still a want in my arms. Something was missing. Something was always missing.

She raised her curls out of her face. "I figured out how I'd do it."

"Do what?" I had to stall, hear her words again, make sure I was doing the right thing.

"End it," she said. She was talking peppy, like she might say, "Go team," even though Carla was no cheerleader.

"How?"

"Car."

"You drive?"

"Duh, I'm eighteen, and besides, my dad bought me a car the day he got killed. We fought about it right before. Fucking-A, that was weird."

She never softened or slowed when she talked about her father.

"He never bought Doug anything. Doug loved cars better than girls, way better. Lots of times Dad bought me necklaces, microscopes, fancy shoes, fancy art. I mean, the car was amazing, but I just wanted a real dad, a brother and dad. In the middle of our fight that day, I told him to fuck off, and I ran to my friend's house. That night, *bam*, he was gone. Never leave things unsaid."

"Oh my God." She moved up and down on the couch. "Bonus. Just thought of that. I had the-missing-the-curve part. But the-crash-in-Dad's-car part? Awesome."

She was into a movie she was making in her head. "Harm to self and/or others," like White's voice on the phone, was the audio tape in a loop in my head.

"Look, Carla," I said, "it's time to stop."

"Stop what? Really, Taylor, you got to get this."

We're back on a first name basis, I guess.

"Really. Think about it." Her hands were cupped over her mouth, like a little girl trying to stuff her giggles down. A little girl in a full-grown body. A bile rose in my throat.

"This weekend I get permission to go to my mom's. I pick up my car. Late at night, when my mom is boinking her latest boyfriend, I take all the origami Kyle and Jack Song folded in the car with me, and drive to the shore where the road curves around, and on the way, *bam*, I miss a turn. Looks like I fell asleep at the wheel. And everything will go up in a fiery blaze. Death and cremation, two for one. Perfect." She bounced against the back of the couch and clapped.

Everything around me was sand, white, crystalline, fine. My hands weren't big enough. My fingers were twigs.

"Did I tell you Kyle had a crush on me?" Sand was falling everywhere. I couldn't keep it from spilling.

"Yeah, so, I'd been getting these notes all folded up, and each one was signed 'Donny Zurkus,' like he could fold. But the last one said to meet him in the cornfield before dinner. So, I'm like, 'whatever,' and I think, 'shit, the biggest bully in the school, but he's tall and cute if you like that sort of thing,' so I go. And I walk out to the middle of the field, and Kyle goes, 'Boo!'

"'Fucking-A, Kyle,' I say. Kyle was smiling like crazy. Such a little-little." Carla smiles now, and her eyes are seeing the cornfield and Kyle.

"'Scared you, huh?' he says. In his gray sweats, you know, and his pea coat, he was, like, a possum, little eyes, big teeth." Kyle was definitely like a possum.

"So, I say, 'What're you doing here?' Donny Zurkus hadn't shown up, and if he did, I didn't want Kyle around. For Kyle's sake. And anyway, three's a crowd. But I don't say that.

"'What're you doing here?' he says. You know that really annoying repeating thing he does. Maybe not." I know exactly what she means. Kyle repeating the words I said, Kyle and I in the cornfield.

"He stiffens up, and says, 'I mean, what brings you out here?' He got over the repeating thing.

"'Looking for bugs.' It was the only thing I could think of.

"'Yeah, right,' he says.

"So I say, 'Following a lead.' And that sounded lame, even to me.

"But he went with it. 'Like a tip? Like a private eye? A tip from who?' Kyle folds his arms behind his back, leans forward and takes three steps one way all stiff-legged, turns on his heels, takes three steps back. He is fucking Sherlock Holmes. Oh, sorry." Kyle pretending to hold a magnifying glass, pacing back and forth. The little guy pretending.

"I try to be all cool. 'None of your business, punk,' I say.

"He says, 'Oh, come on, Carla, you can trust me. Honest. I'll be your private eye. I've even got a magnifying glass. See?' And from an inside pocket of his pea coat, he pulls a real fucking Sherlock Holmes magnifying glass. Sorry.

"'Kyle,' I say, 'you're one strange-ass kid, you know that?'"

There was no one as strange at St. Tim's as this boy. This little boy with greasy hair.

"He puts the round magnifying glass to his eye, bends over, and pretends to look at cornstalks. He bends way over."

"'Cut it out,' I say. 'I'm meeting someone. Do you mind?'

"'Oh, some guy,' he says. He straightens up, but keeps the magnifying glass on one eye. His blue eye is killer big. "'You've got a date. Ooh.' He is grinning that toothy grin. He crosses his arms behind his back again, leans forward, and says, 'Let me guess.' He goes Sherlock Holmes again. 'You're meeting Harrison Ford to look for the Lost Ark.' He turns and takes three steps back. 'No, that's not it.' He gives a little smile, pulls one hand from behind him, puts his fingers to his chin to think, changes the direction he's walking, and says, 'You're meeting Grover?' Then he tries to say some things in a grouchy, Oscar voice.

"I am rolling. Who knew this weird kid could be so funny.

"'Okay, okay,' he says. 'You're meeting Donny Zurkus.' And he stops, like dead-in-his-tracks, and he looks right at me. No shuffle. No toothy smile. No Sherlock Holmes.

"'How did you know?' My insides spin around, got all jammed up.

"'Clairvoyant,' he says. I barely know what that means.

"'Who told you?'

"He says, 'Nobody.'

"'Fuck you, Kyle. Don't make fun of me.' I can't figure out how he knows. There's nobody I told. Besides, nobody talks to him. Talked to him.

"Then, Kyle gets totally little. 'I'm not making fun of you,' he says. 'I'm not. I know, that's all.'

"'Tell me how,' I say.

"'Because I have abducted your brain,' he says in his me- chanical, Martian voice. 'Hee, hee, hee.'" Carla pulled back her lips and says the words with a combination of mechanical and hissing sounds. For a moment, Kyle is in this room.

"'Hey, I'm out of here,' I say. This kid is jerking me around. Usually, he's there for me and listens. I like talking to him. He likes the music I like. He likes bugs, but he goes too far.

"'Wait, wait,' he says in a high voice, no metal machine. 'I'll tell you. It's me you're waiting for. Me.'

"'Stop kidding around,' I say. My insides are jammed up with trying to put the pieces together, the notes inside the ori- gami, the things left in trees.

"'I'm not kidding, not kidding, honest. I folded the bat and everything. You wouldn't come out here just for me, just be- cause I wanted. I meant what I said: You're the best bat in my cave.' He was talking so fast I had to watch his lips.

"'Donny Zurkus has it all. He's tall and handsome. And I'm a little Second Former. I can't compete, but I thought if I got you out here, if you came to the cornfield, I could tell you.'

"'Tell me what?' I asked like a total doofus.

"He is pacing back and forth, not because he's pretending any more, but because he's scared or something.

"'You're the best,' he says. He looks at his feet, those sneak- ers. 'That's all.'

"'You pretended to be Donny Zurkus to say you liked me?' Poor little-little, weird little geeky guy. I didn't tell him how good that made me feel. I didn't tell him he was smart and cute in his own geeky way. I didn't tell him anything.

"Then, he goes Charlie Brown on me. He tips his head back like he's looking at the sky, and he says really loud, 'Good grief,' and he tosses something up in the air and runs away. His baggy sweats slow him down, and his pea coat's too big, so he looks more like someone pretending to run than really running. He runs away from me where I am in the cornfield, down the mud path, his hands in the air, his elbows out.

"That's the last time I see him. The little-little with a crush on me, leaving with more things unsaid."

"I'm sorry," I said. For a second she looked down, and her body went concave, melted into the couch. She might cry, and we could talk for the rest of the time left for breakfast, and I could call off the alert and she'd go to class, and I'd go to class, and the day would keep going.

"He didn't think about people finding him," she said.

"He was in pain, trying to get out of pain," I said. "What did he throw before he ran away?"

"A tape."

"Have you listened to it?"

"Can't."

"Yeah."

"No way. You don't get it," she said. "I killed him."

Her arms were not crossed in front of her. They were slack at her sides. Her voice was not animated like a cheerleader any more. The words were soft and simple. She stated them as if they were fact.

"No, you didn't, Carla. Absolutely not." She looked up as if she were rising out of a pool in summer waiting for me to wrap a towel around her, as if she had no curls, nothing to hide her, her face only eyes and hurt. But when she saw me see her eyes without the curls, her look changed to dry and ready to play another game.

"Whatever."

"Do you hear me?"

"Yes, sir, Sarge." She picked up her hand and with two fingers, saluted me. "Besides, I've got it all figured out. No problem."

"Really. You have to stop."

"I'd do two things at once. Awesome," she said. "You know, miss a turn, go bye-bye."

"Forget it!" I said. "It's time. Got to go." Standing up made the room change. The couch was so big it made Carla small.

"What?"

"You," I said. "You've got to go. Now. Get out." Everything was adrenalin. "I'm tired of you jerking me around. I can't take it."

One hand pulled her curls out of her face, and her eyebrows, dark and long, moved up her forehead. It was her eyes so flat in their light, so beaten; they showed how little she expected, how much I fit what she knew of other adults.

She dropped her curls in her face. "Not you," she said. She shook her head back and forth. "Fuck off."

To get up, Carla used a hand on the armrest, pushed her hips first. She brushed by me without touching. Before she turned the corner to the hall, she stopped. Out of the pocket of her hoodie, she pulled something that filled the palm of one hand and left it on the desk. The screen door slammed behind her.

She took twenty steps out my door, and I picked up the phone, dialed the nurse, and said it was time. The nurse had the car waiting.

In another forty steps down the flat black driveway under maples with no leaves, Carla walked, and a car pulled up beside her. The car that slowed to a stop. She bent at the waist to talk to the driver of the car. Since it was a maroon St. Tim's car, the driver was surely the nurse. That's when the back door opened, and before she got in, she turned toward my dorm. Her right hand went high in the air, the wrist rotated, a finger extended from the hand. A hand flipping the bird.

On my desk a perfect crane topped my pile of papers. Crimson, with gold-leaf shapes. Sharp points to the beak, to the tail. The wings were symmetric, the neck the right thickness, the body of the bird in proportion.

# Song / **Earth on Us**

SCOTTISH PEOPLE MUST HAVE Korean in them. The bagpipe, air forced through small opening, is like *gok*, the wailing we do. Westerners have no stomach for it. We do it for days, and best part? Guilt and regret forced out of our systems. Tim-Tim's is most Scottish at memorials.

This chapel in the basement is more cave than cathedral. The place is packed. No surprise in the front row: Mr. Oral-Fixation White with Mrs. Busybody, next to small Japanese woman and frail white guy, next to Rev. Moose. Classes canceled. Everybody's here. The next row is, listing to his left, Mr. Herbert of the Library, Rower-Man Jeffers, and Rower-Dyke Alta, next to Terence, and the rest of the remaining Second Formers. Some parents came for them. Some didn't.

Behind the rows of teachers, more students, like Rambo, Donny Bad-Boy Zurkus, and Buttons Daly. Behind the students, no parents. American parents are different from Korean. The character in Korean for *hyo* is son and earth. *Hyo*, filial piety, is the earth on the son. The parents are the son's world and carried on his back. What is the Korean character for parental responsibility? I never learned that one. Should be: earth on parents.

What is Tim-Tim's responsibility? Earth on us.

Rev. Moose takes the podium, the bagpipe stops wailing, and we're off.

The Rev reminds me of the teacher in the Charlie Brown comics. Can't help it. Too many holidays on Kim's hospital bed, the specials on the tiny screen. "Wah, wah, wah, wah," the voice goes while Peppermint Patty and Charlie Brown sit at their desks.

The one thing I hear: He invites Kyle's parents to speak.

Bent-over white guy, Mr. Devoted, turns to Asian wife, shuffles up in his baggy corduroys, black blazer. Rev. Moose touches the guy's elbow as he takes the steps. Kyle's father, Mr. Harney, is a little man. The hand he uses to tilt the mic is disproportionate, huge, the fingers bent different ways.

"Hello," he says too close to the mic. It echoes behind me in this cave. He backs away. Bends forward. "Hello, my name is Derrick Harney. I'm Kyle's father, and I hail from Detroit." He backs away again and looks up. His eyes squint a little.

"Kyle's mother is Niki Harney, and she hails from Nagasaki." He tilts his head to the left of the mic and nods at Mrs. Harney. She raises one hand barely off her lap, no wave, lifts it, and nods her head.

"We want to tell you about Kyle," he says. He's got the hang of the sound now. His face has deep lines in it, around his mouth. Too many lines for a small man, not old man, late fifties.

"Mrs. Harney and I met in war, married in peace. Kyle was our blessing when he was ten months old, and we were never so excited to adopt this child, this tiny boy. His whole life he was way ahead of us. The Mrs. and I tried catching up with him. All he wanted was books. That's why we were so excited he could come here, thanks to the Whites."

Mr. Harney's eyes squint, and his lips curve up, not much of a smile. Right then Japanese Mrs. Harney bends down to reach her purse. Not enough room to bend without falling forward out of the seat, her head almost in Dorothy White's lap. Reaches into her coat on the back of her seat. Nothing. Dorothy White to the rescue with a tissue.

Mr. Harney's voice is slowing down. He looks at the mic. "Niki and I never could catch up. Seems he's gone ahead of us, again. We'll miss him so much. Thank you, what you did for him." He bows his head quick in polite informal Japanese style, and turns to the steps from the podium. The Rev isn't fast enough to help him back to his seat.

Derrick Harney lowers himself down. To help him down, Mrs. Harney raises her hand to his shoulder. Spots are all over the back of her hand. He takes her hand as soon as he settles into the seat.

Next it's Head-Honcho White.

"Thank you, Mr. Harney, you and Mrs. Harney bless us with your presence."

Ever the grateful.

"As you all know, Kyle came to us as a Second Former only a few weeks ago."

Eleven, to be exact.

"And from the moment he arrived, he made his mark."

Euphemism: He was odd.

"He excelled in all his classes."

Understatement: He blew them away.

"For instance, Ms. Alta made special note that Kyle's project on South Africa was the most creative and thorough presentation in the class."

Which he destroyed with a mallet.

"Mr. Song noted that Kyle was always helpful in the dorm . . ."

Misdirection: He stuck by me because he was afraid to be anywhere else.

". . . and Herbert Hofmeister mentioned he'd never seen a student so enamored with the reference section of the library."

Misplaced kindness: Kyle listened to the drunk.

"While Kyle was with us a short time, we'll miss him."

"As if," Carla would say. What I'd really like to do, besides yell and throw things, is to interrupt this farce to give a demonstration.

I'd say, "Excuse me, ladies and gentlemen, I'd like to show you exactly what this headmaster has done for Kyle. Mr. White, would you agree that the staff at St. Timothy's is *in loco parentis* to our students?"

He would nod, of course.

"And as the local parent, what did you do for Kyle?"

Like a dog, he'd raise his ears and tilt his head.

"Nothing, that's true," I'd say. "Now, please be seated in this chair before me."

And Wyatt White would look at me with a half-grin because he's polite, after all. And he'd do what he was told because everyone was watching, and appearances are good for admissions. He'd take a seat in front of the podium, his wool trousers, his Tim-Tim's blazer flapping open.

"Thank you, Mr. White. Don't worry. This won't hurt a bit." The audience would giggle.

Then, I'd take six really thick books, like dictionaries, science textbooks, the school dress code, and pile them on his head. Then, as Mr. Physics-Man, I'd have to stand on a chair behind him, white lab coat, my glasses on, and steady the stack for him. With one hand to steady the stack, my other hand would put a board on top. From my lab coat I'd pull out a nail. One hand would steady it perpendicular to the board, ready to be nailed, and the other hand would get out a hammer from a pocket in my lab coat.

"Now then," I'd say, "tell me what you feel."

At this point, Mr. Polite might squirm. "Very funny, Mr. Song, I'm sure your demonstration has merit," he'd say, "but I think we've had enough."

I'd press the stack down harder so he couldn't move. "Oh no, Mr. White, we've had far too much. Sit still."

That's when the hammer would hit the nail. Over and over the thunk echoing in the chapel. The nail inching down into the wood, through the wood, into the first book.

"Feel anything?"

"Why, no," he'd say. And he'd try to turn and look at me, but he wouldn't be able to.

"Of course not, Mr. Idiot," I'd say. Politeness is not a part of the demonstration. "The force of the hammer is resisted by the books. The books provide the inertia. This is your brain at the bottom of the stack. This is your brain on denial. You felt nothing. Still don't. You don't miss Kyle. We've had far too much inertia." And I'd whack the hammer again for dramatic effect.

"Don't pretend you feel anything," I'd say.

I don't know what would happen after that. But even thinking of it helps me get through whatever else Mr. Inertia is saying. He's left the podium. The bagpipe's back. Buttons and Rambo are crying. Carla is nowhere in sight.

Mrs. Harney helps Mr. Harney get up from his chair, but then, Mr. Harney puts her hand on his forearm. Mr. Inertia and the Rev dwarf the little couple from behind. When they turn to come down the center aisle, that's when I see her. Niki Harney has pink, puckered skin across her face, almost the yin-yang symbol, one eye sagging. The telltale keloid scarring. Mrs. Nagasaki, probably she was Kyle's age when Bockscar dropped the Fat Man.

Sir Kyle, young prince of his mother's protection.

Mr. Anti-Nuke, with nuclear annihilation on his notebook.

Not to see the TV show *The Day After*. Not tonight. Not ever.

Bent-over Mr. Harney and radiation-poisoned Mrs. Harney shuffle down the aisle. I meet them with the wrapped package of a hundred cranes.

"Mr. and Mrs. Harney, my name is Jack Song. It is an honor to meet you," I say.

Mr. Harney straightens up. His eyes are blue dots in deep wrinkles. He takes his hand from behind his wife and extends it to me. His hand is callused and fits my hand like a pipe wrench.

"Mr. Song," he says, "we've heard a lot about you."

I pull in my elbows, make my feet parallel, and bow low

from the waist to Mrs. Harney. The eye that doesn't sag is bright. She smiles and bows back slightly, both scarred hands laid flat on her skirt.

"Please accept these from our students who folded them." I hold out the box, and Mrs. Harney's eyelashes descend over her eyes, the eyes glowing white with cataracts. She knows what the box contains.

Mrs. Harney says, "*Arigato Gozaimasu.*"

"You're welcome" in Korean sounds like "Chairman Mao." I bow again, the arms-to-the-side, head-down-to-the-knees traditional bow, long enough to feel the pull of hamstrings, the need for a haircut.

From students' hands to my hands to their hands to fire, what we couldn't give Kyle in this lifetime will fly into the next. Earth on us turns fire, then flight.

# Taylor / **Nothing to Say**

DURING THE THREE DAYS Carla was hospitalized, TV crews in the parking lot of Winn Dixie, Norma's Family Restaurant, and Bi-Mart kept us from driving the flat black driveway through maple trees to the world outside. On public property, the reporters talked to residents of Surrey, Delaware, especially ones who worked at St. Timothy's. Members of the kitchen staff and custodial staff and local contractors talked to reporters. The cameras caught Mr. Leonard, the bartender and handyman and mentor, going into True Value Hardware, but he brushed by them. He held up his hand, said, "No comment," and kept walking. On TV his gray hair was short and clipped perfectly. His face was lined, though, and his eyes tired. The loss of a student was hard on everyone.

But from those interviewed, the whole country soon learned of bruises and pranks and flies. St. Tim's was Castle Elsinore, where plots were devised and carried out and young men died. Fiction was fact.

In the three days after Kyle died, students had nightmares about flies in the whites of eyes rolled back. The Second Formers said that's how they knew Kyle wasn't kidding. Three nights I went from dorm to dorm and from room to room. One student, feeling guilty, tried to remember Kyle's face, the grease for hair, the small eyes and teeth, and couldn't. Another student, trying to forget, was guilty of jumping Kyle's back and pounding him, holding him down to the lab table, or ignoring him on purpose.

Tommy Underwood dropped out the day of the memorial service. The grapevine reported he wasn't eating, he couldn't sleep, and, if asleep, a scream jerked him awake.

Maggie Anderson took it all on. She said she should have been nicer. Most of us figured there was something we should have done, too, but Maggie said it out loud.

"If only I had talked to him, really talked," she said. At one in the morning, she wrapped her arms around an enormous stuffed dog, one of the many stuffed animals making her bed a zoo of soft, furry forms. I sat on the floor and wrapped my arms around my knees.

"And what would you have said?"

"I'd say he's smart." She didn't wince at the present tense. "And I'd listen."

"But Maggie, did Kyle talk? Remember his head on the desk?" My smile tried to pry her eyes off her fuzzy slippers.

And we played "what if" for awhile until she slept.

It was Terence who was both still and rushing.

"Ms. Alta," he said, "what if Kyle survived?"

On the bench under birch trees, we overlooked the lake, the lake where the crew didn't row any more, the lake where I didn't look for Sarah.

"You mean, came to?"

Terence sat at the edge of the bench, his legs tucked under, his heels moving back and forth with his toes dragging on the ground.

"Yeah, what if he didn't die, and he remembered Tommy and me bumping him, and Mr. Jeffers trying to save him, and the ambulance?"

Terence looked across the lake where the fog crept up in the morning. His cheek was smooth, and his forehead smooth. Our down jackets made us round and soft in the December cold.

"You got me there, Terence."

"I think he'd be the same way." Terence didn't look at me or his feet or anything. His chin was up, and he held steady the far shore. "I think he'd talk typewriter, say, 'Ter-ence, you-should-have-cut-me-down, Zip, Ping!'"

Terence had the metal voice, the movement of the chin from left to right, the staccato words. Kyle's voice through Terence made my fingers tingle.

"We would have talked like that." Terence kicked the dirt under the bench. "But maybe people would've helped him after that."

His eyes left the far shore, and he looked quick at me, then looked down at the dirt. "You know what else we did?"

"No idea," I said. Their spending time together was news to me.

"We fixed Donny." He took one hand out of the jacket pocket and covered his smile with it. His dark hand didn't quite cover his whole smile.

"You mean the thing with Donny when we flew kites?"

"Yup, that was us."

"What do you mean?"

Terence's feet were swinging under the bench, and his shoulders were forward, and his hands rested on the bench on either side of him.

"Well, you know how Donny was testing *Hamlet*? Kyle wanted to test something about ghosts and revenge and subliminal suggestions during sleep. Mr. Hofmeister let us check out a tape recorder, and every night we made tapes." He covered part of his smile again, and this time his pink gums showed bright.

"One night Kyle said Donny's uncle was going to kill his father, and that he was going crazy. One night I said he was going to pee in bed and he better go to the bathroom. And he got up to go. I swear." Terence looked at me, then tried to make his mouth not smile.

"Problem is he didn't make it to the bathroom. He peed in the hall. Somebody saw him, and the guys, you know, called him 'bed wetter' and 'baby' and stuff." Terence wasn't smiling any more.

"Where did you put the tape recorder?" I said.

"Outside his window, under his bed, in his closet. We had to change how loud we talked."

"How did you get in his room?" Fifth Formers would notice Second Formers.

Terence shook his head. "I got a lot of tardies to dinner." He smiled down at his feet.

"So, that's why Donny couldn't sleep?"

"Yup." Terence puffed out his chest and sat up on the bench. "I know Donny really knocked Kyle hard. I kind of should have said something."

"And get shoved, too?"

He shook his head. "Donny came to the cubbies that night before lights out, before the wrestling. He found the library card for the tape recorder with our names on it. He figured it was us."

And that must have been the tipping point for Donny, the boys kidding him, him not kidding the boys. Second Formers had made a show of him, Second Formers, Kyle, the weirdest little bright boy.

"Him and the others," Terence said, "they filled up the commons. Donny didn't do much, mostly pointed at Kyle, like his arm was a rifle. Stupid stuff. He went, 'No one messes with Donny Zurkus. Not Zippy. Not Song. Not nobody. I'm going to get you for good.' A regular Godfather. And Kyle giggled. He thought Donny was funny. Or something was funny, anyway. Donny left. That's all."

Terence's feet skimmed the dirt under the bench, one foot at a time. There was so much going on in his legs and so little in his face.

"You know you didn't make Kyle do anything," I said. The eye in the profile of Terence's face was a window into classrooms he and Kyle shared, into dorms, into the dining hall where they sat small in their chairs.

"Didn't stop him, either."

"He'd made up his mind."

"Maybe."

That's all he said.

Leaning back on the bench, I crossed my legs, swung my foot a little faster than Terence's feet swinging under the bench. We faced the lake, the wind picking up, the sting of winter on our faces.

His legs swung. My leg swung. The lake was all there was.

"Aren't you cold?" Alex Jeffers said. He came around the bench from my side and blocked the breeze picking up. The scent of lime and sweat wrapped around me. Looking up at the tall guy so close was too hard, so I smiled hello and dropped into looking at the lake.

"Not yet," I said. Terence stopped swinging his legs.

"It's freezing out here," Alex said.

"Yeah, going in," Terence said. With his palms around the end of the bench, he pushed off. He didn't look at me. "Later, Miss Alta." Terence folded his arms in front of him, closed his St. Tim's blazer around him.

Alex walked in front of me, blocked out the lake, then sat beside me, one arm around the back of the bench. "He okay?"

"Not really."

"Sorry."

"You?" I said. Alex's jawline was cut sharp. The muscle flexed and relaxed. He looked down at his enormous hands.

"Not really," he said.

"I wonder why," I said.

His thin lips spread into a smile. "No reason."

"Yeah, kid dying, no sleep, no problem." My weight shifted toward him, and his arm left the bench and draped around my shoulders. He leaned his weight toward me. And the warm of his lime and sweaty body on one side, his arm heavy on my shoulders pushed out the cold breeze lining my right side.

"I have just the thing." A brown paper sack, crumpled, came

out of his blazer pocket, and the bottle of Jack Daniel's inside looked small in his hand.

"Shit, Alex," I said, "on campus?" Suddenly I was underage and sneaking and sure I'd get caught.

The angles of his face softened. "So let's boogie," he said. His smile was young, too.

"Now? Leave?" There had to be something wrong with what we were doing.

"Sure," he said. He put the bottle back in his pocket. "No study hall. We're free until check-in." He had a point.

"Deal," I said. His hand outstretched was warm in the lake breeze. His hand made my hand small. I wanted something big to wrap around me.

Walking past the bench on the way to the parking lot, we dropped hands. In a boarding school, we're never alone. Except we're always alone wherever we are, but there may be someone watching. The loneliness we feel is as sure as water. It changes into fog and rain and a frozen lake, but it's always water. No matter where we are on campus, we see the lake, the water caught by an evening breeze on the way to winter. And someone else sees what we see. We don't know if they're there for us. We're alone. Someone else is alone, too.

It must have been in the eighth grade, about the same time of day when light is strained and cold, when Phil Fenton told me he had something to tell me. It was carpool and time to go home. Phil Fenton had blond, curly hair, played lacrosse, and wore jeans with rips in the knees. Under his straw hat his long blond curls hung down the sides of his face.

"Over here," he said, and he pulled me into Mrs. Wishert's room, the eighth-grade English class.

"What?" I said. "Mrs. Harris is here, carpool, got to go." There was something in my chest that wouldn't let me breathe. It was cold, like scared, like dark when you go outside to let the cat in and the street is too quiet. Something else in my chest was too warm.

"Back here," he said. I couldn't see.

"Phil, where are you?" My hands weren't completely out in front of me, out to the sides a little.

He didn't say anything. And the heat of him was close. The sweat of him was close. The sweat was old socks. "Here," he said.

I didn't know what his hands were doing or where to stand or what he wanted to tell me. His hands on my hands were squirmy, and his hands led mine around his back. And his hands around my shoulders turned me around, backed me against the wall of Mrs. Wishert's classroom, and his body pressed me back, and his mouth was all wet on my face. My mouth found his mouth.

This was necking.

Phil Fenton and I necked every afternoon before carpool for two weeks. And then, one time there were hands and sweat and something more in him. My back was smushed against the wall, and he pressed against me harder, and there was a power that wasn't there before. It made the room darker and farther away from English class and white chalk on the blackboard. I was smaller. My hair stuck to my neck, his mouth was wet on my neck, and his squirmy hands were rough. It wasn't like necking any more.

I didn't know what I was supposed to do. There was a feeling in my chest that wasn't warm or cold. There was something rising in my chest.

"No," I said. It came out really loud, like a school bell or something.

Phil jumped back.

"Damn," he said. "What's wrong?" His voice was sleepy.

"I don't know. Got to go," I said. My hands checked my shirt and pulled my shoulders on right. There was heat coming off Phil, and I went around him, out Mrs. Wishert's door.

There was something so wrong in me it filled my chest. It was wrong all the way down the linoleum hall, down the sidewalk in the winter dark, into the warm car with Mrs. Harris driving home.

There was something wrong in this ride to this Delaware town, Alex driving a red Toyota Celica down the flat black driveway under maple trees, out the brick entrance of St. Timothy's. On the highway to town, he pulled out the bottle. With one hand he held the bottle and the steering wheel, and his other hand twisted off the cap. The half-pint bottle made a tap on the steering wheel. Turning toward me, he made his eyebrows do Groucho Marx up and down. Then, he tipped the bottle and took a taste. He handed it to me. The whiskey bit my throat, but warmed me all the way down. The thing in my chest felt warmer.

Town wasn't far, and it wasn't big. The one family restaurant was Norma's, and it served steaks with fries, biscuits and gravy, and real southern fried chicken. Every dish came with corn pone and coleslaw, like it or not. About the same time as the waitress in her orange-striped apron and tiara-type cap came to take our order, a man with polyester pants and blue floral shirt pushed onto the bench seat beside me.

"Mind if I sit for a minute?" the man with the polyester smile said. He almost sat on me. My legs were touching Alex's legs under the table, and for me to move over, Alex had to turn sideways. "My name is Marshall," he said, "Marshall Wayne Murphy." And he stuck a hand across the table at Alex. His hand hung above the table until Alex shook it. "Pleased to meet you," Marshall Wayne Murphy said. He didn't offer his hand to me.

"I work for the *Delaware Star*," he said. He put a pad of paper on the table. Alex and I looked at each other. Alex with his blond cropped hair, his chiseled jaw, his button down shirt, me in my St. Timothy's blazer and khaki pants, my button down shirt. We were the bull's-eye in his scope.

"I understand you work at St. Timothy's," he said. The pages of his spiral notepad flipped up as he licked his fingers to pluck them. The lined pages were light green, long and thin. He dug into his inside pocket to find a pencil.

"We have nothing to say," I said to his notepad still flipping.

"Really." He stopped plucking the pages and looked at Alex.

"That's right," Alex said. He looked at me.

"You have nothing to say about a boy hanging from the rafters and a teacher accused of abusing him? That's fine." He picked up the top cover of the notepad and slowly closed it. His hand had manicured nails, glossy, perfectly shaped.

What Alex looked like must have been what I looked like. Mouth closed, eyebrows crunched up, eyes shifting back and forth.

"What teacher?" Alex said.

Marshall Wayne Murphy was quick to open his notebook. "Oh, want to talk?" He looked up and grinned. "Oriental name. Let's see here."

There was only one teacher with an Asian name. My stomach with the whiskey in it was a cannon ball.

"Here it is," he said. "Jack Song, Physics."

"No," I said.

"You're wrong," Alex said. The muscle of his jaw was sticking out.

"Another student gave great details. Told all about showers and this guy Song tucking the boy in." He winked at us as if we shared secrets with him.

Alex was turning so red that his hair looked white. "What student?"

"Well, let's see," Marshall Wayne Murphy said. He licked his manicured fingers and turned pages again. "I know I've got it: Donny Zuckhaus. I think you call juniors 'Fifth Form.'"

Alex bit down, turned his head to the wall. The jaw muscle flexed, released, flexed, released. My hands went to my forehead, my fingers digging into my hairline. Fiction makes fact look simple.

What could we say?

"The student lied," Alex said.

"Can I quote you on that?" Marshall Wayne Murphy licked a finger, pushed pages aside, raised his pencil.

"Forget it," Alex said.

The feeding frenzy of polyester and floral print reporters

would hit Surrey tomorrow. More reporters. A lot more. A suicide was good enough for national news. A sex scandal was even better. Poor Jack.

"Excuse me, Mr. Murphy," I said with a smile, "could you please move? We're leaving." I shuffled toward him on the bench, actually pushing him. I threw money on the table for the meal we wouldn't eat.

His mouth opened, but he didn't say anything, grabbed his pencil and his pad and moved off the bench. Once he stood, I was out the small space between his polyester pants and the table. Alex was right behind me.

On the way out of Norma's, I didn't look at the breakfast bar or the other booths by the window. The glass door with the metal handle across the middle, the decals of credit cards they accepted on the glass, this was the exit. Outside, the parking lot smelled like chicken fat. Five steps on to the blacktop, and I turned to Alex.

"Holy shit," I said.

"Holy shit."

Both of us raised our hands to our foreheads and bent over, turned in opposite directions. We were in some weird *Star Trek* episode with sound waves crushing our eardrums. What we heard was too hard.

This must have looked great from the windows of Norma's. I stopped.

"Oh God," I said, "let's go."

On the flat drive back to St. Timothy's, Alex and I didn't say anything. My left hand spread flat across his thigh, his thigh warm, pressed into my hand. We passed the whiskey between us. The only sound was the radio, some Talking Heads song. The lights on the dashboard made the car red inside, and Alex's hand giving me the bottle, me giving him the bottle, was like the black wand of a radar in some control tower moving back and forth. Intruders were entering our space from all around us. And there was nothing we could do.

At the brick entrance to school, Alex screwed the top back

on the bottle, and wrapped it in the wrinkled, brown bag. We had finished it. Maybe Herbert Hofmeister was right at that faculty party on the lawn stretching down to the lake: If you're going to teach, you're going to drink.

Alex pulled around my dorm where the light over the parking lot was too bright. After putting the car in neutral, he reached his arm around the back of my seat and leaned toward me. His face big, I could reach it with my lips. Maybe his face was the forever place. Maybe his face could fill the crack in my chest. Some part of me wanted to pretend, wanted to be a part of a school with stone blocks this way and stone blocks that way. I wanted to want Alex. I had led him to believe I wanted him. But the car smelled maple, the two of us large in the little car, close. The whiskey was warm in me. The smell of sweat and maple and chicken fat from the diner was too close. The ceiling of the car was inches above my head and caving in.

"See you, Alex. Thanks."

"What about Song?" he said.

"Talk to him. Tell him that we know Donny is lying. Tell him he's not alone in this." The little handle was somewhere on the door. It was more like a D-ring than a handle, and I almost broke it off trying to get out. The ground felt farther away, and instead of blacktop, it was riverbed, uneven, changing. The pavement sloped toward my back door, and someone sat on my doorstep, the entry light orange above.

The Toyota sprayed pebbles as it pulled away. The person in my doorway sat up.

"Taylor?" she said. It was Crisco rising in my doorway, her big shoulders turning orange in the entryway light.

I said, "You're here."

"Of course, I'm here." I missed a step and fell forward. Crisco caught me, leaned back, and spun me off my feet. Her body was tight, held me like a fitted sheet.

"What're you doing here?"

"No news like bad news," she said.

# Carla / **Tape #1, Side A**

TEST. TEST. 1-2-3.

Awesome.

So, if you're listening to this, then I'm dead, too. We're to-gether again in our cornfield. You shouldn't have left the way you did. That totally sucked.

I haven't listened to your tape. I'm sorry. No can do.

So, anyway, can you see where I am now? Fucking nut ward. Fucking Alta. Unbelievable. Group therapy three times a day. Meds twice a day. Individual therapy once a day. The shrink who's kind of okay gave me this totally old tape record-er, like huge, ancient, and she said I have to get stuff out, stories and stuff. With all the meds my mind goes fluffernutter, but talking to you, that works. All I can do in group is picture you in the cornfield, hanging in the dorm, your greasy hair. And I imagine the one-liners my brother, Doug, would make to the kids in the group, like "Shut up" or "Life's a bitch," to the loser kid who flubbed his suicide. Missed his brains and shot his ear, van-fucking-Gogh. Or the Whiner whose momma never pays attention to her. Bor-ing.

You'd like Doug. You two were kind of alike. He and I had this pediatrician growing up, all pasty white and crew cut. Like the shrink in charge here: Dr. Do Little. He's sitting across the circle from me, tweed jacket and bow tie. Dr. Do Little turns to me in group, his round glasses all smudged, and I'm like, "I don't know," to everything he asks. He's always asking what I feel. The way he says "feel," it sounds gross and slimy.

Do Little says I should let it out. He doesn't say what "it" is. In the prison cell they put me in, hospital room, they give me a journal, no lines, and a tape recorder with a blank tape. Bonus. I can't help but think that they erased somebody from the tape to use it again. I haven't said a word to anybody anywhere so far.

Okay, there was one time I talked. Had to.

That time the Whiner, sucking on her gross hair, is next to Do Little, her body all stretched out, like she's a board some-body propped up against the chair. The loser, van Gogh, is talking about his miserable life in this nasal voice. I hear him say, "wah wah wah nobody cares about me wah wah wah, poor me." So, I don't know, I just lose it. These kids are like Tim-Tim kids, stupid and spoiled.

"You know what's funny?" I say out loud, and the room goes dead. Dr. Do Little pushes his glasses up with his finger and looks at me.

"Carla?"

"No, Mabel," I say.

So, I start in, and pretty soon the Whiner isn't sucking her hair, all wet and gummy, and van Gogh's jaw is dropped.

"Yeah, so, I figure he got me alone for like eight years and did whatever he wanted with me out there in the peach trees and in my room at nap time. Trouble is I don't remember a thing about exactly what he did. All I know is afterwards, I had big bruises. I remember those. But later I got cool things, like a car."

Do Little says something nerdy, "Your brain protected you and compartmentalized the experience."

Whiner tilts her head, keeps her soggy hair in one hand. "What kind?"

"Mustang."

"Awesome."

I don't know why I blabbed. Had to show them up. Dad must have done it to Doug too. Dad was totally fucked up.

I remember this one time in the summer, it was so humid that we were dripping, standing still. Doug and I kept sticking our heads in the fridge. Mom yelled at us, so we pretended to help her in the kitchen.

"Here, Mom," Doug said, "I'll get the butter." And he had that shaggy brown hair in his eyes, but his eyes were crinkled with that big smile on his face. The light from the fridge made his eyes black, his nose long, his neck forever. His hand on the fridge door. The cool came from the fridge in waves, like someone breathing winter, and he stood there.

"Yeah, Mom," I said, "I'll get the eggs," but I was too little to reach that shelf.

"Kids," Mom ended up saying, "out of the kitchen." Mom cooked when she got hot, cooked in the stinking heat. Flour made her hands doll hands. She pushed her hair back with her forearm, and her hair stuck there.

It was Dad who called us from their bathroom.

"Kids, get in here." His voice was Father-Knows-Best and Elmer Fudd, both.

Doug stood there so long in the fridge light the waves didn't come out any more, and his eyes went away from mine. His shoulders went down, the way a dog goes down when it knows it has to do something it doesn't want to do. His face turned toward Dad's voice. "Coming," Doug said.

Our parents' bathroom was huge, bigger than a bedroom at St. Tim-Tim's. The spray on the tiles was all the sound there was in the room, and Dad was wavy behind the shower glass. He was moving all around like some shadow in cartoons. The glass door popped open. He was in there, his hair flat not curly, the khaki pants sticking to his legs, his shirt wet paper sacks on his chest. His way of getting cool around him.

His big voice, "Come on in, the water's fine."

Doug bent over to take his shoes off, and Dad grabbed him by the waist, pulled him in, butt first.

"Shit," Doug said, "shit, shit," and Dad let him say "shit" because the water was cold.

"Come on, Carla," and both of them held out a hand to me.

I jumped in with my shoes and clothes, and the three of us squeezed into the shower and jumped around. The cold felt good, and we arched when the spray hit us. Then Dad had his arms on either side of Doug, his hands flat on the tile, like a bull hooked his horns in him, and Doug couldn't move. Dad blocked the spray with his back, the spray bouncing in my eyes, and I couldn't see Doug. The water hit my head and made two rivers around the front of me, my T-shirt was my skin, my sneakers soggy by the drain. The smack of the water wasn't as loud any more. Dad stood like a bull does, before it charges. I know that now, Kyle. But then, I went around him and got between the two of them, did a little Ring-Around-the-Rosy dance. Doug's head was the height of Dad's armpit, and Doug turned in circles right where he was, little tight circles, his eyes closed, not touching anyone.

That was weird. Creepy weird.

So, I guess the point of a nut ward is to keep you living your miserable life. Like van-fucking-Gogh is supposed to be boring, and Whiner is meant to whine. Doug's still in his lock-down place, you're dead, and I'm stuck for eternity at Tim-Tim's. That means walking those freezing halls with fucking Jack Song and that pathetic Alta and that echo of where you used to be.

A gray moth.

A lump in the cornfield.

Origami animals out my window.

Doug would like you.

If I could be the tie around your neck, I'd rip. Every thread would snap and curl. The tie would tear across its stripes, and you'd thud down on the floor of your cubby. You'd still breathe, and I'd be the tie piece, hanging from the rafter.

And the cornfields would be good. Uh-oh, I better be quick.

The tape is squeaking.

And I could look out my window and see something besides cranes.

# Song / **Sneaker Wave**

WAVES TRANSMIT ENERGY OVER distance. They travel through the medium but do not displace the medium. So, through a dorm room wall, people can hear others talking, but the wall is not affected by the sound. The speed of a wave depends on the medium through which it travels. Rumor through media moves faster than rumor through people. The speed of a sound wave through air is generally 343 m/s under normal circumstances, but increase pressure and intensity, and one has headline news.

Mr. Zurkus was in my parents' living room in San Diego within minutes of the news release, his muscle-boy body in a new suit riding up the screen. My parents never fix their vertical hold. Bad-Boy Zurkus, his new suit flapping as he walks through reporters.

Today I'm sitting in Oral-Fixation White's office. Suspension from teaching means house arrest. I walk inside the apartment in circles when students go to class. Bad-Boy Zurkus says I killed Kyle by touching him.

Today White is a smoke machine. Back and forth, back and forth in front of the windows. Far below is the lake. On the lake the water is the medium for waves. The wind causes energy to move through the water.

"You must have done something."

White stops, puts both hands on the back of his wingback chair.

Virginia tobacco. Not enough air in the too small office.

"The teenage mind is untoward," I say.

My parents will not answer the phone today. My parents will not leave their kitchen. No visitors. My mother will fill the rice cooker, and steam will rise from the bubbling pot. The pot will rattle, and the switch will flip when the rice is done.

White, King of the Phone Calls, his secretary holds calls while I'm grilled. School attorney calling every five minutes.

"You did nothing and Donny does this?" He holds his pipe to his mouth. "Unlikely."

In North Korea, justice is based on loyalty to the state. Every family is placed in a class: core, wavering, or hostile. If hostile, no possibility of hospital or education, little food. If caught talking to foreigners, you disappear. Interrogation is kneeling with metal rod held between thighs. It drops, and they use it on you. No nice-nice, like talks with pipe-smoking lion pacing in his cage.

"Mr. Zurkus needs help," I say.

He stops. No more Doppler effect of the sound. When the source of the sound wave moves, the frequency and wavelength depend on that motion. The sound appears to bend. Now, it's a direct hit.

He turns, faces me. "What the hell is wrong with you? Your career is ruined, the school is smeared all over the TV, and you think Donny needs help? God, man."

Who can say what teenagers do? Some of them study, take notes, go to Harvard; some lie awake and devise pranks, Young Sirs of Mischief and Misrepresentation; and some hang from rafters.

"Maybe he's stuck in *Hamlet*," I say.

"Come again?"

"Ask an English teacher, ask Alta."

"Song, don't be glib."

"Glib, I'm not."

Mr. Headmaster looks away, moves to his desk. His shoulders are rounded. He leans over the mess of his desk. The lines around his eyes are deeper; the circles are darker. What Administration means is barrier reef. They keep storms off shore. What happens when a storm is too big for them to keep away? Crashing. Destruction. What Administration forgets is the flesh. Donny is a boy, perhaps malevolent, certainly misguided.

And waves have anomalies. The sneaker wave can occur anytime, anywhere, in moderate and dry conditions. Undersea depth irregularities often focus wave energy, waves from offshore storms encounter shoaling, strong currents exacerbate incoming waves, and sneaker waves can snatch a grown man as much as 100 meters up the beach. Never turn your back on the ocean.

Sneaker-Wave Zurkus.

"We have to do something and do it now. Couldn't come at a worse time." He lights another match, sticks it in the pipe. Ugly habit.

"Suspending me from teaching is not action?"

"Not enough," White says. He sucks the flame down the pipe.

What action could quell the hunger of reporters? In Korea there were incentives for neighbors to rat on neighbors. Too little food makes everyone conniving. Saying that someone sat on a pile of newspapers with pictures of leaders on the front page meant that person disappears. Saying someone plots to leave North Korea, the family disappears.

"What do we know about Zurkus?" White says. "Christ Almighty, his father is Union Textile."

"Didn't you go to school with him or summer in the Hamptons?"

White looks up, the stupid pipe sticking out from his mouth.

Who in this century smokes pipes? He's staring at his bookcase.

"No, he's not a Princeton man, but Stanford." White turns to me. "Didn't your friend Okinawa go there?" His eyes are hot blue in the middle, like flames from Bunsen burners.

"Sam? Omura? Yes."

THOSE WHO GRADUATE FROM private education are one percent of the population. They become the top ten percent who run and own the country. Behind the scenes they operate a very simple wave model, called Destructive Interference:

Two scientists hold either end of a string. One yanks his end down, sending a wave, while the other pulls up by exactly the same amount. When the waves meet in the middle, each will cancel out the displacement of the other. The tricky thing is that the waves will not dissipate. The waves will pass each other and continue on their merry way.

In other words, each wave may lose its original intent, but each will be satisfied. That's how it works. Donny and I don't talk. Other people make things disappear, even though the energy keeps moving.

Sam Omura, the top donor to the sciences, the top alumnus. Mr. Teacher of Teachers. He might know Bad-Boy's father. He might know the right words to say.

White says, "I'll make the call. Sam Omura and Charles Zurkus III are a good match."

# Taylor / **The Turbine**

AFTER ALEX AND HIS maple smell and Crisco tucking me in, taking the couch, I slept hard. You'd think I'd dream of Song and dodging reporters, of Kyle and his smashed city. But no. Water was white and everywhere.

Big water, churning, a turbine. The noise was a dump truck with gravel on a washboard road. It was the middle of the Delaware Memorial Bridge at rush hour. It was bigger than sound, no sound, just Sarah and me. Her hair was this way and that way out from her head, no weeds caught in it, yet.

Her face was shining like she was glad to see me, the big cheeks, the eyes going almond, doing the thing they do, stars for eyelashes. We could have been on the rug in the college dorm, laid out, facing each other, looking at each other, which we did sometimes, chins on crossed hands. Except we were in a turbine. Except we were in the Schuylkill. I knew that.

And in the dream we didn't say anything, looked at each other like we were mirrors. It was like we were skewered, a metal rod through our stomachs as we faced each other, looking in our eyes, at cheekbones, at chins. The two of us pierced, turning over and over in the middle of the Schuylkill.

And with her cheeks pulled into her smile, Sarah said to me, "It's okay," and her brown eyes did their star thing. And she started to move backwards off the skewer, backing away.

And as soon as I moved my arm to reach for her, she turned into a crane, a red paper crane, crimson with gold shapes, folded perfectly.

And as soon as I saw the origami crane, the sound came back, and I was sucked into the turbine, tossed around, the water up my nose, white everywhere, the sound inside me, a wave taking me under, up, spinning, and there was nothing I could do.

# Song / **Not There**

MR. ORAL FIXATION MADE the call to Sam, related by college to Donny Zurkus' dad. The old-boy network. This time I'm connected. Vectors of relation. While the old boys do what they do, make things go away, play Ollie North, White sends me to Rehoboth Beach, a Board of Trustee member's summer cottage, away from reporters, carnivores of carnage. Call me Mr. Roadkill.

"TAYLOR, THIS IS SONG. Please excuse the intrusion," I said into the white phone with the little note taped to the table next to it: *Please use your own long-distance calling card.* Of course, Miss Cheapskate Cottage Owner.

"Song, where are you?" Ms. Rower said.

"On holiday."

"Right. Just a little vacation," she said. Sarcasm. Smart for a rower.

"Of sorts. I'm calling about Carla."

"You heard." Ms. Rower's voice went quiet.

"Bad news, you know."

"Mrs. White loves to talk."

"Queen Gossip."

"Well," Rower said, "Carla's in the psych ward."

"Wilmington?"

The shiny linoleum, the fluorescent lights, the smell of Pine-Sol that takes a half-life to get out of your nose, all floors are the same. The blood unit. The psych ward. East Coast hospital, West Coast hospital, all the same.

"She went last week, should be out soon." Her voice didn't rise, a flat wave.

That's what we always said about our grandfather, "He'll be out soon," from the concentration camp, Total Control Camp No. 7. When my father and his brothers were very young and very hungry, my grandfather stole a beet root on the way back from his fourteen hours at the mine. He was arrested on the spot, and that's the night my father and the family left for China. Then, they made their way to South Korea, came to the U.S. That's the story. Somehow we learned where my grandfather was taken. No one ever saw him again.

"For what?" I said to Ms. Sounding Guilty.

"She said she was going to kill herself, had it all planned out."

"And you believed her?" These new teachers, gullible.

"Heard of contagious suicide?"

"Psychobabble."

"You weren't there, Jack."

"No, but you aren't exactly there, either, Taylor." The dinners where she stopped her fork midway to her mouth, didn't pass the gravy to Eager-to-Feed Second Formers, walked through the halls with her long rower arms hugging her books like they were life vests.

"What are you talking about?" Ms. Rower's voice goes up. More air, less space to pass through.

"You're a new teacher. You haven't taught a year."

"But I know what she said." Ms. Rower's back in grade school.

"How can you be sure?" My father's voice in my mouth, the riddles, the twisted logic is the ventriloquism of age. No science in that.

"What's your point, Jack?" Young Rower turns resistance.

"There were options."

"Maybe for you."

"Meaning?"

"You know her. You know St. Tim's. St. Tim's knows you," Alta says in her high voice, too little air through too few years.

"Empirical evidence suggests the school knows little of me." I point out the obvious. "I will always be the outsider."

"You've been there awhile."

"That's true," I say. The weight Newton failed to measure transfers from Rower Dyke's shoulders to mine. "And you are too new to know what twists the adolescent mind will take. Carla is like Kyle, too bright, too different."

She takes a breath. "Exactly," she says, "Carla is too much like Kyle." And Alta turns into a planet, creating gravitational pull. I might explain G or any number of things I didn't tell Kyle. The power of connection, through blood, diseased or not, the *hyo* of loyalty between siblings or students, all of it collides. The vacuum created by collision is filled by responsibility, mine to Kyle, mine to Carla, and the greatest, to my family.

"You're right, Taylor," I say.

Houston, we have touchdown. Ms. Rower, the teacher, has landed.

# Carla / **Tape #1, Side B**

ME AGAIN. OTHER SIDE. Day Fucking Four.

One of the most awesome things about tape recorders is the clicking, especially with used tapes. This huge, old recorder really catches the sprockets of the tape. Click, click, click. You know what they remind me of? You're going to love this. The deathwatch beetle. They bore into wood, like in old houses, and their name comes from people who were waiting for their loved ones to die and couldn't sleep, and they'd hear the bug doing its thing at night in the quiet. These tapes? They're my deathwatch. Thanks for being on watch with me.

Do Little wants to know how I feel about death. You die, *c'est fini. Es el extremo. Das Ende.* Life sucks in lots of languages, ya know?

Reverend Moose says humans create what they need for the afterlife because life lived is too much to bear. What d'you think? You've been dead for how long? What's your afterlife? From where you are, do you know what Doug's is? I know he's not dead.

Last time I saw Doug, he was my age. The judge opened

the paper, *guilty*, and the courtroom turned totally flashbulb and people standing up, and Mom standing up but not saying anything, reaching for him, and Doug in his orange jumpsuit and that hair, not shaggy any more, officers leading him away. He didn't look up, except at the door. He turned like he was trying to get the hair out of his eyes, and he looked right at me, not Mom, and he put his lips together like he was saying something, and he smiled, a little, mostly in his eyes, his eyes in my eyes.

I don't know if I got what Doug was saying.

It's been years since then, and they still won't let me see him. Too dangerous or something. Was he saying, "You"?

I hate death, but I'm not going to tell Do Little. He'll lock me up like Doug.

The poser van-fucking-Gogh says he's not afraid of death. Why'd he miss his brain? The Whiner says everyone would be better off if she were dead. *C'est vrai.*

I don't want anybody dead. Dead is lonely.

Alta and I should be closer because of dead. All I wanted to do was talk about it. But when I get around her, I get mosquitoes inside.

In her apartment before she narked on me, the mosquitoes were like old war movies, Pearl Harbor. When we watched old movies, Dad turned off the lights, and all four of us were on the couch in front of the black-and-white TV, and out of the dark, there was the buzzing sound, closer, closer, loud, all of us huddled down, and we cheered for the Americans and booed the Japanese.

You're Japanese or half Japanese or something, right? Or adopted by Japanese? You would've hated my dad for lots of reasons.

Why wouldn't Alta talk about it? Can you read her mind, Kyle? Can you let me know? I'm all twisted up about her, hating her, and other stuff.

It all makes sense when I think about that day way back. The town beach. I was maybe ten, little for ten, and Doug was maybe fourteen. Doug and I stayed after everyone else had gone home. We were out there by the cattails looking for bugs. He always loved the water ones, even more than me. Perfect time for crawdads and skimmers. A little dark, a little cool.

We had our backs to the beach, didn't see him coming, and anyway, he might have come the whole way underwater. But all of a sudden, a big iron arm goes around my middle, and I'm up in the air, pressed flat to his wet chest, and he slides his other hand under my robin's egg swimsuit, the one Mom bought me at Macy's, with fish on it. I screamed and kicked, and Doug's eyes were big, and I saw the lake and the night and heard crickets, and Doug was scared.

"Put her down, Dad," Doug said. He was such a boy.

"Why should I?" Dad said, and he rubbed his nubby chin into my neck.

Doug's hands went to fists, but Doug was a twig in front of us. Dad's hand was crawly and hard under my suit. The sun setting and his arms squeezing me, I could barely see Doug.

"Cut it out," Doug said.

"Make me," Dad said. And he lifted me higher.

Doug didn't move. His chest caught the light left on the lake. His chest was concave.

Dad was breathing slow and regular. He moved me a little up and down. He took deep breaths. My back got prickly rubbed against his chest.

"Tell you what," Dad said. "I'll make you a deal."

"Leave her alone," Doug said. His voice went up like it did when he was mad.

"You," Dad said quiet, "for her."

Dad's arm let go a little. I pushed down, tried to wiggle out. His arm tightened back, and his other hand let go of my suit and came around my neck. He squeezed.

"Shhh, stop," Dad said to me, like he was tucking me in. I stopped wiggling.

His hand was so big on my neck, his fingers all around. I couldn't breathe.

"Okay," Doug said. "Okay let her go." Doug came toward us.

Dad said, "Good. That's how it'll be from now on. You for her, and no one says a word," and he tossed me up in the air behind him. I flew, and *splash!* I dropped underwater. Water up my nose. Didn't know which way was up. I swallowed. My feet were rubbery. Then, I found the sand, and the splash stopped rocking me so much, and I stood up.

It was darker, and I couldn't see where Doug was.

Doug said, "Go," from somewhere in the reeds.

Running was hard with rubber legs and sand and beach, and Mom was in the car in the parking lot with the lights on. Mom was supposed to pick us up. Dad was supposed to be at the gallery.

I was wet and breathing hard, and Mom said, "Where's Doug?"

I pointed to the water.

"What's wrong?"

"Doug," I said, and that's all I said. It was cold. Mom looked at the lake, got out of the car, and took a few steps toward the beach.

She said, "Doug," like somebody might call a lost dog.

Right then Doug walked out of the dark, the horizon barely light behind him, a flat crack far away, and the crickets loud.

"Sorry, Mom," Doug said. He got in the front seat.

I got in the backseat. I was shaky and wet, and we never talked about it. And we didn't tell Mom. And after that I didn't go in the peach trees.

After that, Doug was quiet and lifting weights. He got big, weird big. He hung out at the gym with other boys with weird big muscles.

Do Little would scribble all over his yellow pad with his pencil and still try to make eye contact with me if I told this story. He'd draw lines to connect the dots: bad dad to abused brother to suicidal me.

But it's not that easy.

Never is.

So how would your chart go? Kid tormented to suicide? Too easy.

Maybe if I can go back to the courtroom, I can figure out what Doug's mouth said. I know he cut Dad's throat. He took the tree saw, the pointy teeth of it, and dragged it across Dad's throat. He did it that night after Dad gave me the car, after I told Dad to fuck off. At least, everybody said Doug did it. If I'm back in that courtroom with the shiny benches, everyone standing, and Mom reaching for him, if I see Doug's jumpsuit and his hair cut short, him turning to me, I think he says, "You." I think he killed Dad for me.

Tell me you didn't hang yourself for me. Tell me you didn't kill yourself because of me. Give me a sign.

# Song / **Resistance**

NEAR WHERE I GREW up, there are beaches like these, shallow waters and sheltered expanses. Destruction of rocks and continents, sediment washed out by streams, carried to shore by littoral drift, the long parallel current caused by waves crashing at angles, and then the packing of sand by oscillating waves moving perpendicular to shore. Rehoboth Beach, playground of the elite, and their teachers.

No lab books to grade, no students to tuck in. Young men of distant parents, we teachers *in loco parentis*. But not any more.

Little notes on index cards everywhere in the house: *Please take garbage with you*, and *Jiggle handle if toilet runs*. Loopy handwriting, most polite. A woman's writing.

A shoal, a sandbar. My mother for me. In Korea sons are shoals for their parents. My parents in San Diego now buffeted by the rough media.

I was no shoal for Kyle.

From this bench on the boardwalk, built so long ago, this beach the stomping ground of D.C. dignitaries, not merely the boarding-school set. Low tide, and the beach stretches almost to the horizon. The earth's curve. Should have brought Second Formers here to learn *shoal, tide, refraction,* and *drag*.

Once I met Carla here at a cottage. Similar loopy notes, *Please leave shoes outside,* with shaky pen drawing of Dutch clogs. As if some candy would magically fill them by morning.

Countries have strange customs.

*A woman and a dried fish have to be bitten every three days.*

Not some index card. Old Korean saying. Confucian yin-yang mumbo jumbo about forces opposed, the wearing down of resistance. In this case women are food, the stuff to be consumed, swallowed, beaten. Women are rocks; men are waves, pounding. Used to be that Korean girls were raised in the family of the boy with whom they were matched. Boys married at fifteen, girls at twelve.

Carla was seventeen when we met at this beach, eighteen when she sneaked into my apartment.

Confucius taught girls silence, compliance, obedience, and then Catholics taught them to serve. Double trouble. Somehow my mother lived differently, learned to think from Catholic schools, work equally with my father, equal status. Her mother, though, was beaten every day by my grandfather. She said he smiled when he beat her with a walking stick. He liked beating like he liked crispy fish. Good for circulation.

After Kim died, my blood pooled. Bad *chi*. I needed shelter. When Carla came to Tim-Tim's, her stiff walk, her curls, her questions and bugs, something felt the same. Carla so different from my sister, but the same. Not trying to love my sister that way, just something familiar, a trace. The habit of sheltering was the only way I knew to love. Shelter for shelter. Caring for others is a good way not to feel for yourself.

The very first day when Tim-Tim parents drive their station wagons around the circle in front of the main building, students pull out backpacks and boxes and pillows and milk crates, little packrats of their teenage years. Arms full, they walk into the stone building, and leave behind their age and grade. They become *Formers,* not *graders*. Carla became a Third Former.

Parents in their sports coats and skirts, matching colors, all things J.Crew, packed in with kids carrying pillows and stuffed animals and crates of homemade tapes, the Doobie Brothers, Metallica, and other hideous bands. No one had Grateful Dead.

I was inside the main entrance with a clipboard looking for the boys, the space too little for too many boys, Mr. Maze Director, sending them to their dorms, their new lives in rat living.

But there was this girl, black curls falling in her eyes, no parents around her. She carried a plastic milk crate in front of her. No stuffed animals. No pillow.

"Table for two?" Curly Girl said. She leaned toward my clipboard.

For a second I looked for *T* for *Table*. Mr. Gullible.

"Name?" I said.

"Hungry."

"Well, Miss Hungry," I said, "Try Miss Check-in, standing over there." Her arms were hyper-extended from the crate she carried. In it were rows of tapes, Grateful Dead, each tape numbered in thick black marker. All the tapes lined up the same way, numerically ordered. Fastidious. My nod to the other entrance in the dark hall sent Miss Hungry to check in. Carla walked like someone learning to walk, straight lines and pulleys and wheels. She didn't look back.

Who knew she would row with such power, run such distances, lie with me on a couch.

Last summer, between her Fifth and Sixth Form years, we came to Rehoboth for the weekend. Her father made a deal with a local artist for a show in his gallery in exchange for some weekends at the beach. It had been a long summer, very hot, and the beach is always cool. And months had gone by with letter after letter. Carla can write beautiful things, and my reasons for not going sounded weak. In the end, I was weak and said yes. She drove the red Mustang convertible her father gave her and stepped stiff-legged out of it, Miss Mannequin, with a book bag on her back.

"Traveling light?" I said.

"Clothing optional," she said.

Her height, my height, almost the same. Raised two cultures apart and similar builds. A decade apart.

Our shoulders touched when we walked to the front door. The pulse of a wave can last until the drag or resistance changes the energy.

Inside the cottage she threw her backpack on the couch and walked back toward me, arms open.

"Alone at last," she said in a mock movie-actress voice.

"Let's hit the beach."

Most of the day I dodged her. Walking on the beach, we bumped each other, barefoot in the light sand. This sand the grinding of shells and granite, washed and washed over the shoals. At one point she played bull, making me the matador.

Bending at the hip in a right angle, she put one finger on either side of her face, extending from her temples, and she pawed the sand before charging me. Ms. Bull charging. Waiting, waiting until she was inches away, I pretend-pulled the cape, stood up on my toes, turned sideways, and let the charging bull pass. Mr. Matador. Her heels dug into the sand. When she stopped so quickly, she fell on her butt. The pretend-cape danced. She looked up. It swung and swirled above her, her head tipped back, the curls off her forehead, those eyes of well water. I drew the cape behind me in a twirl about my waist, around and around, faster and faster until I keeled over beside her, and we laughed. Bulls don't fall butt-first, and matadors don't drop beside them. Teachers don't sleep with students.

Too much opportunity with no obstruction. Internal reality obstructing external possibility.

*A woman and a dried fish have to be bitten every three days.*

Toward evening Carla walked backwards in front of me. We were two blocks from the house, with groceries in our hands. Her curls bouncing around her head each step backwards.

"You're avoiding me," she said with a smile.

"Not really."

"Yes, really." She kept backing up, synchronized steps with my steps forward. "You're a wuss." I hate that word.

She spun her body to walk beside me, her low grocery bags following centripetal force and clipping me at the knees.

"Teachers don't do this."

"That old line. Pathetic."

We piled up trying to get in the door. Enough space but too much emotion. Before I could turn the key, she was pushing the door, grocery bags banging against the wood. In the kitchen, she slammed the cupboards closed, threw containers in the fridge. Ms. Impatient.

"Carla, come here," I said and took her hand. Her fingers felt like they had an extra joint they were so long. I tugged her to sit down next to me. The couch was too soft, so we fell back against the wall. We laughed, but she wouldn't look at me.

"I'm sorry," I said, and she curled into my chest, her forehead beneath my chin.

With my arms around her, I rocked her, her hair smelling of sun and ocean and, faintly, cotton candy.

"You're not some weird father-figure thing, you know, for me, anyway," she said into my chest.

"And you're no child," I said, but the way she curled into a part of herself made a part of me wash away. Her hair and her long fingers and her eyes, they were concrete and real. While entropy takes us to decay, her presence was vital, and in her presence, I forgot loss.

But shoals don't kiss, and beaches don't lie down.

But we did. It started with the way she folded into me, and her kisses on my neck, and my chin showing more of my neck and my arms loosening and her turning to face me, crawling into me, and my hands moving down her back, and then we were lying on the couch.

If Carla tells the psychiatrist in the psych ward about our weekend at the beach, no matter what we did and didn't do, what will the Old Boys do?

Option 1: I am prosecuted to the full extent of the law.

Option 2: They turn a blind eye since they realize that I did not have relations with a boy.

Option 3: Can't think of a third option.

The Old Boys would understand that saying: Women are to be eaten, discarded. Old Girls are bitten every day. But I couldn't do it.

In the middle of her on top of me and her shirt up enough that the skin of our bellies dragged, I stopped, sat up, turned my body sideways on the couch. I didn't mean to, but I knocked her off. Mr. Coordinated.

"What was that?" she said. Her face was big and smiling, and her curls were everywhere.

"I can't do it."

"You're kidding." Her eyes held no light, reflecting. "You're kidding, right?"

"I can't do this." It seems I can only go so far. Inside me there's resistance, matter that obstructs the energy moving in one direction.

"Then what're we doing here?"

"Good question."

That night we slept in separate beds in separate rooms. The heat outside was the glass of sand holding energy from the sun; the wind was the moisture from the waves. Inside it was soup. There was a note card near the electric clock by my bed: *Please disable the alarm.*

The thought occurred to me to leave my own note card: *Don't bring students to bed.*

Note to self: *Don't underestimate students.*

Muscle-Boy Zurkus is bright for a jock, Mr. English Assignment torturing Kyle on the lab table. Melting wax into the ear. Mr. Hamlet in his revenge play, informing the Carnivores of the media. Old story, though: school master preying on innocent boy. But Carnivores don't care what they eat so long as it draws other scavengers.

Old Boys won't like Tim-Tim's in the spotlight. Though

they've been the ones to tell me at the reunions and mucky-muck fundraisers: Bad publicity is good for admissions. Name recognition matters most. The Old Boys are like meat-eating media. They don't care what the cause, so long as Tim-Tim's is fresh on the mind. At least Sam Omura will speak for me. His outsider-ness like mine, but his mass carries more density, offers more pull than mine. Sam Omura is a prince among men.

So, what bargain will Oral-Fixation White strike with Union Textile, Donny Zurkus' dad?

Option 1: Donny will get a glowing letter of recommendation to the college of his choice if he retracts his statement.

Option 2: Donny's dad stands by his son and revels in my demise.

Option 3: Can't think of Option 3.

The morning after we slept in separate beds, Carla was Ms. Slammer. Every cupboard, every drawer, sent energy through the whole house. Couldn't have slept if I wanted to.

"Good morning, Ms. Sunshine." The distance between the breakfast table and me was tiny. The red chair slid out from the table barely enough for me to squeeze in the seat.

In sweats and a T-shirt, she was a girl, but when she turned toward me, her face was the picture of a screaming face painted on a wooden toy.

"Can I help you find something?" The silverware in the slammed drawer sounded like breaking glass.

"No." She slammed the next drawer.

Option 1: Put my arms around her, which was not the wisest move yesterday.

Option 2: Try to reason with her.

I finally thought of an Option 3: Walk out.

"Carla," I said, "can we talk?" Option 2.

"All you want to do is talk. We talk about your age, we talk about your responsibilities, and we talk about when I graduate. And after talk, talk, talk, we make out. What am I supposed to do?" Her hands were by her side, palms out.

"If you think of it as a wave, it travels up and down."

"Shut up," she said. "Don't go science on me." She crossed her muscle arms.

"What I'm saying is that there is nothing constant." Everything made me sound like a wuss.

"Tell me something I don't know," she said.

It didn't take her long to pack her backpack. In the doorway to the kitchen, she leaned like a pile of sticks and looked at me. Her eyes were miles away, the light taking light years to travel the distance between us.

# Carla / **Tape #2, Side A**

Hey, Kyle, it's Day Eight. Still here, the loony bin.

Remember Saturday nights? I bet you don't miss seeing *A Separate Peace* or *Psycho* for the millionth time. What's it like where you are?

Did you ever sneak out of the dorm at night? Piece of cake. After the dorm parents shut down, like 1 a.m., we put masking tape over the latch of the outside door. I'm sure you did, too.

One time last year Donny swiped two six-packs from home the weekend before, and he, Rambo, and I met at our spot in the woods past the cornfields. We ran for it. When we got there, Rambo set a big flashlight upright so the beam of light went straight up, made the trees naked. It was cold, maybe February, and our breath sometimes floated through the light beam.

After a couple of beers, we started to warm up, and Donny made us do Beerhunter.

"Scared?" he said.

Rambo grabbed one of the Coors and shook it. Then she started moving the beers around like they were peas under cups, and I couldn't tell where the shaken one went.

"Okay, Macho Man," Rambo said, "You start."

All three of us sitting on logs around a flashlight pointed straight up, we could have been Boy Scouts camping. Our foreheads were light, but our eyes and mouths were shadows. Donny held the Coors to his temple.

"WHAN that Aprille with his shoures soote," he said. He hated Chaucer. His eyes closed, he popped open the tab. The click and fizz were quick. Donny's eyes opened. He survived.

In this nut house, you see a different shrink every few days. The girl-shrink says that what I'm doing with my life is playing roulette. Whatever.

I told her about Jack and Alta. Not everything, but some.

I told her that you were the only person to get me, more than anybody, even Doug.

And I told her everything I touch dies.

What a loser.

She told me I had choices.

Does a stonefly choose to molt twenty-five times as a nymph? In three years, which is the same amount of time most kids are in boarding school, the nymphs stay submerged in water. That's what it feels like, boarding school. A kid is down there in the muck where shit happens and looks up at something he thinks is sky, a place he can breathe although he doesn't know what breathing is. And every time he tries to get up there, his skin falls off. Twenty-five fucking times. That's boarding school.

If I could choose, I'd be the female stonefly dancing on the river top. I'd flutter and splash to get my eggs out, and that would attract one single steelhead. That would be Alta.

If I could choose, I'd be her food.

So I choose not to tell Ms. Shrink about this thought, and she tells me how Ms. Alta had no choice but to inform the authorities about my suicidal tendencies. *Harm to self or others* is the line I crossed, and law bound her to report me. Fucking-A.

Ms. Shrinko is wrong. Alta feels it, too. It scares her shitless. That's why she turned me in. Right?

You can tell me.

# Taylor / **Finish Line**

ONLY 250 METERS TO go, but it feels like a thousand. Usually when the buoys change from white to red in the last 250, you know you'll survive. Christmas vacation starts in two weeks, but I swear the buoys are still white.

Carla came back yesterday. At least, that's what Rambo told me.

No school car has come to pick me up and whisk me away, so she must not have told anyone I kissed her. No quarantine like Song's. Maybe she didn't feel it. Maybe she thought my lips were little bugs on her neck. My teaching's done. *The Children's Hour* plays in my head, and Shirley MacLaine keeps crying. Back so soon can mean that I was wrong, can mean that Carla tricked them. While she was gone, no students visited me. No trust.

There are only two entrances to the dining room, one by the Wyeth with all those faces the same, and the other, the dark archway on the far side. Seconds before Dorothy White gives the blessing, Carla walks in the far entrance, leading Donny Zurkus by the hand. The way she leans forward, she is a tug boat, and Donny is the load she tugs.

Two weeks in a psych ward, and she comes back in order to tow Donny.

Two weeks away and she's showing off how normal she is.

Normal and straight in two weeks.

They find seats a couple of tables away, and Carla sits so she can't see me. She knows where I am.

WHEN I WAS IN college, after late rowing practice each afternoon, there were always two seats waiting for Sarah and me at any dinner table in the cafeteria. We were a package. Everyone knew.

A few times a year Sarah brought Mark to dinner, the formal dinners: Homecoming, Winter Carnival, Spring Formal. Mark driving from med school, his hair clipped just right, and Sarah with eyelashes doing their star thing, they came in the cafeteria holding hands, stopping at the door to scan the whole place, and they'd find a table with other couples. Not with me.

At formal dinners, I sat with the rugby girls, ex-rowers who wanted to party more than train. By dinner, I had four shots of tequila, and by dessert, I had seven. By the time dancing started, I was on the floor doing push-ups with a clap in the middle. Sarah and Mark didn't get to the dance floor until after I was taken to my room.

Carla with Donny is like a giraffe with a crocodile.

My eyes keep moving to her back, the black curls falling over her collar.

After mystery meat slopped by gravy, peas, and lumpy potatoes, after the Second Formers clear the dishes, I head back to my apartment. The outside door is heavy like a vault door, and the cold comes hard and chokes me. December is piles of leaves and clear nights and clouds of breath in the lights along the path.

Of course, they're there between the dining hall and my dorm. Of course, she's pressed him against a tree, and they're sucking each other's faces. She picked the path I'd walk after dinner. Carla is sending a message, of course. She's normal. I'm not. She's straight. I'm not.

I have no message to give her back.

The path with leaves and bare trees spins. The path back to the main building is a chute I fall through. Crisco told me it would be hard.

This is hard, like catching my breath right after the finish line. This is hard like being dumped. But how hard can it be to do the right thing, to turn away from something I shouldn't have done in the first place?

AFTER THE WHISKEY AND the reporter asking about Song and then Alex kicking up gravel with his car in front of the dorm, after Crisco helping me inside, I pinned her against the wall. Crisco's breath was strawberry and soft. My smell bouncing off her skin was the way the beach smells after the tide goes down.

Unlike walls in a dorm, walls in people are unstable. Booze or loneliness or loss can bore through them. Teachers are supposed to have walls. Solid ones.

Crisco did a head-fake-sideways move.

"Whoa, tiger," she said, "You've had a little too much."

"Too much what?" I said.

"Everything."

The door to the bedroom was on the same wall, and Crisco's big hands, with big rower calluses, took my shoulders and put me in my room, on the covers of my bed.

My hands on her forearms, my eyes in her cornflower eyes, my hands and eyes a question. Crisco said, "Not this way."

Beets. The color inside me was beets, the bile rising in my throat, the rosary and Father M in the background.

"What an idiot," I said.

"Idiot, you're not," she said. "Cheap date, maybe." Her sunflower face was full and moved away from my face.

That night I had thought of trying to make Alex want me, thought that whiskey-burn in the throat could make my thighs feel slick and warm, thought Alex wanting me might make St.

Timothy's feel like a home I had never known. Alex might fill the crack in the middle of my chest.

And whiskey and driving and raging against the reporter worked. Alex wanted me, but I was still that girl caught between her mother's voice and her body, my mother saying, "You just haven't met the right man," and "You're just different," and my body saying, "Wrong." My blood through its veins dragged, the drag filling my body with weird energy. Attraction was great to take me away from school. Alex was good for that. But when it came right down to it, my body kicked in, the body with all its weird messages.

My head, with Jack Daniel's, still knew that the way through schools with stone blocks this way and stone blocks that way was to find the right man, the right look, like Alex with his sinew-rope arms, his fresh-cut hair. But my body, weird with booze and flight, wasn't held to dress codes and St. Timothy's. My body, wanting its own thing, said, "Crisco."

And my body wanting girls was prickly, the blood too thick for the veins. My mother's voice, "You're immoral," and the way my insides turned beets.

"Carla" was not what my body said. Carla was beets and my mother's voice and the silence when Sarah left my dorm room after I came out to her.

If I could kiss a student, I could show everyone how bad I was. But they already knew.

# Carla / **Tape #2, Side B**

KISSING DONNY ZURKUS MAKES me go Gila monster. I want to lie in the sun and flick my tongue, and I want to swallow small animals whole. It's both at the same time. He's a jerk, but when we're walking around, I feel monster big.

You don't mind my hanging out with the guy who was the meanest to you. Sure, he's a bully, but his mean is, like, kryptonite. People with power lose it around him. The loony bin was bad, but now I'm back, and all I can do is make these tapes, number them with Magic Marker. Mr. Hofmeister let me have the tape recorder from the library. No check out. Perks of being loony. And if my roommate walked in and heard me talking to you, she'd turn me in just like Alta. So, I wait till I know she's in class. I don't know if you're listening. Give me a sign.

So, one time Alta saw me with Donny. It's not that I saw her see us. I smelled her. Kind of. We were on the path back from the dining hall to her place, the only path, and me pressing Donny into the trunk of the tree, we took up the whole path. Somebody came toward us. Somebody turned and walked away. Flick. Flick. Gulp.

The weird thing about being back is no Jack. Gone the same two weeks I've been gone. If it were last year, we could have used two weeks together. Maybe we could have stayed two weeks in Rehoboth. Maybe we could have walked on the beach and cooked meals and taken showers together. Maybe we could have made up stories to tell people why both of us were away, but those stories, the ones we made up, they couldn't possibly have been better than the ones that are happening this year.

Nobody told me Jack was removed. A loony bin is a separate planet. No space stations. No communication with earth. How could anyone think Jack touched Kyle? No way. Sure, I hurled the idea at Jack. Why not? I was like a grasshopper under stress. That's what they do: vomit to discourage predators. My vomit was an accusation. It was a defense, not a truth. I vomited at Jack.

Jack is tiger swallowtail, yellow and black. He flew away from me, but he did the right kind of flying away. The teacher-thing, adult. He wasn't creepy weird like my dad. He didn't do me because he couldn't go against his grain. That Asian honor thing. He was there for you, there in a way that no one else was: adult. Jack Song did nothing to you.

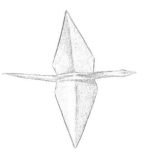

# Song / **Angle of Re-entry**

MR. ORAL FIXATION SAYS before he hangs up, "Stand firm, man. Buck up. We're working this from every angle, and we'll take care of it. Our people are talking to the Zurkus people. Trust me." There's no platitude like those of the uncomfortable to the inconsolable.

The white phone with the note taped to it doesn't ring very often, and when it does, the news isn't great. After two weeks of living in this beach cabin, I'm ready to blast out of here. No teacher can relax. Always more papers to grade, more lessons to prep, changes to our field of study. Here I am without a library, without my lab books, with nothing but notes taped to every cabinet and drawer. One black-and-white TV with rabbit ears and one station. This cabin owner? The queen of skinflints.

Angle of re-entry is what Kyle never got right. He was a rocket ship, trying to come back to earth, to the mother ship. His mass traveling from space back to earth had to accelerate to a certain speed and hit our atmosphere at a certain angle, descending between 30 and 35 degrees. Less than 28 degrees and the traveler bounces back out into space. More than 38 degrees and the traveler burns up.

Kyle hit it just wrong. Young Sir Nihilist, he couldn't make us understand the perils of nuclear bombs, couldn't protect himself from predators, couldn't face being in one place in one time. More than 38 degrees. His place and time were other, were motion, and entering the realities of this world, which is what the young men and women of this nubile age do in boarding school, put too much drag on his system. Reality burnt him up.

That's not to say our guilt has been expunged.

Two weeks in this beach cottage, and I've folded every beetle, bug, and bird I know. Give me a sheet of paper and a half an hour, and I can fold just about anything. The skinflint cottage owner keeps wrapping paper in a trunk in the attic. Pretty and thin and musty. Each crease will make spider webs of creases. Each fold must be considered. No margin for error.

So far I've filled half the trunk.

Every morning before sunrise I walk the flat shoal of Rehoboth Beach, the tide changing each day, the low tide so low it expands the land mass of this isthmus by half. On one side the Atlantic, on the other the bay. There's always someone out there, someone with a dog, the dog alert to gulls and its master. Carla and I never walked the beach in the morning.

By lunch time I'm inside folding or reading or writing something down, something for a class if I ever get to teach again. Mr. Finished at finishing school.

By afternoon I'm walking the shops, finding the Satsumas or the fresh scallops or stargazer lilies. No one knows my name despite the earnest greetings by the shop owners.

Back at the cottage, I nap, wash the fish, cut up vegetables, arrange the flowers. A single man cannot afford to skirt domestic chores. After a nap, something I've learned to do in the last two weeks, I turn on the news from the black-and-white set. That voice on the news is the first I've really heard all day, the first I want to hear.

Tonight I hear my name on the news.

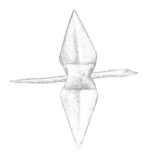

# Taylor / **River, Tide, Ocean**

A DAY IN THE life of a boarding school teacher is race to breakfast, one set of clothes, race to class, another set of clothes, race to practice, another, shower, race to dinner, another set, back to the dorm, relax, grade, check the dorm, relax, grade, bed, another set of clothes. My bedroom is piles everywhere. My living-room-part-kitchen is books and papers and folders and dishes. My TV is rarely on, except to catch the news with Dan Rather. Tonight I'm not assigned dorm duty, and masses of sophomoric examinations of revenge versus justice weigh down my knees. Pen in one hand, a cold beer in the other, and the local news get me focused.

Channel 6 Action News anchormen come on too loud with their exaggerated voices, statements sliding up to questions. The field reporter is interviewing someone familiar, a couple, one man gnarled and old, the woman with scars on her face. She looks through a drooping eye at her husband, both surrounded by reporters.

She says, "We are confident that he was in no way responsible."

Channel 6 Action News reporter says, "Mrs. Harney, how do you know?"

"My son would have told me."

"Did he say he was harmed in any way?"

"Yes, he did." She turns to look at Mr. Harney. He straightens to meet her look. At the same time without saying anything, they break their gaze at each other and look down. The reporters push their microphones toward her.

"Kyle told us about other boys pinning him down, punching him, playing tricks." The reporters interrupt, jabbing their questions. Mr. Harney turns to shield his wife from the reporters.

She says, "Boys are not kind. He wrote us about that. He wrote us about Mr. Song teaching him good things. The day he died he wrote us." Her voice a whisper and the reporters a mob.

"What did he say?"

"Did he say who did it?"

"The school did nothing?"

"He said he was better off, that Mr. Song tried. We know that Mr. Song had nothing to do with our son's death. There will be no investigation. And that's all I will say." She backed away, held up her hand as if her hand could ward off judgment, could mete out justice. Mr. Harney stepped toward her, took her hand, put his arm around her. They turned away from the reporters.

Pushing off from my chair with the papers pressed to my thighs, the beer still in hand, like a hunchback, I cross the living room and reach for the knob to click off the TV. Still hunched, I backed to the chair with my papers pressed to my thighs. My living room was books and folders and the refrigerator kicking on. My left hand was wet with the warming beer. In three gulps it was gone.

I was rock on the lakeshore. I was rock under ripple. I was ripple.

All these papers about Hamlet and Claudius and Sir Francis Bacon, and I saw how much Donny Zurkus learned about power. His father, Union Textile, and his words about

Song brought the country to St. Timothy's. Donny, his lanky
limbs, locked in desks built for Second Formers, walked into
that dining room last night with Carla like he was Claudius,
the sweet taste of revenge on his lips, his own form of justice,
at once private and public, to repay the injustice he believed
Song caused him for his suspension and sure rejection from
the most elite colleges.

Now, justice played in someone whose wounds were not
green. Kyle's mom did not seek revenge. She sought to clear
Song's name and Kyle's name. She didn't even want to blame
the boys who picked on Kyle.

Mrs. Harney is river. Mrs. Harney is tide. The ocean is as big
as her grace.

AFTER CHANNEL 6 ACTION News at 5 p.m. and the same
news at 11 p.m., I was reading Sir Francis Bacon and Freud
and Shakespeare quoted and regurgitated in some Fourth
Form jumble like the BeeGees playing Mozart. The spring in
the screen door stretched before there was a loud knock on my
door. Papers fell from my lap and fanned out. After 11 p.m.
meant lights out and locked dorms, and Carla couldn't possibly
be standing there.

And Carla wasn't there. The white print on the black label
spelled "Jack Daniel's" through the windowpane of my door.
Alex Jeffers was pointing his big, rower finger at the bottle and
grinning into the door. The whiskey splashed in the bottle that
Alex held. He had started a while ago.

"Jack for Jack," he said. He walked in when I opened the
door.

"Come right in." He brushed by me.

"Can you believe it? You saw the news, right?" My sweats
and socks and unwashed hair, my eyes blurry from reading papers, I blinked at his ebullience.

"Sure."

"We should celebrate." He looked at the kitchen side of my
living room. "Glasses?" he said.

The way he talked, the words had more Ss than they needed. "At it awhile?"

"A bit." He spun toward me. "Caught the early news." Over
six feet tall, the muscle-bound man shrugged, looked six years
old. Spinning toward me was a movement too quick, and he
kept spinning, leaning on one leg.

"Easy, big guy." I stepped toward him. And the momentum
he had when he spun kept him moving, and his arm wrapped
around me. He folded me into his chest. My face slammed into
his pecs, and I breathed in the smell of cake frosting from the
whiskey seeping out his pores.

"Mmm," he said. My head turned to the side so I could
breathe. My arms dropped. I had papers to grade, and the questions he might ask about how I kept my hand on his leg during
the drive to and from town, why I scrambled out of his car, and
who the woman was on my doorstep the other evening were
pieces of debris floating in the wreck of the last few weeks.

"Alex," I said, "you have to go." When I leaned back, he
didn't let go.

"But this feels so good." His chin sank farther down my
neck.

"It's late." His hug felt good the way sun feels good in winter. He was the big man who tried to save a Second Form boy
and the boy died. He was that kind of guy, the one who rushes
toward a fire when other people run away. There were lots of
reasons to want his arms around me.

"Don't you like this?" His arms moved in circular motions
on my back, the bottle somehow landing upright on a table.
Last week this hug might have been a door, a place to enter the
St. Timothy's world and prove I belonged. Last week I wanted
his hand on me.

"Yes, but," I said.

"But what?" His head left my neck, and his hands took my
shoulders, and his eyes in my eyes were too close. "What?"

"Nothing." Going farther with Alex might have made the
dress code, the drinking, the implicit agreements of boarding

school make sense, but in this past week, every code broke.

"You don't like me?"

"It's not that." My head bowed to keep my eyes from him, and his hands squeezed harder to keep me from backing away. "You're, this, great," I said. The six-year-old in him, blond and pink cheeks and dizzy.

"You're special, too," he said with way too many Ss.

"Thanks."

We stood there in my living room, and he folded me inside his arms. And when he swayed, I held him in case he leaned too far, and the two of us were warm in my living room with papers and books, an old TV, and my empty beer bottle. Outside it was December cold, the branches of the maples clicking. For a moment the last twelve weeks stopped splitting apart the crack in my chest. For a moment the cold stayed on the outside and didn't make a draft inside me. I wanted to stay in this moment of someone taller and stronger and acceptable wrapping around me.

His hand was big on my back, his enormous hand, moving slowly, pressing my sweatshirt, my sweatshirt turning circles. When his hand moved under my sweatshirt, under my shirt, I reached around and pressed his palm flat to my back. "Not a good idea," I said.

"What?"

"This," I said. I pressed his hand for emphasis.

"What?" He pulled his hand away from my hand. "What?" he said and reached farther up my shirt. The smile on his face was in his words, his head higher than my head. Alex, as strong as he is, could take what he wanted if he wanted, could turn my apartment into a desert with the two of us the only people for miles. Lucky for me, Alex was more boy and more drunk.

Stepping away from him, I pulled his hand from behind my back and brought it between us. With my hand I held up his hand, as if it were a rabbit from a hat, and with my other hand, I pointed to it. "This," I said.

"Oh, that little thing," he said. "If I've told it once, I've told it twice."

"You've told it a thousand times," I said, and the old line became trick and charm and truce.

"Hands have a mind of their own," he said. "The little buggers."

With my hand on his wrist, Alex started to fall. I grabbed his hand with both of mine, and leaned away to slow his descent to the couch. "Sorry," he said, "guess I needed to sit down."

"Guess so," I said and knelt down on the carpet in front of the big man leaning back in the too-soft couch, the couch where Terence had slept the night when Kyle died, the couch where Carla insisted she killed Kyle. "You okay?

"Fine, thank you, and you?" Alex said in a perky St. Tim's voice. His head rested on the wall behind the couch, and his eyes were closed. He rolled his head back and forth.

"Can I tell you something?" I said. On my knees I wanted to apologize for the signals I sent.

"Anything," he said, "as long as you don't expect me to remember it." His big hand covered his mouth as he yawned.

"About the other night."

"After the diner when you ditched me?"

"I wanted to," I said.

"You wanted to ditch me? That's not what your hand was saying." A big smile followed the *S*s in what he said. "Little buggers."

"About that." I tried to say more, but he kept going.

"All I can say is you sure know how to confuse a guy." He swept his hand over his forehead and combed his fingers through his hair.

"I'm really sorry, Alex," I said.

"Forget about it." His big hand waved the air, pushed the thought aside.

"No, I can't."

"You can't what?"

"I can't, I can't . . ." I said. Now I was the one shaking my head back and forth. The reasons for wanting him and not wanting him, the reasons I couldn't tell him about Crisco and who I was, the fears and apologies and admissions all stalled inside me.

"Be with me," he said. He brought his head forward, off the wall, but his eyes were half closed.

"Yes."

"You can't be with me because there's somebody else?"

An easy way out was something I hadn't imagined. Here was an apology without vulnerability. Here was open water, no boats challenging, fans cheering.

"Yes," I said.

"That somebody the other night?"

"Yes."

"Lucky girl."

Did he mean me? Did he see Crisco in the half-light of the parking lot, Crisco with her big muscles and boy-shape? The taste of beets, the way students would look at me, the way I'd be fired filled my throat. My hand reached for his knee.

"I am," I said.

"You are," he said. And his head swung back against the wall.

For a while there was nothing in the living room but the sound of the refrigerator turning on, the maples clicking outside in the cold. The wind had picked up, and it swept the cold from the lake against the stone buildings.

Without telling Alex how much I wanted to want him, how my hand on his leg in the car had been a way to keep hold of the living, how those smiles at school dinners and passing in the halls were like buoys along a racecourse. They kept me on a course, a course for which everything in my life had trained me. Tonight I wanted to apologize for the flirting, the start flag of a race, for the stops I made.

In this moment, Alex falling asleep on my couch, the wind and cold in a Delaware December, the buoys fell away. I had no cox'n to steer me, no boats in lanes on either side. The course was no longer what I tried to want. It was gone.

# Song / **Equal and Opposite**

*HYO* IS ALL THERE is between parents and sons. *Hyo* can keep a boy in a country where his parents are, can make a boy leave a country to find honor for his parents. There is no word for parents honoring sons.

Mrs. Harney, Mrs. Courage and Honor, did what Kim didn't get to do: Speak up. Asian women are bound by silence. Maybe Japanese women are different from Korean women, not as much shame beaten into them. Mrs. Harney spoke out loud to reporters. Her words weighed more than Mr. Harney's, for she was the face that would sway the public. And she is Mother, the primal force. The district attorney, moved by her mass and action, dropped the case.

For Kyle, Mrs. Harney was iron, at one time malleable and soft, at another time magnetic, rigid, untarnished. She is the clash of culture. On her body is written the old Japan and the new Japan. The old Japan was collaborative, relational: no value without the family, no bonds without honor. The new Japan is competitive, self-actualized, driven by shame. As a child in Nagasaki, Mrs. Harney was caught by the world trying literally to forge itself new. The Western world tried to blast its way into peace, and the Eastern world tried to save its face. Mrs. Harney, with her yin/yang scars, the keloid markings of radiation, saves my face and her son's face by speaking up, defying the role for Asian women, escaping the lascivious clutches of the media by speaking not what they wanted, but the truth: Her son died because we did not protect him. Kyle did not die because I touched him. I didn't touch him.

What is the equal and opposite reaction of violence done to Kyle? Violence done to himself.

Mrs. Harney has iron in her spine to speak up. She made moot the old boy network. My honor saved by acts of two Japanese friends. Their actions contrast the sphere of influence my father and grandfather suffered. My two Japanese defenders resist the forces acting beyond my control; they are heroic, Newtonian, awesome.

To return to St. Timothy's after two weeks, to drive through the reporters at the school's entrance, there will be nothing but drag force on me. My velocity will meet the resistance of time and speculation and judgment in this formula:

$$F_d = -\frac{1}{2}\rho v^2 \, A C_d \hat{v}$$

Of course, I won't be moving that quickly, but if I wanted to calculate the drag coefficient, I'd start here.

I'd end, knowing it's huge.

# Carla / **Tape #2, Side B, Continued**

THIS MIGHT BE KIND of disjointed, Kyle, but I'm pissed. Totally. Like Shrinko said, I have to make choices. I choose to talk to you.

So, there we were, out in the spot in the woods past the cornfields, the place where Donny and Rambo and I go sometimes.

"Shut the fuck up, Donny," I said to him.

Total loser.

"Fuck you, Carla," Mr. Mature says back to me.

"I'm not the one who went to the press. What were you thinking?"

"Hey, not my fault." Donny's voice goes girly.

"Oh, well," I say, "some other guy called the reporters? Some other guy blamed Song?"

"You don't know. You weren't there." Now he's up from the fallen log, the sacred circle of logs around the upright flashlight, the beam going straight up into the canopy of trees. He's tall enough to be one of those trees. What a waste of a good body.

"And where was that?"

"In the fucking dorm."

"No shit."

The stairwell smells of soggy paper bags, the door to the hall opens thick like a vault door, and Jack's door to the right is black and shiny. No way do I know the dorm. Right. But I haven't told you that part, yet. That's history.

"I saw them." Donny puts his fingers into his black hair, pulled it straight back from his forehead, held on to it like he could pull it off.

"Saw them how?"

It was cold out there. Midnight sucks in the woods on the far side of the cornfields. December totally sucks.

Donny turned his whole body toward me, his elbow still out, his hand still pulling his hair.

"One time Kyle was in the hall, all curled up on the floor and shit, and Song was touching his foot, just sitting there with his hand on the little guy's foot. It was weird." Do you remember that? Did you think it was weird?

"Oh, total abuse. I see what you mean."

"Fuck you."

"You're kidding, right? You did this whole thing because Song touched Kyle's foot?"

"Wait. One time right before curfew I see Kyle slip out of Song's apartment, make sure the door didn't slam, look all around."

"You've got to be kidding me. This proves what?"

"Wait! You were the one who told me Song cared too much. You told me he went too far."

"Oh, great. You went off that? I didn't mean Kyle, you moron."

"What do you mean you didn't mean Kyle?" Donny looked right at me, and I didn't make a move. "Quit screwing around. Song is a perv, and everyone knows it."

"Like who?"

"The guys."

"Why?"

"Think about it. No girls. He's how old, not married, no dates. He's a perv or fag. Same thing."

The beam of light made Donny's forehead white since he was leaning toward me, his arms out in big gestures, as if his long arms could make me believe him. Loser.

"He's not like that."

"Right."

"No, really, he's not like that." At this point, I'm grasshopper, wings tucked.

"How do you know?" Donny stepped toward me. He was so close I couldn't see his face any more.

I could have saved Jack. I could've told him.

"You asshole. You just want to get back at him," I said.

Startling is a great defense. In Mexico a tiny black-and-white grasshopper has crimson wings. Predators run scared when it startles.

"Do not." Mr. Mature came back.

"Ever since he caught you, you've tried to get back at him."

"He got me suspended." Suspension can mess with all kinds of things, like college, like career, like Daddy.

"Yeah, like you had nothing to do with it."

"I'm out of here." Donny leaned over and grabbed the flashlight. The beam went sideways, and off he went down the path, the beam of light all crazy in the trees.

There's nothing like midnight in the woods with no moon and no stars. Awesome. The leaves were down, and I waited so long I could see the gaps in the trees. I waited long enough I could hear nothing, what nothing is.

Out there so long, I wondered if I waited out there long enough, would someone find me? Jack is gone. You're gone. Taylor is all I have, and she doesn't get me. I had Jack. Jack had me. He wasn't after boys. He's not like that. And he's not the other kind, either. Since I was eighteen when he did the thing on the couch, and since, anyway, he stopped. He's no perv.

It was fucking cold out there. The trees out there, round

pieces of dark, different than midnight dark, are all secrets. It was just me and those trees. Are you in those trees, Kyle?

# Song / **Consequences**

Not Kyle spinning on the lab stool, once, twice, three times. Before I open the door to the Marsh Road Diner in Wilmington, the breakfast counter is framed in the diner door. A compact man with no gray hair faces the controlled chaos in front of the grill, the waitresses reaching and cooks flipping eggs and orders hanging from clips. No one else sits at the counter, and Sam's not charming Nancy at the moment.

"Sheila forbid you drinking coffee?" I take the stool next to him at the counter. Start with family. Work toward harder topics like Tim-Tim's, like Mr. Bad-Boy's dad.

"Can't get service," Sam says. His shoulders go up when he turns toward me, and that's when I notice the backsides of the waitresses lined up. All the aprons are tied with perfect bows. I never could tie an apron on Kim with a bow like that. Nancy is two meters away, and ten galaxies.

"Not even water?"

"Nada," Sam says. He faces the line of bows.

"Hey, Nancy," I say to the bow, second from the right, "How about coffee for your favorite professors?" When she turns part way around, her right hand holds a Mr. Coffee Thermos, but the steps she takes move on a vector away from us, around the end of the counter, to the booths. No smile, no wisecrack, no how.

"It seems that bad press overshadows good," Sam says. He spins toward me on the stool.

The Taiko drum hits me inside. "Suuu," the drummer yells. My parents walk every day to the grocery store, my mother chatting to the clerk as she rings up fish and vegetables. Will the clerk in San Diego know the news? Will the clerk close her line before my mother unpacks her cart?

"How could they," I say more to the counter than to Sam, "think such a thing? Nancy knows me."

"What do they know, Song? You're a customer, that's all." Sam lines up objects near him on the counter. The napkin dispenser. "And you're not from here." Salt. "And you're a Jap." Pepper.

"Right. I forgot." Teacher of teachers, Sam grew up in Delaware, grew up next to Tim-Tim's. He knows how people think. In Delaware, all almond eyes are Oriental eyes. And he doesn't say the other thing, the thing the waitresses think but don't say to us. The women turned away from us do a syllogism inside: Song touched boy. Boy killed himself. Song killed boy. If one piece is fallible, the whole is fallible. The only true part of their syllogism is the middle one: boy killed self.

"Let's get out of here," Sam says.

Without our usual goodbye to Nancy, we leave Marsh Road Diner. There's a McDonald's down the street, and the bright orange and plastic inside are perfect for a couple of guys who don't want to spend time in the place. We take a booth.

Nancy and those waitresses contain the wave in them. The wave does not pass through. They are the middle of the rope suspended between two bodies. The wave continues to undulate, and they do not break its pattern.

"Sam," I say, "I'm sorry you got dragged into all this."

"Me, too," he says, "I like that place. Good sausage." His

dark eyebrows rise when he looks across the orange table at me.

"Maybe Sheila will thank me."

"Maybe."

"How was talking to Charles Zurkus III?"

"A lot like eating broccoli," Sam says. He takes the salt shaker and shuffles it between his small hands. Back and forth, the glass bottom on plastic table, lots of drag.

"Did you know him at Stanford?"

"Not much, but enough. And you know how that goes, alumni stick together. Besides, his company does some work on the side for our company." CIA Sam doing covert work with Zurkus III. Textiles and engineering somehow saving the U.S. from the Soviets, and both forces colluding to protect one man's son and one man's friend. Sam's force exerting more influence than Charles' force. No science can explain relationships.

"What did you say?"

"The truth, that his son has an active imagination." The salt shaker was more hockey puck, back and forth.

"And Daddy agreed?" Hard to imagine a parent backing down so quickly. Puffy Zurkus III, all bluster, no bite.

Sam looked through his bushy eyebrows at me, "That and a little reminder that I'm in charge of the contracts his company has with us."

"You didn't threaten him."

"No need." Sam shakes his head.

"I can't thank you enough."

"Again, no need," Mr. Magnanimous says. The salt shaker stops in his right hand. My eyes move to his left hand out of habit. "The boy, the one who died, he's the one you told me about, correct?"

"Yes. And you know," I say.

"I know you did nothing," Sam says. "His mother? I saw her on the news."

"Yes, Nagasaki."

"Terrible."

"The boy was adopted, but he had *hyo*. One boy army trying to save his mother from another atom bomb. Trying to save all of us."

The salt shaker still fitting the palm of his hand, Sam says, "That's a lot for a little kid."

"Too much."

The Big Macs come in their orange baskets, and Sam is licking his fingers and attacking his fries before I have picked out the pickle and tossed it away. After finishing his fries, he looks at mine until I push my basket toward him.

"Help yourself," I say, and he does. He finishes my fries, and I finish my Big Mac, and he asks questions about Tim-Tim's and what the Whites did for Kyle and what they didn't, if they knew about the bullying when it was happening and if they took steps to stop it. He shakes his head about the Second Formers still at the school, about the press conferences, about the rat maze cubbies that house those boys. Neither of us has answers, but we both know that kids away from home are earth on us, earth on the school.

"Next time let's get a real meal," Sam says, and we pick a day to meet next month. We'll find a new place to eat, some place with omelets that hang off the plates and plenty of sausage.

# Taylor / **Kinds of Cold**

TEACHERS ARE NOT SUPPOSED to be outside the students' dorms. Teachers are not supposed to be drinking on school nights, either. Maybe I'm not supposed to be a teacher.

It's easier to be outside than in. My living room still has papers and books all over, and I can't be there. The cold out here, almost Christmas cold, is a make-you-walk-straight kind of cold. There's nothing like rowing-on-frozen-lake cold.

One time in college, cold came early in autumn. The varsity crew was out on the lake where we practiced, but this afternoon our coach cut the ice with the motor from his launch. Every stroke was supposed to be a glide up the tracks, but splashing from the oars had filled the tracks with freezing. We had to pull ourselves over the bumps of ice. And then, when we exploded on the catch, we broke the ice. Every time. And our hands? No gloves. With gloves we can't really hold on to the oars. Without gloves our hands froze, and we couldn't hold on to the oars. Oars were flopping around and splashing. Each splash was a slap to the face. Water froze on windshirts in front, sweat condensing on the backs.

You were trying to keep us going. I broke the rowing protocol of no talking in the boat, not ever, and started singing "My Favorite Things" really loud.

Everyone joined in.

In our wood-composite shell in the middle of the lake at the beginning of winter, eight rowers and a cox'n were singing at the top of our lungs from *The Sound of Music* while ice formed in the tracks.

Sarah's head turned to the left, and I could see the corner of her smile.

But she's not here, and I'm not looking for her.

It's December 1983, and I don't know what I'm looking for.

From the outside, a dorm looks like a cruise ship, something huge and looming, most windows lit up and music leaking out closed ones. There's a world in there, people acting in their stories, allegiances and vengeance and plots within plots, whole countries won and lost, and I'm outside looking in. But it's so late right now there aren't many lights on.

Carla's room is upstairs, the corner room with the lights out.

Maybe Jack is right. I haven't been here, not really. Crisco said that I couldn't reach the students from so far away. Since Sarah died, I haven't been anywhere. Maybe I was too far away to see Carla just trying on the idea of suicide rather than ready to do something.

Maybe I can be here for her now.

"What're you doing out of your dorm?" A voice trying to be low came loud behind me.

"Sorry." I jumped.

Carla raised both her hands to her mouth to quiet her laugh. She doubled over, collapsing in half.

"Damn it, Carla," I said, "You scared me." And I couldn't help but smile. Everything was funny.

After she straightened up, she slapped her mittens on her thighs and doubled over again.

"And just what're you doing out of the dorm?" I said.

"I asked you first."

"I'm faculty."

"And your point?" Carla was so quick. With beer and cold, I wasn't keeping up.

"You're supposed to be inside. What're you doing?"

"Freezing my ass off, just like you." Carla was curl.

"No kidding." That's what I'd say to a friend, not a student.

Carla walked up to me and raised both her hands to my shoulders. She turned me toward the light from one of the windows on the first floor where two girls were still up, each at her desk. I couldn't see Carla so well, but she moved her face toward mine. Her face gave off heat, and she smelled like leaves and December. Her close was good close.

"Hm, has Ms. Alta been drinking, perhaps?" Carla held me with both arms, blocked my vision with her face.

"Hey," I said. I twisted out of her hands.

"Oh, she has." Carla's smile was big, her hair kept back by her stocking cap. This Carla was the one before Kyle died, the one who was sassy the way Red Hots are, something more kick than anything.

This cold, this heat from a face so close was the cold the first time I kissed a girl. The summer before that movie with Sarah in college, I was eighteen and a Girl Scout counselor in a rundown Girl Scout camp in a rundown area of Nevada. Never before had I been a Girl Scout, in Nevada, at camp, or gay. It just happened. An older counselor looked out for me, showing me how to tie ties and put on pins and set up tents, and on the two days off we had each camp session, she took me to softball games, bars, and eventually, hotels.

One night in the first week of camp, we snuck out of our cabins and met on the banks of the creek that ran through camp. We weren't supposed to be out in the mountains because there were cougars and bears and things a girl from New England knew nothing about. It was cold, the air was juniper, and she put her arm around me. It was easy to turn into her, easy to meet her lips, hard to know how the ground still held when I walked the next day. She was my first girl kiss.

The next day thinking of her lips made me dizzy. Thinking of someone finding out made me sick to my stomach. When I got back to college that fall, I didn't tell anyone, especially not Sarah.

Turning away from Carla, I stepped under a tree. Less light. Carla followed, and we were both in the shadow of the tree, the building. The sky carried no moon.

"Were you out with Donny tonight?" I said.

"No way."

"Who were you meeting then?"

"Whom."

"Carla," I said. I was rock on iced lake, boot through thin ice, boulder in pond.

"So what if I met him?"

"You could get in a ton of trouble."

"Like sent away?" Those words were the ones I dreaded.

"Do you like him?" These were the ones I tried not to say.

"Sure," she said, "he's cute." I had to hear those words.

"Cute? Donny Zurkus?" I turned away. "Oh, sorry."

"Do I detect judgment, just a smidge?" she said. Her mitten raised toward my face. Her fingers inside were probably pinched forefinger to thumb.

I pushed her mitten away, but then I stepped into her, put my arms around her, pressed her down coat into my coat.

"Taylor," she said. My name was a sigh.

Her dark coat and my dark coat and a night with no moon. I held her outside of her dorm, under a tree with no leaves, outside a window with no light. I held her, and we breathed in and out the same. I was there. Something must have happened to the anger, the flipping-off Carla that the nurse picked up that day when I turned her in. Some switch must have flipped in the hospital. What switch can happen to make someone live?

Before I pulled away, I squeezed her, down coat and all, as hard as I could.

"I have to go," I said.

As I stepped away, she said, "Are you jealous?" Her arms were at her side.

"Of what?" I said. My steps backwards, away from her, were steps taken inside and out. "Good night."

# Song / **Boundaries and Bending**

"SETTLE DOWN, SETTLE DOWN, Misfits of Physics," I say to the Second Formers. Can't believe I missed the miscreants.

Before I continue, Peter Frankel jabs his hand in the air, "Mr. Song, Mr. Song."

"Yes, Mr. Wrinkled Shirt."

He looks down at his shirt and tries to smooth one side with the palm of his hand.

"Is it true that you're related to Mrs. Harney?" Unabashed. Little air through little opening gives high pitch, but no hindrance.

"Let's get right to the point, shall we?" The five boys left in the Second Form after Kyle, after Tommy Underwood left the school, and Maggie Anderson still here, lean toward me from the lab stools. "I am in no way related to Mrs. Harney. She is Japanese, and I am Korean. Now, to the lesson at hand."

At the beach I had plenty of time to think about lessons, arrange them, walk through them, list the ingredients needed.

Before pairs of students, a rope is coiled, a thicker half meshed with a thinner half. All ropes and materials are on the black lab table the students surround, the table donated by the Du Ponts, the table where Kyle was pinned. Good thing the Second Formers didn't see Kyle as a specimen, a frog.

"Before you, you will find a rope. Notice one half is thick, one half is thin. In pairs, stand up. One person hold one end and the other hold the other end. Very good. Now. Reach back into your vast memory to our discussion of waves, and tell me what will happen if the person on the thin end starts a wave motion."

Like kindergartners standing at recess, they hold the ropes between them around the table, each student a study in disarray. Of course, one student starts a different kind of wave, both arms extended above his head, his whole body bends forward as if paying homage to a god, and the next student picks it up, and pretty soon the wave of football games and mob scenes pulses around the class.

"Ah, yes, my little football fans, I see. A wave passes fluidly if unobstructed." The students can hardly believe their cleverness. "But if you will notice the ropes in your hands, there is an obstruction, a boundary."

Like criminals, the pairs raise one hand each in unison, as if the rope were shackles. Their enthusiasm is underwhelming.

Peter Frankel says, "You're calling the end of the fat rope a boundary?"

"And what would you call it?"

Peter says, "A border or something."

"Terence, what will happen if you start a pulse on your end of the rope?"

Terence looks at the rope in his right hand, and then he turns his face to me. There is nothing in his eyes, two marbles, no questions, no concern.

Maggie Anderson, Miss Subdued but Eager, says, "I know."

"Miss Anderson, do tell."

"The pulse will travel from his hand to my hand." She points from Terence's hand along the sagging rope to her own hand. The boys erupt.

"Way to go," "Yank it," and "Hubba hubba" are some of the comments between laughter. Maggie Anderson, forever the lone girl.

"Enough," I say. "Clearly, you have not left the gutter in the two weeks I was away. Tell me, what is refraction?"

Terence speaks like giving a report, "What you told us, bending." If he flattened his voice, if he chopped the syllable, he could Kyle-speak.

"Brilliant, young man," I say. "Bending a wave. When a wave hits a boundary, the wave changes speed and direction. In this case when the wave hits the boundary from the thin rope to the thick rope, part of the wave continues and part of it comes back. In other words, boundaries change the wave, and some of the wave reflects. Try it."

Two by two the Second Formers step away from each other and draw the rope taut. One whips the rope, and the other can barely hold on. Another just barely shakes the rope, and the other feels nothing. Terence and Maggie make machine motions. Jerk rope up, jerk rope down.

"Smoothly," I say. "Make waves. Be waves. Make the ropes wave."

Misfits of Science, they smooth out their motions. They try, and they try, and eventually, they see the little refraction of the wave.

"Cool," I hear, "Awesome," I hear, "No way."

The rope between Carla and me is now slack. The boundary of age and propriety refracted the wave. Some came back to me, some to her. The rope should not have been between us. The wave in the rope between Kyle and me has no boundary, no drag. The wave will not end.

"Remember, my little scientists, there is nothing without Newton. There is no action without an equal and opposite reaction."

"IT'S DONE," MR. ORAL Fixation says. "No charges. Donny

Zurkus has retracted his statement." These wingback chairs, the sun through the closed windows after classes, today's tobacco makes me sick. Way too sweet.

"So, it can be undone," I say into pipe smoke.

"I'm not sure what you mean. Let me just say I pulled every string, called every trustee. Trustees called every connection they had in the DA's office. Alumni called newspaper rooms across the country to quell the story. The only thing we could hope for was some distraction like, I don't know, satanic worship at Hotchkiss or some god-awful thing. Your friend, Sam, was a key ingredient. Good heavens, man, wise up." His words came out sideways since his pipe was in his mouth.

"And what have we done for Donny Zurkus?" I say.

Earth on us, the word that isn't *hyo*, earth on son, but related. *In loco parentis.*

"What have we taught him?" I say.

The pipe is placed carefully in the ashtray.

"That little ne'er-do-well?" the King of Compassion says.

"What'll he learn?" I say.

"Frankly, Song, I'm surprised at you. After all we've done to clear your name." Mr. Headmaster pulls out his tobacco pouch, taps the pipe, fills the bowl.

"Mr. White, it was the misguiding of youth that brought attention to St. Timothy's." Two boys misguided, misguided as vectors of light, their waves speeding out of the atmosphere unimpeded.

"I don't think I like the implication, Song," he says into the pipe. His face close to the desk. Flames bend from the lighter into the bowl as he sucks the pipe.

"No, I'm sure not. These are boys, and as long as I am able to teach here, I will protect them. Donny Zurkus is mean, sneaky, and misguided. But he should be taught."

"Too late, Song. His father has had him picked up, and that's it. Donny's out."

My hands on the arms of the leather wingback chair, I hold on.

"Another child we've lost, Mr. White. Two this fall. Shame on us."

Losing children in Korea is worse than losing limbs. Kyle was *inyon*, soul of my soul. Donny was a negative valence, but his negative keeps electricity flowing. Donny was doing all he could to avenge himself, to protect his pride. His choices were decisions we could have discussed. As parents, we were supposed to help.

Through the window behind Oral-Fixation White, the light is at its December angle. We are as far away from heat as we will be, and we will spin into the new year as far away from our responsibility as we'll ever be.

Shame on us: 수치스러운

# Taylor / **River**

JONI MITCHELL'S "RIVER" ISN'T the best song to play in December. My mother hated her.

"Shut that crooning," she yelled from the bottom of the stairs up to my room. One of my five records, *Blue,* played until the grooves wore out. My older brother had tired of Joni Mitchell, James Taylor, and a few others. So the used records, with the scratches I knew, became ropes to hold my siblings close after they left for boarding schools and colleges. After my father left, I played the records to keep my mother out of my room. In the whole house, it was just the two of us.

"She's Canadian, Mother," I said down the stairs.

"Oh," she said, "shut the Canadian crooning."

December light came in one wall of my apartment. Maybe it was the lake or the cornfields, but the light was more rust-colored. It was the color of Wyeth's *Christina's World*, a painting my mother hung in her bathroom after my father left.

Saturday at St. Timothy's meant grading exams and preparing lessons. On weekends St. Timothy's is a wasteland. Students packed off in vans to local malls or studying in groups in the library or on weekend passes to God knows where.

It's hard to believe it's been three weeks since Kyle died, one week since Alex stumbled into my apartment and said "Lucky girl."

Since Kyle died, Tommy Greenwood and other boys left. Terence still wakes up screaming, and Maggie Anderson carries a journal she won't let go.

Since Kyle died, the U.S. survived the airing of *The Day After* and the Soviets going on full alert thinking NATO was going to attack, but St. Timothy's didn't watch the TV show. Herbert, the librarian, is sure we're going to all die from Soviet missiles, but his drinking might keep the Soviet threat and state alive.

Since Kyle died, Jack Song is back, and Donny Zurkus has left. Carla no longer tows a boy into the dining hall.

Since Kyle died, I can't sleep.

Every time I open a door, I think I'll see him swinging.

Outside, the light through the trees along the lake is diagonal. There's no rowing, no one out there. The lake is filling with ice. Overhead a goose calls. With each flap of its wings, it calls into the sky.

Kyle is gone.

Sarah is gone.

I can't eat. I can't run.

Too many evenings a six-pack helps me sleep. A six-pack of Hamm's and a walk very late at night get me from awake to no-dreaming asleep. Delaware cold isn't like New England cold, but the crisp air and the white of my breath fill my lungs with something besides the sound I want to make, a yell louder than what you might yell when you're lost. "Anybody there?" is chilled out of my lungs.

One night about three in the morning, I stood outside Carla's dorm, which was lit up like a cruise ship. The maple was light on one side because of Carla's desk light through the window. That maple outside her window is old, and without leaves, its trunk and branches are a sea monster crawling out of the water. Carla looked up from her desk and stared out the window; she stared and stared like the glass could tell her something. Her lips didn't move. She didn't ask it anything. She just stared.

But then she leaned closer to the glass. She leaned so far she had to get up to get closer. She put her hands on the desk, but she wasn't close enough. Up on the desk on her knees, she cupped both hands around her eyes, put her hands on the glass.

With her face up to the glass, she might have seen me in the moonlight, but I stepped back against another sea-monster maple. Three or four times she put her hands to the glass and then leaned back. There was something in the crook of the branches in front of her window. She looked around her room. Maybe she was trying to see if someone else could see what she was seeing.

The next night the tree outside Carla's dorm room was dark on both sides. At four in the morning I knew no one would see me, so I climbed up to see what caught Carla's eye. The cold in my lungs, the thick branches, the way you leverage your weight between feet and hands to climb high, it was good to climb a tree in the middle of the night.

And what I found I could barely see in the moonlight. It was yellow. It was paper. It was soft from the dampness that night and other nights, but it held its shape. And someone had left it for her, high in this tree. I left it where I found it.

Carla, who lost her dad and brother, lost Kyle, had someone who sent her a sign, a bright, folded paper, that only she would see. Someone folded the figure, climbed up this tree, caught Carla's eye. Someone wanted her to keep looking in trees, to keep looking for bright things, to live. A yellow crane in a tree was a sign.

A knock at the door sends the papers on my lap flying on the disgusting carpet in my living room.

"Come in."

The door opens. "Anybody home?" The voice is a Christmas choir, a sunflower, spring.

"Crisco, no way."

"You can run, but you cannot hide," she says. Her smile brings butter light into the Delaware day. She wraps her arms around me, and I sink into her. If Christmas had come, I wouldn't have noticed. If spring had come, I would have bloomed right there.

"You're such a loser," I say. "Nobody leaves Philadelphia for Delaware."

"From what I can see, you're not doing so hot." She lets me go and takes a step, leans into my bedroom where clothes are in piles, takes a step to the edge of the papers and folders and books hiding my living room floor.

"Busy," I say.

"Bull," she says. "I'm getting you out of here."

"This isn't a prison, Crisco. Thanks. You don't have to spring me out." I can see her dark turtleneck, dark pants, dark stocking cap and gloves. She's got a sack over one shoulder, and she's hunched, looking out windows to see if the coast is clear. She takes big steps, raising her knees, placing her feet on tippy toes, better not to make sounds.

"Listen, pal, you're stuck here. I get that you made a commitment, but we have to get you unstuck. I don't know all of what's going on, but it's no good."

"Thanks, really, but we just have one more week. I can make it. You know, 'just ten more strokes.'" Rowers know the worst thing a cox'n can do at the end of a race is tell you how many more strokes there are left, so you pull your guts out for that exact number of strokes, and then, they say, "Just ten more strokes." You hate it, but you reach inside yourself some place and pull out some strength you didn't know you had for exactly ten more strokes, and then, they say, "Just ten more," and you think you may die. Rowers have no idea where endurance comes from or how much they can endure.

"This isn't a race, Taylor." Crisco puts her big hand on my shoulder, and talks to me like she might talk to an old woman who isn't sure where she is. "This is bigger. You've been through too much. It's time."

It might have been the way the light mixed the red of the cornfields with the sunflower of her smile. It might have been the geese calling overhead. But I'm sure it was her hand on my shoulder and the way her words were slow and soft.

I buckled. She helped me down to the ground, and curling into a ball, I pressed against the carpet. The smell of dirt and popcorn brought the whole semester back, all the crew parties, the girls dancing and laughing. All the late nights grading papers and preparing classes, the juice glasses with water or whiskey, the phone calls from Sarah's mom, the quiet filled my head, and my head rested on the carpet. The night Terence stayed on the pull-out couch was milk in a glass, no spill. And then, the night of Alex stopping by and the dance we did around our relationship was a racecourse without buoys. Crisco's hand made circles on my shoulder. She didn't say anything. The refrigerator kicked on and off. And geese called overhead.

# Taylor / **1984**

NOW THAT I'VE TOLD this story, now that the boy isn't hanging in the dorm any more, and the way he built a city to destroy it and named the sparks between fur and amber, and the way he wanted to protect Carla and me and his mother, will that boy come to mind when the geese take flight, when one call from a lone goose breaks the sky?

After Crisco came that Saturday in December, I packed my things in the dorm with stone blocks this way and stone blocks that way, the dorm made for farm boys to learn more than revenge plays and Newton, and drove through the lawns on the driveway lined by maples where once a kite stuck, a kite made by a boy who brought an ancient art of kite flying to a school built by Du Ponts. Out the gate and through the flat, frozen cornfields of Delaware, to the fields of Pennsylvania, Ohio, Indiana, Illinois, I kept driving west and north until I came to this lake, one in the middle of a city, one where I row each morning, and the geese come in low.

Crisco came, too, and she trains for the Olympics, the ones after the ones that didn't happen in 1980. On Lake Washington she rows in an eight that aims for Mount Rainier, the cox'n calling tens for each rower, each rower giving more than she knows she can endure.

Will the girl who knew bugs and origami, the girl whose wants couldn't fly or molt or swim, will she take her own shape one day?

Will the Korean American man who could fold just about anything, given enough paper and time, who tried to trade his blood for his sister's, whose honor turned a school into a parent, will he keep teaching young people to measure the forces acting on them, name the types of resistance to their motion?

I didn't want to tell all this, the story of how cruel boys can be, the way loneliness tastes sweet and makes you think it's love. I wish desire hurt like a hangover. I want adults to see past their want and loss. But all I can do is tend a crack I still carry around, a crack that will never fill.

When autumn arrives in Seattle, I take out a single scull on Green Lake. Sometimes when a flock of geese comes in low in the morning, I slow the shell to stopping, hold the blade handles together to keep steady, and I lie down. Under my back, the lake rises and falls. Above me, the gray sky is line after line of geese. In all the sky gray, a boy I remember is a lone goose flying home.

# Acknowledgments

IF I COULD SHOW you what community means, you'd see a herd of wildebeest and zebras stretching beyond the horizon. Writing groups, like the Dreamies (Cecily, Jackie, Yuvi), like the Pinewood Table, have looked out for me, protected and fed me on this journey. Especially J Rose and Stevan Allred. And so many dangerous writers. *Asante sana.*

If you could hear the silence where I've written, you'd know Hedgebrook and Soapstone writing retreats, the people who have put up with me in their homes, who have lent me their gorgeous spaces. A tiny house in Cannon Beach gave me the opening to the novel. It was there I sank into Tom Spanbauer's words and kindness. At the Oregon Extension I heard the wind like a train through the pine. A motel in Maupin along the Deschutes gave me the ending. In Mosier I've written and rewritten to the thrum of wind. My siblings have been so patient; my family instilled a love of language, justice, and benign pranks. My Aunt Priscilla was always eager for news of my writing when we kidnapped each other for lunch. Thanks to my fellow dang poet, Aloise. Thanks to Sharon and Mike, Nan and Jan, all those who tended me, cheered me on. Thanks to the ODDies for their faith and patience. Thanks to Coventry Cycle Works who helped me work out characters and plot points by helping me stay on the long rides out there in the quiet.

If I could show you teachers who don't stay quiet, who witness and act, who know how to hold difference in their hands like water to drink, you'd see the English department at work at Clackamas Community College. You'd see the majority of boarding school teachers. You'd fill with pride and longing, with the reassurance that what happened to that little boy at St. Timothy's won't happen today. My colleagues at CCC are the finest teachers I've ever known.

And since we're in Oregon, I can mention rain, and you'd know the green and the rivers and the salmon, and if you knew the renewal of water, you'd know what friends do. A group of friends came to my house month after month and listened to the novel read out loud, and ate great salads and pies, and asked questions and heard what I was trying to say. They came to readings and book signings. My friends are such water.

What is air and fire and earth is Cheryl. Always she says, "Write. Go write." She has listened and questioned and cheered. She has wept and cajoled, helped me discover the secrets and successes of the characters, missed them when I wasn't working on the novel. She's cooked dinners and made postcards and massaged shoulders and made connections I never would have. Without her there wouldn't be this novel. I can't imagine what there'd be without her. Thanks to Kendra for naming Taylor.

And it was Hannah who believed in the story in a big way. It was her yell across the continent that told me the book was real, and her generous sharing of experience and faith. And it was Laura who got it all. Her reading of the book puffed the cranes to the right size and shape. Her complete understanding of the intention surpassed my own. Her ideas, her careful comments, her belief took the book and made it fly. And with her came wonder women, like Gigi, Mary, Diane, Annie, and Tracy. Thanks to Bob Troy for his generosity and physics.

If you could put one foot in, push off from the dock, settle into the seats of an eight, you'd know Kippy. This year marks thirty years that she's been gone, and I'm all the more grateful I knew her for five. There's really nothing like someone who is a stroke in an eight. To her sister and mother, I am so grateful for their love and friendship. To the crews who have rowed together, who still row together:

let er run . . .

blades up . . .

balance . . .

# About the Illustrator

GRAPHIC DESIGNER GIGI LITTLE is the creative force behind Forest Avenue Press' visual identity. Outside of the domain of Forest Avenue, she has written and illustrated two children's picture books and her fiction and essays have appeared in anthologies and literary journals. She lives in Portland, Oregon, with her husband, fine artist Stephen O'Donnell. Before moving to Portland, Gigi spent fifteen years in the circus, as a lighting director and professional circus clown. She never took a pie to the face and never got stuffed into one of those little cars, but she is a Rhodes scholar on the art of losing one's pants.

# About the Author

A ROWER FOR YEARS, Kate Gray coached crew and taught in an East Coast boarding school at the start of her career. Now after more than twenty years teaching at a community college in Oregon, Kate tends her students' stories. Her first full-length book of poems, *Another Sunset We Survive* (2007), was a finalist for the Oregon Book Award and followed chapbooks, *Bone Knowing* (2006), winner of the Gertrude Press Poetry Prize, and *Where She Goes* (2000), winner of the Blue Light Chapbook Prize. Over the years she's been awarded residencies at Hedgebrook, Norcroft, and Soapstone, and a fellowship from Oregon Literary Arts. She and her partner live in a purple house in Portland, Oregon, with their sidekick, Rafi, a very patient dog.

# CARRY THE SKY

## READER'S GUIDE

# Author Kate Gray in Conversation with Jeb Sharp, Producer of PRI's "The World"

*Jeb Sharp is an award-winning public radio journalist based in Boston. She has churned out hundreds of news stories in her time, but finds novels better than journalism at describing the human condition. She too once rowed crew at an East Coast college. She met Kate Gray at Hedgebrook, a retreat for women writers.*

**Kate, why did you write this book?**

This story is based on my experiences thirty years ago. The bullying I witnessed at a boarding school, and didn't recognize, has stuck in my body. I wrote it to try to forgive myself for not stopping the suffering when I was a quivering pile of emotions. I was a scared baby-dyke in the highly competitive straight world, which grew me up and spit me out. The story wouldn't stop wagging me. I had to write it.

**What was the process like?**

Arduous. It started when I was teaching with Tom Spanbauer and the Dangerous Writers at a summer writing program on the Oregon Coast. One night I wasn't sleeping well, so early in the morning I woke up, and this voice came in my head, not the crazy kind. It was the way that Tom describes it: some friend, in a bar with loud music, pulls a chair up to you as close as it can go, and this person is talking into your ear so closely that you can feel her words, her breath, her lips on your ear. That was how the story started, a prologue that addressed the reader as if the reader and I were two friends in a bar, sitting as close as we could. I returned to those first three pages over and over when I would lose a sense of the intimacy and pain in Taylor's voice. Then, the prologue became unnecessary, and I didn't include it in the final version.

Without a doubt, the weekly writing group run by Joanna Rose and Stevan Allred was the support and driving force behind completing the novel. Every week each writer brings a maximum of six pages. For a couple of years I got up at 5 a.m., wrote for an hour, then started my work day. Once or twice a year I would segregate myself somewhere and write more than that.

After I had written and rewritten a complete draft, received rejections when I sent the manuscript out, my indefatigable partner gathered a group of twelve friends to our house for potlucks once a month, and we read the entire draft out loud. Their questions and insights were invaluable. Reading the whole thing out loud let me hear the gaps, the promise.

**How long did it take you?**

The first draft took eight years, and the rewriting took two years.

**Did you always intend to tell it in alternating voices/ narrators?**

Originally, Carla was the third voice. And no, there wasn't the regular alternation. Some of the feedback I got on the second draft was that Carla and Taylor's voices were too similar. So, I rewrote it a third time and inserted Carla's voice where I could. But I always had multiple voices in mind because everyone who experiences the same thing tells a different story. I have five siblings, and each of us has a very different version of the same experiences.

**The novel is partly based on tragic events in your own life—what was it like to weave hard truths into a work of fiction? Was it even more autobiographical to begin with? What was the ratio of pain to catharsis?**

When I finally finished writing the first draft of the novel, I was in a tiny hotel in Maupin, Oregon, which is a tiny, gorgeous town on the Deschutes River. It was spring break, March, and that's the real anniversary of my friend's drowning. That part of the story is true: this woman I loved drowned in a rowing accident on the Schuylkill. To this day on the anniversary of her death I try to spend time by water. After ending with that image of the crane in the tree, I walked down to the Deschutes and sat on the riverbank. Once before I had asked the spirit of my friend for a sign that she was still looking after me, and I did this again. At that moment a salmon leapt out of the rapids up the falls. I'm not making this up.

When you write to understand, to go more deeply into truth so that you can bear it, the pain is part of the redemption. In the story there's a lot of truth, and you're right: it became more fiction as I wrote it and rewrote it. When you write witness literature, you shift your own trauma. The writing process doesn't necessarily heal what you felt, but it opens a pathway between your brain and your heart; you have the words that probably weren't there during the experience.

Was writing the book painful? Yes. To me the most intense scene was Carla telling the story of her father with Doug in the water. Something like that happened to me, but when the attacker tried to bargain for the other, older person, that person left me. In writing the story I was able to move the shame, the anger, and the silence of that experience. In fiction you get to write a different ending to your story, change the factors, make different things happen. By telling these violent vignettes, I'm hoping the reader can feel less alone with his/her experiences of violence, can find images that give comfort.

**Talk about what rowing means to you and what it was like to write about it.**

Rowing is an art, a religion, a way of being. Before I rowed in college, I had done many field sports. There's little like rowing. It's the ultimate team sport: you transcend your own body to become one with the others in the boat. To write about it was to relive it, to appreciate the beauty of it, to feel gratitude for the twenty years I was able to row.

**There are so many powerful vehicles/themes in the book—rowing of course, but also physics and origami. Are they also in your life, in your past?**

Initially, I went to college to major in Physics. Calculus III during freshman year crushed me. But physics and poetry are not far apart. In both there is associative or intuitive logic, and certainly there is elegance. One of the joys of writing this novel was researching the physics and trying to wrap my brain around Jack Song's lesson plans. I've rarely done origami, but I love the peace of it. A few times I've made cranes with friends, and that process was powerful.

**What was it like writing a lesbian character and in particular evoking a time (not that long ago) when people were more closeted?**

My friends (most of whom are over fifty years old) and I talk a lot about how much things have changed. My partner and I are celebrating our recent marriage, and marriage is something I never thought possible. The external world sometimes moves more quickly than the internal one. Evoking those times was not difficult because a) it's still dangerous for queer people, and b) those marks of fear and hatred are indelible. From high school to a few years ago, I omitted pronoun references in conversations, rarely talked about my family, didn't reply when stories were told about husbands and wives and vacations. Over the years I've had death threats, been spat upon, had my car vandalized, been stalked, been falsely accused of being a sexual predator. When you've had to protect yourself, it's hard to let go of your ways of hiding. What is wonderful is seeing younger people freely express themselves without self-consciousness. Their way of walking in the world is perfect, beyond what we who grew up in the eighties ever imagined possible.

**If I close my eyes and think of the feeling of the book, I'm surrounded by images of water and birds. Can you talk about those descriptions and metaphors?**

I spent quite a few years sculling on the Willamette River in Portland, Oregon. When you are on the water as the sun comes up, when you are sculling, there is nothing between you and the sky. In every stroke you open your body as forcefully and fully as you can. You throw yourself across the water, over the water, under the sky. The sky at 5 a.m. is full of birds. Water and birds have been sources of comfort and joy for me even in the darkest times. Once I opened the bay door to the boathouse just in time to see an osprey hurtle headlong into the water ten feet in front of me. I counted to five before the huge bird surfaced with a fish and lifted off from the water and almost crashed because the fish was so big. I laughed so hard with the surprise and magic of that act.

**How much research went into the novel? What was familiar territory and what wasn't?**

There was a lot of research into physics and Korea and the Cold War. And when you live through an era, you don't necessarily remember the phrases or TV shows or bands that played. The internet provides glossaries of the eighties, for instance, that helped me use authentic terms, exclamations that the students would have used, that we used to use at the time. And those phrases and shows took me right back to that time and those places. I could then remember the clothes students wore, the conversations we had, the haircuts. Research was critical to creating the world as the characters experienced it.

**You write about tough, tough themes and yet with such wit and redemption. How do you approach grief and pain and fear in your writing? Who were your teachers/influences in that?**

If you want to find models of complex and deeply textured emotions, read African American poets. Maya Angelou spoke at my boarding school and saved my life. In her classic presentation, she gave the audience a reading list, and I consumed everything she mentioned. Writers like Countee Cullen and Mari Evans and Paul Laurence Dunbar gave me permission to feel and act and write with a range and mess of emotion. And then, I gobbled up Sharon Olds, Sylvia Plath, Marilyn Hacker, and Adrienne Rich. The Confessionals paved the way for the Dangerous Writers in the Northwest, who believe that writing what scares you is a gift to the reader because you let them know they are not alone, you eliminate the distance between writer and reader, and you say the really hard things so that the reader doesn't have to. You go first.

And Toni Morrison's *Beloved* is still the most important novel in contemporary American literature, I believe. Reading her book over and over, her way of using multiple perspectives on one traumatic experience got inside me, and her way of creating the presence of the horrible collar forced on slaves so much more powerfully by the absence of naming it gave me the idea of not providing Kyle a voice. I'm hoping the presence of his voice is stronger in its absence.

Elizabeth Rosner's *Speed of Light* showed me how to tell the story in two tightly-intertwined voices, how to write prose that was poetry.

And I come from a family of writers who can tolerate almost anything besides a lack of humor.

**You write about sexual violence and bullying and other overt trauma, but you're also tackling the more ambiguous and taboo subject of what teachers and students feel for each other, what it means to act on those feelings, what the lines of transgression are—what was it like to put those words down on paper? Is it hard as a writer to free yourself enough to impersonate someone pushing and even violating those boundaries?**

The tired adage for writers is "write what you know," and another piece of that is to extend what you know, push it by taking the other person's role, to write the stuff that scares you. By putting myself in the heads of people I might despise, I find some measure of their humanity. It's hard. Sometimes after writing scenes with those transgressions, I biked long distances to figure out how those lines blurred, to make sure those feelings were not stored in my muscles, and to work through the residuals, like disgust and shame and surprise.

**It strikes me there is a profound lack of privacy in this prep school setting. Were you consciously evoking that feeling or is it simply a byproduct of writing about that environment?**

Boarding school teachers have no privacy and work around the clock, especially if they live in apartments within the dorms. Two of my sisters and their husbands have spent their lives working at boarding schools, and I began my career as a teacher thinking I could do the same thing. In one year I gained so much respect for what boarding school teachers do and enough experience to realize I wanted a different lifestyle.

**You are a poet as well as a novelist. How do you think that affected the writing of *Carry the Sky*?**

Since I didn't know how to write fiction when I started, I may have taken more leaps in language and made more associative connections than most fiction writers. Sound often determined my word choice. As a poet, I had to learn things like plot and dialogue. And luckily for me, Forest Avenue Press is a haven for quiet novels, ones that are character and/ or language-driven more than plot-driven.

**What's your hope for the book and its readers?**

My hope is that the book makes a difference in one person's life. I hope that one young gay or lesbian person feels less alone, that one person who has lost someone to suicide or accident or prolonged disease finds comfort in knowing that she can recover, that he can recover in the way that he needs to. I hope readers read plays like *Master Harold … and the Boys* and *Hamlet* and Francis Bacon, that readers connect literature with the complexity of who we are and can be. I hope someone flies a kite. I hope someone hugs someone she knows who might be like Kyle. I hope someone talks about feeling lost and someone listens and finds that person. I hope readers ask great questions like yours, Jeb.

# Reading Group Questions

*Carry the Sky* takes an unblinking look at bullying. What's unblinking about it? Talk about moments where a character makes a bad choice, and the author doesn't sugarcoat the results.

What are some of the ways "difference" is explored in *Carry the Sky*? How does the Wyeth mural act as a symbol?

Has the educational system changed since 1983 in terms of accepting or encouraging difference? How has social media changed the way bullies attack weaker peers?

What are the social, religious, and personal forces that made Taylor feel shame about her sexuality? Do you think those forces are as prevalent today for GLBTQ people?

Jack Song is one of the only people of color on staff at St. Timothy's, although he has an ally in his friend Sam Omura. How are the depictions of race in the book reinforcing and/or resisting stereotypes?

What do you think about the author choosing two teachers as the point-of-view characters? How would the novel change if the headmaster were telling the story? Or Kyle? Does hearing the perspectives of Taylor and Song, as they try to tend these students, change how you think about your educational experience?

Does Taylor's grief for Sarah affect her ability to teach? How about the conflicted emotions about her sexuality? As a more seasoned teacher, does Song manage his grief and outsider status any better than Taylor? Do you think Song will stay at St. Timothy's?

Carla is nearly, but not quite, a point-of-view character. How did the author's use of dialogue and tape recordings, to get her voice on the page, affect your response to Carla's experiences? Do you wish she had a point of view or were you glad for the distance?

Carry the Sky is about bullying, but it's also about loneliness, how being different can isolate individuals. What are some of the ways Kyle reached out—or could have reached out—to the people around him? Who tries connecting with him? Are there characters you hold responsible for what happens to Kyle? If so, which ones?

How did it change your perspective on Kyle's choice to have his fellow dorm mates find him? Where were all the adults?

Honor and shame are two big themes in the book. How does Song act honorably? How does he act dishonorably? What about Taylor? Which characters—adults or students—have positive influences on the other characters?

How does the Cold War backdrop impact the story? Why do you think the author set the book in 1983?

What are some other boarding school books you've read? How are they similar to Carry the Sky? How are they different?